G000126309

Louise Burfitt-Dons is an author and a screenwriter of TV movies shown on television networks worldwide. She was born in Kuwait and has lived in the UK, Australia and France. Louise is married with two daughters and one granddaughter. Her home is now London with her husband Donald.

Stay up-to-date with Louise at:
www.louiseburfittdons.com
Twitter @LouiseBurfDons
Facebook /LouiseBurfittDons

Praise for the Karen Andersen series

'Taut, hardboiled, detailed and funny. This is thriller excellence!' Charlie Flowers, *Riz Sabir Thrillers* and Convenor, London Crime Writers Association

'A tense, vividly-characterised political thriller, with finely nuanced dialogue, that starts off like a hissing, slow-burning fuse that leads inexorably to a climax of heart-pounding suspense...' Jared Cade, *Murder on the London Underground and Agatha Christie and the Eleven Missing Days*

'Louise Burfitt-Dons writes a political thriller which is authentic and gripping.' Kathy Gyngell, *The Conservative Woman.*

'Page Turner! A cracking political thriller. The insecure, paranoid world of the political candidate collides with the equally insecure and paranoid world of a Jihadist bride recruiter. It's twisty, clever and a real page turner.' Emma Curtis, *The Night You Left*

'The knowledge and perspective of the different characters/elements involved in this highly political "fictional" thriller was brilliant! Louise definitely knows her stuff.' Hazel Butterfield, Women's Radio Station

'The world of British Jihadi brides and internal bullying of political parties. Domestic violence, trafficking, sharia law... a terrific book for our times.' Harriet Khataba, *Her Story Matters*

'Ambitious, fun and chillingly real.' LBC

'Jihadi Terrorists and Tory Party politics combine in a thriller written by an insider.' Goodreads.

'The complexity of the terrorist threat undermining British society today ... Original, compelling.' RSA

'Great political story built around politicians, radicals, Muslims and Islamists --- who want to become martyrs.' *Crime Reader*

'A wonderfully written fast-paced political thriller! Brilliantly constructed plot and fascinating look inside the villain's mind.' Ellie Midwood, *Girl from Berlin*

'I was really desperate to get to the last few chapters of this book to find out how everything tied together! Intense and teasing.' Vine Voice Reviewer

I was gripped from the beginning! I had been reading in the news about the Jihadi bride trying to return to the UK and enjoyed watching the Bodyguard series and suddenly I was in the middle of Louise's story. I was enthralled by Zinah, her influence over women and the terrorist threat she presented. A very real story of modern day Britain. A great read. I can't wait for the next Karen Anderson book.' Amazon Customer

A fascinating behind the scenes of politics, feminism, jihadi recruits which grips from the start.' Waterstones reviewer

'Contemporary Britain, portrayed with as much vivid setting and attention to detail that Christie gifted to her Marple books. A convoluted and clever plot. An exceptional read.' Goodreads.

'A well-written insightful thriller with several threads that fairly hums along. The author's description of the inner workings of the Conservative Party is an education in itself. Add to this the view of life in post-Brexit Referendum Britain from the viewpoint of a private investigator, a born-again jihadist and the numerous other protagonists and you've got a recipe for thrills that reaches a climax at the Party Conference. Looking forward to another Karen Anderson novel.' Amazon Customer

'A current, relevant read. Karen a private detective, finds herself caught up amongst ISIS extremists as well as corrupt politicians. A read that was close to home literally as I reside in a London Borough. The author embraced the relevant issues and created an interesting page turner.' Amazon Customer

Also by Louise Burfitt-Dons

FICTION

The Missing Activist

NON-FICTION

Moderating Feminism

PLAYS AND SCREENPLAYS

Kidnapped to the Island
Mother of All Secrets
Your Husband Is Mine
The Ex Next Door
Christmas in the Highlands
The Counsellor
A Christmas Riddle
Act Against Bullying Monologues
The Valentine Card

THE

KILLING

OF THE

CHERRYWOOD

MP

LOUISE BURFITT-DONS

Published by NEW CENTURY

nc

A Paperback Original 2020
Copyright © Louise Burfitt-Dons 2020

The right of Louise Burfitt-Dons to be identified as the
author of this work has been asserted by her in accordance
with the Copyright, Designs and Patents Act 1988.

All rights reserved. No part of this publication may be
reproduced, stored in a retrieval system, or transmitted
in any form or by any means, electronic, mechanical,
photocopying, recording or otherwise, without the prior
written permission of the copyright owner.

This is a work of fiction. Names, characters, places
and incidents either are the products of the author's
imagination or are used fictitiously. Any resemblance
to actual persons, living or dead, businesses,
companies, events or localities is
entirely coincidental.

A CIP catalogue record for this book
is available from the British Library

ISBN: 978 1 91 644912 1

New Century
Duke Road
London W4 2DE

About Jihadi Brides

Beginning in 2012, hundreds of girls and women travelled to Iraq and Syria to join the Islamic State of Iraq and the Levant, becoming brides of ISIL fighters, known as Jihadi brides.

While some travelled willingly, others were taken there as minors by their parents or family. Some of those women subsequently acquired high public profiles, either through their efforts to recruit more volunteers, their death, or because they recanted and wished to return to their home countries.

Commentators have noted that it will be hard to differentiate between the women who played an active role in atrocities and those who were stay-at-home housewives.

*To those who work to counter
all forms of terrorism*

CHAPTER ONE

IT WAS SOMETIME around four in the afternoon on 12 September 2016. Two ISIS soldiers collected the hostage from his cell. In a private room, he came face to face with the chief captor. And his missus.

'Answer these questions. My wife will ask them.'

A camcorder in the corner recorded the interview.

The wife was head to toe in black, with just her eyes uncovered, so the hostage couldn't see what she looked like. She spoke in a hifalutin English accent when she said, 'Hello Greg. My name is Basilah.'

Her voice reminded him of a presenter on the BBC Breakfast show. Kinda sexy. At long last, he'd met one of the infamous British Jihadi wives. Basilah from Bagshot.

He said nothing.

'You need to give us answers so we can let your family know you are still alive.'

He searched her covered head for clues. A tremble of a smile. Maybe movement of the shoulders. Some positive body language. To ask and test on intimate detail was a standard technique used in kidnap negotiation. Yup. There was hope for his release. Bags of it.

'Who was your tennis partner at school?'

'Philip Cross.'

'What was your father's job?'

'Racing journalist for The Post.'

'Who was born first? You or your twin?'

'My twin. He's older than me. And half an inch taller. And better looking.'

She laughed. Did she have a sense of humour? Could he build some rapport?

The husband showed him out of the airless chamber. Greg expected to return to the cramped housing he shared with twelve other western hostages. Perhaps beaten, or subjected to more waterboarding. Greg could take punishment. He'd accepted the treatment by now. The bullying games they played. Starved and threatened with beheading by one group, later handed on to another who fed them cake and boasted of freeing them.

So, what would happen next? Where would ISIS show this film? He knew the media wouldn't get it unless ISIS allowed it. If the families disobeyed, they would murder a captive. Everything was stage-managed. These recruiting videos inspired hundreds of warriors from around the world.

As they led him away, he glimpsed at what appeared to be the storyboard they use in advertising. Or for creating film programmes. Two men poured over the plan of how the video would unfold. One raised his arm in complaint. The lighting was wrong. They argued in Arabic. What should be the next shot in sequence? They flipped the page. He saw a cartoon character bent double and bowing with a black-clad figure standing over, wielding a knife.

Realisation dawned. His eyes bulged at the sight of it. Surely not him. Wasn't he about to be set free?

Outside, a truck pulled up. The husband shoved him towards the back, as wifey, Basilah, looked on.

She'd done her job. Two of Greg's comrades were already inside. Their tense posture and silence did the rest; told him they were all about to die. The door slammed. Chief got in upfront and the vehicle shot off into the desert. When it stopped, four fighters undid their shackles and dragged them one by one down onto the hard, caked sand.

'Put these on. Please.'

It was after they'd fitted orange jumpsuits that their captors retied their hands behind their backs. That's when Chiefy introduced the nice guys who would behead 'the infidels'.

The three killers could have been actors from Hollywood's Central Casting. Tall, muscular. One from France, the other from Belgium. And a 'Brummie'. Keen as mustard for the moment that would transform them into social media heroes like 'Jihadi John'. Executioners' photos made great avatars on Twitter.

No doubt they would clean themselves up during the process. Cut off their heads and immediately afterwards scrub up. Back on camera for the post-execution scenes. He'd seen so many of the videos and there was never any blood splatter. The bastards loved showing their prisoners these little movies.

Thirty-five-year-old CEO of Gibb Construction was the first to be forced to his knees. Sand looks soft but it can be harder than rock. Like his stomach. His mouth was as if he'd been sucking on a rusty can.

Not now. Not now. It can't end this way.

A sweet, dusty earthiness filled his nostrils. He recalled a construction site after the rain.

I can cope. But how will Dad?

His teeth locked solid. How long would this hell go on for? The engineer from Birmingham did his best. But Greg Gibb was a big guy. It took several goes to sever the head off the gentle giant, who his father had once nicknamed Midnight, after a winning horse. The smell of fresh blood wafted across the desert.

They spared the others. 'Maybe tomorrow for you. *Inshallah.*'

Glen Gibb attempted to sleep. But it was useless. It was still two hours until dawn on 10 April 2019.

Over a hundred minutes more to stare at the walls of the claustrophobic basement. Sweating into the sheets. The video of his twin brother's last moments played over and over in his mind. He couldn't stop them.

Why Greg? It shouldn't have been him. It should've been me.

He had to break the tide. Stem the flow of images. It wasn't good for him. Look what happened to his father. The news of his favourite son's death drove the horse-mad Garth to an early grave too. To down his hundredth bottle of bourbon and crumple up with heart pains. Good riddance. But Greg deserved better than a brutal passing. That's why it should have been Glen in Greg's place.

Garth's nicknames were apt. Midnight was the winner. Also Ran was the loser. The dodger. The one Dad belted when he'd drunk too much. The one Midnight protected when Dad belted Also Ran when he was off his face.

It should have been Also Ran. When he'd read about the girl from Syria, it'd set things off again. Why should she be let back into the UK? Had Midnight come back? The news sparked it all up again. The horror. The guilt. Why not Also Ran?

The longer he tossed and turned, the more preoccupied he got with revenge.

A female white recruit to the Islamic State had witnessed Greg's last moments. Taunted him before the execution. Asked him about his twin. 'He's older than me. And half an inch taller. And better looking.'

What was she called? Basilah? One day he'd find her, and she would also pay.

Along with all the other Jihadi brides who were hiding in obscurity. He would shame them. Rattle their perfect worlds.

Humiliate them on the internet as ISIS had done to Greg. Like he'd done to Tessa Clark.

The race was on!

CHAPTER TWO

AT TEN TO nine, the morning of 10 April 2019, Karen Andersen, Private Investigator, stretched like a cat. The flat was a tip, but it was a warm place. It smelt of fresh bread from her trip to the shop on the corner, which bakes their own.

High pressure and mid-Atlantic winds had brought unseasonal temperatures to London for spring. But today it was starting to cloud over. Ever since a bout of depression after a failed love affair, she'd been clawing herself back to normality. At long last, despite the foul weather, she was her sunny self.

Karen's flat doubled as an office. In the far corner was a desk with a PC and two separate screens. Another laptop on the kitchen bar whirred away. Trappings of the world of the 21st century. A flatbed scanner. The chassis of an ancient IBM. Motherboards. Kindles, iPads, voice recorders, smartphones. It meant she could work all hours of the day and night, trolling sites like Open Corporates, doing director checks and not having to set foot out the door.

Andersen Investigations was run from here. It was where she held meetings and probed the net. She could call the spare bedroom into use when, and if, she required extra help. So, files and books covered every surface. Crammed solid.

An easy-going nature is a bonus in security work. And Karen Andersen's job was in the most part checking CV claims, internet fraud, pet thefts. But sometimes it involved finding missing girls or conducting undercover surveillance for Partridge Securities. That's when the cases got messy. Then it required buckets of drive and bottle.

Immersing herself in other people's crap had a tendency to turn her manic. 'When you look at things by extremes, my dear, it's not good for your mental health.' This had been the sage advice of her octogenarian neighbour, Elspeth Cochrane. Mrs C perceived she had the perfect fix to mood swings. 'Music therapy. You need a piano.' Mrs C's brother had died and passed one on. She'd grown tired of it cluttering up her own front room. So, she'd talked Karen into taking it off her.

So, for the past month, the small premises of Andersen's also housed a white Yamaha upright piano. At last the wise advice was working. She was enjoying her outlet. That wet morning she banged out a simple piece of music learnt in her childhood. Chopin, bare-bones version. A battered copy of Scales and Practice for Grade Three was on the top of the piano. She'd get to that next. Everything in moderation.

The sound of someone thumping at the same moment on the street entrance door interrupted her performance. The mystery visitor who struggled up the stairs was a twenty-nine-year-old Filipino woman called Regine Mendoza. She carried a shoulder bag large enough to live out of. Karen recognised her at once. Working as a maid in a hotel, she'd come upon a guest hanging from the overhead fan. It had been staged to look like a suicide.

'Remember I helped you?' Regine said.

Regine entered the flat and threw herself down on the sofa amidst confidential files. She dived into her leather sack and pulled out a series of unsealed brown envelopes. She peeked inside each one until she located what she was looking for. Newspaper articles on the murder case she'd helped solve.

'That's right. Then you went on the run,' Karen reminded her.

Not long before the body was found, Regine had fled an abusive Saudi household, fearing to be in the news in case they pursued her. So, she'd gone to ground.

'You tracked me down. You found me,' Regine replied. It'd been vital evidence that had led to a murder conviction. 'Now I do the same with you.'

Regine was plying the pressure. Over two years had passed. In that space of time, the timid wannabe singer had developed into a mini diva. She wore head to toe Dior; a gold chain bracelet, chain bag and chain boots. She told Karen she'd met a Russian businessman when she was singing jazz-style in a Mayfair hotel. He'd gone in there just after midnight two weeks back to play some Three Card Poker. The rest was history. They were an item, big time.

What Regine wanted from the private investigator was still unclear. In fact, it was a total fog. 'You check him out for me?'

'Regine, how did you get my address?' Karen asked, nervously. The visit had been unexpected.

'Like I say. I found you.' She flashed a flimsy card which read 'Karen Andersen. Professional Investigations.'

There were several types of cases that Karen refused straight off, and one of them was paranoid partners. 'Regine, if this man is so nice and good to you, why do you need to know more about him?'

'I don't want to leave my home until I'm sure he loves me.' Regine reckoned Karen owed her as much as she'd risked her life to help her with a serial killer. 'I can pay you,' Regine continued, drawing out a huge wad of cash. 'He gives me all this money to gamble, but I keep it.'

Even though she was positive he'd fallen in love with her, she went on to explain that he had the photo of another woman as his phone screensaver.

'Can't you just ask him who she is?' Karen responded, impatiently.

'No. He will think I am jealous.' Shades of the other side of Regine returned. Irrational and stubborn. 'He says it's his sister. But I need to be certain. It is very important. You must do it for me. I want you to check him out.'

'What's his name?'

'Ivan.'

'Ivan who?'

'He won't say his other name. Look.' She handed out her phone. On it was a photo of a credit card. 'See? I took this last night.' The name on the bottom of the card was Ivan Koslov.

'What am I supposed to do with that? You shouldn't go around photographing people's bank cards,' Karen replied, getting up and moving to the kitchen area.

'He takes me gambling for big money. Nice places every night. Yesterday we went to the Ritz. That's where I saw your boyfriend.'

'My boyfriend?' The day Karen had first met Regine, she'd been with Haruto Fraser. They'd tracked Regine down together.

'Japanese guy with funny hair.'

Karen's stomach took a drop. How could it be him? Why would Haruto, who she'd thought was wandering the wider world, be back in London? 'Are you sure it was him?' Karen asked.

'Well, he looked like the same guy,' Regine said casually, following her across the room.

Unannounced, Karen's neighbour, Mrs C, sailed in. She closed the keyboard lid of the piano as if she still owned it. 'Did you get through the door all right?' Mrs C interrupted, directing her question to Regine.

'Do you know each other?' asked Karen.

'We spoke on the stairs,' Mrs C replied, using the entrance system fiasco as an excuse to butt in where she wasn't wanted.

'Your intercom doesn't work,' added Regine. In the last year, they'd had a paging system fitted. It was decided they would leave the entry panel outside unmarked for security reasons. Plus, the engineer had fixed it too high on the wall. As had happened so often before, visitors resorted to simply banging.

Karen's mobile started ringing. 'Excuse me, I have to take this.' It was her 'sometimes' boss, Donald Partridge, or Quacker, as he was better known, requesting an urgent meeting. Mrs C then mouthed that she would make coffee, but Karen stopped her. It was a chance to bring the bizarre session to a close, not extend it. This was not supposed to be Piccadilly Circus.

It took another twenty minutes for Regine to collect up her bits and pieces and leave the flat. Elspeth Cochrane followed her. Even then she could hear the two women chatting on the shared staircase. But on the other side of the wall, Karen paced the carpet, an excited flutter rose in her lower stomach. An adrenaline rush. Regine's mention of Haruto had unsettled her. She moved about, unable to stand still. Her mouth was dry. She was no longer sure of what the day had in store. Her breathing was short. The sun did one of those neon tricks of ducking behind a cloud and out again. Haruto back in London?

But this was no time to go sentimental on herself. Quacker had a bee in his bonnet about something.

CHAPTER THREE

AT A QUARTER past ten, Karen left the flat, but without an umbrella. There was no time for shooting back even though it was bucketing down. She splashed her way south down Devonshire Street, and turned into Chiswick Lane. The 190 single-decker bus dropped her at Hammersmith Bus Station where she jumped on the Piccadilly line to Hyde Park Corner.

Quacker, was head of Partridge Security. Karen was just one of his many agents. Officially, he ran his firm from a homely semi-detached house in Acton, which he shared with his nurse wife, Chris. But he spent most of his time flitting around the high-profile hotspots of Westminster.

He was always out and about. Karen had had a summons before to the Park Plaza, Shepherd's Restaurant and a restaurant in St. James's Park. When they'd met at the lunchroom at the National Portrait Gallery, he'd said, 'This is another place where MPs hang out. And even the most obscure cases have some link, however remote, to the top of government.'

The venue proposed today was a first for Karen. The peaceful ambience and elegant surroundings of the RAF Club was a welcome respite from the deluge. It was also a great location, just across the road from Green Park. But something made her think, because of it, Quacker had a heavy case on.

When she made it to the front desk of the lobby, the concierge ushered her downstairs. The wall was a gallery of aviation art. There was a waft of furniture polish mixed with carpet cleaner.

A tall man in a suit and carrying a briefcase was leaving the basement study as she approached the door. This had the smack of the Home Office.

Quacker was sitting back in his chair, studying one of the paintings of a Lancaster; a cherished reminder of Britain's airborne achievements.

'Greetings!' He said as Karen walked in, standing up to greet her. 'Thanks for coming, Karen. Got caught in the rain, did you? Never mind. You look the part.'

Because she'd researched the place, she was wearing a navy-blue suit. The dress code was why she'd not biked it in. 'I haven't been here before,' Karen pointed out.

'They do an excellent curry night here on a Friday. If you're a member, that is. Or know one. Splendid place this is,' Quacker continued. 'The only reason it's still here is because of the committee's very astute decision to purchase the freehold some years back. Coffee?'

There was a pump-action dispenser on the desk and cups on a tray.

'In a minute, thanks. You wanted to see me in a hurry?'

'When you worked undercover on the West Acton Jihadi Brides Club—'

'Your title, not mine,' Karen reminded him.

'What was the Arabic name you gave to infiltrate the Zinah al-Rashid network of girls to the Islamic State?'

13

'Basilah,' Karen stated.

'Wondered how you came up with that. You heard it somewhere, you said. There was someone in the paper a few weeks ago called the same. English woman who'd gone out there as a bride and was trying to return.'

'It's actually a common name.' She'd plucked one that was already driving hard-hitting pro-terrorist messages on the internet.

'You compiled a report for me. It was very concise. And you did well with that,' said Quacker.

'Thank you.' What's with the compliments?

'By allowing us to nail al-Rashid, you stopped British girls making the journey out to a war zone.'

'Probably.'

'Do you know how many of those whose details you established ever went out or had been out in Syria?'

'I'd have to work on that,' she replied cautiously.

'By the way. Your name cropped up the other day. Someone asked me about you for a reference. My comments. She's a brilliant investigator who works out of a base in Chiswick. Usually gets to what you need to know.'

Usually? Karen crumpled. It didn't sound too good.

'I'll get to the point, shall I?' Quacker carried on. 'Remember a young woman called Tessa Clark?'

'Radicalised by Zinah al-Rashid,' Karen remarked. 'Called herself Amirah. Then changed back to her English name. Helped me infiltrate Zinah's WhatsApp group.'

'She didn't go out there though, did she?' Quacker questioned.

'No.'

'Lucky girl. She had a narrow escape, didn't she? Anyway, someone has threatened her over the internet. I thought you'd know who it might be.'

'An online poll done in the States found over a quarter of Americans admitted to having engaged in trolling or other. Probably similar stats for the UK. So, it could be anyone,' Karen shrugged.

'That doesn't help much.' Quacker frowned and toyed with his cup.

'If it's serious stuff, it's most likely a male, low empathy, slightly sadistic. Enjoy causing pain. They love just creating mayhem.'

'Sounds like half the police force,' Quacker joked.

'Some think what they do is funny. When it is not very amusing at all.'

'Motive?'

'Non-clinical psychopathic traits. None other than getting a rise out of what they do, which gives them a sick pleasure.'

'Or hatred of that person.'

'Unlikely. Most trolls don't even know their victims.'

'So, in this case, it's not a troll. It's someone who has the knowledge that Tessa Clark once put herself forward to be an ISIS bride.'

'Who would that be?'

'I thought you might fill me in on that.' Quacker was challenging her.

Karen leant back in her seat. What's all this?

'Other than myself, you and two others from the security services, no one knew she was in the al-Rashid network,' Quacker claimed. 'By all intents and purposes, she presents online as a quiet, law-abiding nineteen-year-old graphic artist with a pet dog and a passion for making cakes. Not someone you'd expect to get rape and death threats.'

This took Karen aback. 'When did all this happen?'

'Two weeks ago, Karen.' Quacker was observing her reaction, whilst at the same time checking his phone.

Why hadn't she heard before? Tessa Clark had originally been Karen's case, not Quacker's.

'Why didn't she contact me directly?' Karen responded, in a more serious tone now.

'I tried to get hold of you myself the other week and couldn't.'

'I left my phone at my neighbour's.' In fact, the local library had phoned to say they'd discovered it sandwiched between two books in the non-fiction section on music. But she wasn't about to admit to sloppiness.

'Security of information is a big thing.' Quacker wrinkled his brow. 'Someone got wind she was once signed up as a potential Jihadi bride.'

What was Quacker getting at? There was an awkward silence. He didn't have to drum it in how the work of a private investigator was confidential. Misplaced mobiles could end up in the wrong hands.

'Well, what's Tessa Clark been doing since?' Karen asked. 'We're going back nearly three years,'

'She designed websites after she left school. Did an online course. Should have got her to do the Partridge Security site, shouldn't I? Might have been cheaper than what I was charged. Absolute fortune.'

'So, she's still in the West Country?'

'But it seems she had a nervous breakdown over this leak. She's now taken a job in a shop.'

Leak? Karen got up and poured herself a cup of coffee to give herself time to think.

'What makes it a leak? The fact someone discovered she was once an ISIS supporter?'

'Yes. Not good,' Quacker remarked. 'And with Syria in the news every day and girls out there wanting to come back to the UK, it's got people's backs up. We can't afford any more lapses.'

The coffee cup rattled. Further lapses? 'It could have been any of the very many people she had contact with back then. School friends. Family.'

'That's a possibility.'

'I'll call her,' said Karen, taking her seat again. 'You have her latest number, then?'

'She said it was the same one she'd had since 2015.' Quacker scanned through his contacts.

She stopped him with, 'In that case, I'll have it.'

'Well, it would be a good move if you could do that for me. Reassure her. Find out what this guy—well, we assume it's a guy—is up to. That's it.'

Karen was halfway between mouth and cup. 'That's it?' she said, trying to hide her frustration. A ticking off? Is that all you needed me here in person for? she thought to herself.

'I'm in a rush, I'm afraid. I've got to pick up Chris from the airport,' Quacker said, nonchalantly. 'I told you she was coming back early, didn't I?' Quacker's long-suffering wife had been renting a holiday flat in Goa with her newly divorced younger sister, but they'd fallen out over their different partying habits. 'But drink your coffee.'

It was nearly half-past eleven.

'No problem. I'll leave it thanks,' Karen uttered under her breath.

The Partridges were rarely apart and Quacker had done everything to make his wife's craving for spending six months in the sun without him a possibility. This could have been the reason he was so short-tempered. Like Karen's day so far, maybe nothing had gone to plan. But as she scurried out of the room, she tripped and fell up the stairs.

Her mind was racing, trying to fill in the gaps in their conversation. And there were plenty. Quacker was definitely off with her. She wanted to think otherwise. But there was no getting away from it. It seemed he held her responsible for some serious lapse in confidentiality protocol.

She had to clear it with him, or she would never work for Partridge Security again.

CHAPTER FOUR

AFTER LUNCH AT midday, Prisoner 378 went back to her wing at HMP Bronzefield. Tammy Bishop had good looks, charm and was a mistress of reinvention. It drove people who shared with her up the wall. Her self-obsession and arrogance. As a result, she'd had five cellmates in three years. Tammy had entered jail as a tough-as-nails white convert terrorist, named Zinah al-Rashid, to serve eight years. Now she was a squeaky-clean reformer. Either persona was the subject of bullying and assault from cellmates and their cronies. Eventually, they'd moved the thirty-four-year-old Jihadi bride recruiter to her own unit.

Butch Bev was waiting to bombard her. She wore her red and black lumber-style check shirt, which stank of smoke.

'Zinah,' she called out.

Tammy felt the slap and weight of Bev's hand pushing down on her shoulder. 'Why not use my number, why don't you?' Tammy shouted back.

'How's single living? Lonely?' Bev was spoiling for a scrap.

'Loneliness is merely a state of mind, Beverly. I'd sooner be on my own than trapped with a serial killer.'

'You only have to look in the mirror to see one of those. Can't be anyone else you're talking about. Zee-nah!'

'It's Tammy, actually.'

'Oh, sorry. Sorr-eeee. Tell me, how many names have you had?' Bev was in her face, hands in pockets. Goading.

'Why, my dear? What's it to you?' Tammy said, staring straight back at her.

'Wondered who you would be next week. Kylie Minogue? Liz Taylor?'

The question made her think. How many names had she used already? She'd been born Tamsin Evans in Hammersmith Hospital in 1984. Her mother Miriam Bishop had divorced Jeb Evans when he'd converted to Islam.

'My name is Tamsin Bishop. In fact, I was always Tamsin Bishop until Mummy remarried.'

'Ooh, Mummy remarried, did she? How sweet.' Bev said, pulling at Tammy's shirt. 'Go, hang yourself, bitch,' she continued, faux-kicking Tammy in the back of the legs. The same old thing as she'd done before.

Butch Bev was not the worst. The other low life scum joined in with her bitchiness. She'd explained all this to every cellmate. Told them her past. Advised them how best to refer to her. Why she now used Tammy and nothing else. How Mummy's second marriage was to a Tory MP called Archie Smythe.

So why not call herself Tammy Symthe? Because ignoramuses pronounced it 'Smith,' which sounded common as dirt. That's why. Mousey Mrs Kell was Awful Archie's downtrodden mother. But Tammy had added the 'Kell' all the same when she'd got herself a job in fancy Harrods. The name badge with Tammy Kell-Smythe on it did wonders for her glamorous London persona. But this was all years ago.

She was planning a new start. Why weren't they all working out what they would do after prison? They should be planning a new future. Give up crime. Copy her fine example. They might even become as famous as she intended to be.

Tammy Kell had been many things in a past life. A political wannabe. She'd also come under the allure of ISIS, operating as Zinah al-Rashid. How she'd been mistaken. Honest-to-goodness she'd changed. Couldn't they tell the difference? Zinah al-Rashid was synonymous with extremism. She'd had time in Bronzefield, time to grow and change. Zinah didn't fit her. Nor Tammy Kell. Yes, it been in the papers. But they linked the name 'Kell' with the murder of a twenty-one-year-old political activist, Robin Miller. And she'd not killed Miller. She'd made the story up to gain status. He'd done it himself. Cut his own throat.

Everything would be clear as crystal after she wrote her book. The title: 'My Life with ISIS: From bombs to bombshell.' After she'd written sixty thousand words of it.

'Tam? Letter for you.' The wing officer turned a blind eye to Butch Bev.

'Did you see what she did?' Tammy said, taking the envelope from the officer.

'It was only playful.' The officer brushed off the bullying as usual. 'She meant nothing by it. Where's your sense of humour, Tam?'

They would repeatedly deny the attacks, she was thinking. But this letter was more important. This was far more critical. She'd written to Robin's family to explain the true turn of events. And at last, a response!

She turned the envelope over. Straight away she recognised her own writing. It was the same one she'd sent to David Miller, the father of her so-called victim. But he'd opened and read it, then readdressed it in blue biro to 'Zinah al-Rashid' at Bronzefield with her prisoner number and the word, 'Liar'.

This was why Tammy Bishop couldn't wait to get out of prison. Everything was so hard in there. If she got the chance, she'd tell him to his face about his son's last moments. A personal meeting would make him believe her.

She'd made requests for visits from people that never occurred. She'd written letters to onetime friends, which came back marked 'Return to Sender'. Now, this.

She told everyone else who'd listen, 'Robin Miller killed himself. I couldn't talk him out of it.' About how his complaint had been dealt with depressed him; he'd accused someone of bullying and the political party ignored it. The Tory Party sidelined him. He thought they'd turned on him. 'Regretted making the fuss in the first place, was what it was all about.'

Yes, he'd sliced his throat open with her kitchen knife. And yes, she'd stored his body in her freezer. But nothing more. Why did they hate her so much for hiding the body?

She reread the envelope. 'Zinah al-Rashid.' They'd avoided using her proper name. It was Tammy Bishop. It was no longer Zinah al-Rashid.

If she got out, she could speak to them at length one way or another. It was impossible from the prison phone. Everything inside was in the hands of others.

In here it was as if she was a kid at boarding school again. Plus, she needed better clothes. And make-up.

I urge you to listen to me!

Get ready for group therapy! Two o'clock. *What a waste of effing time.* In the airless room were four others also doing the course entitled 'What will you do when you leave prison?'

I have to go though, thought Tammy. She'd done a deal with the authorities. To help with the deradicalisation of returning Islamic State supporters. But tell nobody! Inside you spoke about what you'd do on the outside, but never when a release was likely to happen. So, no one was aware Tammy would soon be free.

She hated this group discussion. They were all dreamers and as thick as mince.

Run a fish and chip shop. Be a beautician. Go to university. She was fed up of listening to all this tripe. Who were these people? Two fraudsters, a shoplifter and a teaching assistant who'd once played in a classical orchestra before she'd developed a drug habit and started dealing.

The latter had come into prison with sleek hair, Tammy remembered. Today she sat there grinning with a shaved skull and piercings. What was going through her brain? She blurted out 'I'm going on reality TV when I'm out of here.'

'Tell us more about this, will you?' The counsellor in charge of the group who was nodding off out of boredom woke up with the unexpected interaction.

'Thousands of people audition for shows so you need to stand out,' the druggie teacher informed the group.

'Yes, I'm sure the producers do want someone who stands out,' agreed the counsellor.

'I can't tell them I've been in prison, can I?' added the prisoner, sadly.

Tammy was suddenly all ears. Now there was something to learn from all this, at last!

The difference between her and other terrorist-turned-security-informants was her soft-spoken style. She turned heads. Tasteful understatement had its place. Très chic, at other times she dazzled with the season's most wearable trends. If you've got it, flaunt it.

Unlike other informers who kept a low profile to avoid social media abuse, Tammy didn't want to leave Bronzefield and hide away like a hermit. And it was the teacher who gave her the clue. TV. What a plan. This is how she could make up for lost time and help get the message out about how the UK was being held to ransom by Islamic terrorists. But do it her way. She was a star. But like all aspiring celebrities, she needed exposure.

Big Brother. Love Island? A possibility. Tammy possessed pluck, nerve and ambition for greatness. Unlike the teacher.

'The producers want someone who stands out,' she heard in her head. Yes, it'd be quicker than a book. She'd be on TV and in the papers in no time at all.

'You'd be brilliant,' Tammy lied to the nursery school nobody, who beamed. But not as brilliant as Tammy! Why hadn't she thought of it before? It was a no-brainer, surely? Her mother had been a model, hadn't she?

The group therapy had prompted her to think back on the past. It was all about a fresh start, wasn't it? Put the bad history behind her, pick up on some good.

Who was she really? To discover her background, she needed the services of the private investigator who'd discovered her pseudonym. The woman who'd known her true identity. The one and only Karen Andersen.

'Wow' and 'Love Island would be great.' A couple of women in therapy were now right into the reality show thing.

The group leader looked pleased with herself. She encouraged this kind of involvement, but rarely got it.

'Wow is absolutely the word for it. They are all into diversity,' Tammy said. She was now becoming wonderfully carried away with her thoughts. Smiling as she was scheming. Later, alone in her cell, she'd work out the finer details.

Tammy could have been a success in life, she now thought to herself. She could have been someone special if only her mother had lived. Not died when she was so young. Surely, losing Mummy had been the reason she was in here! If things had been different, there would have been no contact with Mohammed al-Rashid to lead her astray.

The session continued. They talked about the pain of losing loved ones while in prison.

'Has that happened to anyone here?' The group counsellor made her face dark and broody. It dampened the merry mood.

'My grandmother died,' offered Tammy. She knew nobody in the gathering cared less. 'I miss her.' But for a moment she had finally won the attention and a little sympathy, perhaps. 'She had Alzheimer's.'

But once on her own, she plotted how she'd follow in her mother's footsteps. What did Tammy know about this amazing creature? Nothing. Only that Miriam Bishop, an aspiring model, had drowned in an unexplained boating incident when little Tamsin was six. Because of that, they'd left her in the care of Awful Archie with his odd fetishes.

Now here she was, her liberty gone, desperate to know more, everything.

She needed to be out of here soon. *She'd do anything to get out of prison.*

CHAPTER FIVE

KAREN ATTACKED THE Tessa Clark case straight away. By two-thirty that afternoon she had sketched a picture of what could have happened. She discovered the harassment story was a trifle unusual. It was racist, with a twist.

The girl in question had been a white convert to the Islamic cause. She'd received the following details from Quacker. Someone from an anonymous account had written, 'Go back to Syria, bitch'. It had been posted as an indirect message on her Twitter.

What followed was a photo of a young woman in full Islamic dress with the tag, 'This is the Tessa Clark as you don't want to see her.' #TessaClark #JihadiBride #IS #Amirah.

Next off, angry Twitter users had caught on. They piled in strong, to stick the boot in. There were rants from ISIS supporters stating 'She's abandoned Islam!' They accused her of apostasy, the punishment for which is death.

Tessa had since closed down her Twitter account, but there were still plenty of repercussions. She was being slaughtered online.

Karen had expected to have matters sorted far earlier than this. Speed was of the essence in cases like these. Fast action. Close hacked accounts. Put trolls to flight. Move quickly. Plus, she presumed Quacker would want an update by the time he got back from the airport.

If the exposure of Tessa Clark had been Karen's fault in some way, it was dynamite. Quacker never tolerated carelessness. A basic condition of working for Partridge Security was confidentiality.

She needed to clear her name, and quickly.

Alas, it was not meant to be.

Tessa Clark worked in an underwear shop. The first time Karen called, she was out at lunch. The second, in the middle of a bra fit. 'We don't encourage phone calls at work,' said the storeowner, confirming it would be a battle to get through.

But five minutes later Tessa rang back on her mobile. 'Oh, hello Karen. How are you?' Her contented manner seemed misplaced for the situation.

'You should have got in touch with me long before this,' Karen sharply responded.

'Is this about the internet stuff?' The noise of traffic meant she was outside the shop. 'It's horrible what you've done.'

'I've done? I strongly advised you to take everything down that had any reference to Islamic State. Why didn't you do that?'

'Are you trying to suggest this is all my fault?' Tessa screamed back, over the clangs and hoots of the street. 'What's it to do with me?'

'You're posting stuff online.'

'There's nothing more online. I've checked.'

'I've checked too. And I think you'll find there is,' Karen added bluntly.

Gone are the days of a hand full of forums on the internet. Karen knew that, Tessa didn't. There are at least sixty different social media sites that are popular. It was understandable that Tessa had ignored the oldies. With the ultra-fast sharing apps, news placed on old accounts can crop up years later on dubious chat rooms. And when Karen had carried out a full audit, she'd found one.

'What?' No way!' Tessa argued. 'I've gone through Facebook, YouTube, WhatsApp, WeChat, Instagram, and Twitter.'

'MySpace?' Karen questioned.

There was a silence, followed by an audible gasp. 'Oh no.'

'There's a photo of you wearing a hijab and making a Daesh salute. Not smart.'

Karen heard her mumble several 'shits' through the phone.

'Take the bloody thing down,' Karen demanded.

'I can't do it right now. I'm at work. I've got to find the login and password. I don't know what it is.'

'Do it straight away. Or you'll have no job to return to. Look at what you're advertising. There are school buildings in the background. Girls in green uniforms.'

'But I'm not there anymore,' Tessa contested.

'Anyone can still track you.'

'I haven't thought about MySpace in years!'

'It still gets fifty million visits a year.'

'I didn't know that, did I?'

'Call me at five when you've found your login and password and done what I've asked you.' Karen ended the call.

Twenty minutes later Tessa Clark called back. She'd done as Karen had told her. She feigned illness and ran home to dig out the password to her old account.

'I've found it.'

We all make mistakes, thought Karen. Tessa Clark's blunder of not removing the photo had caused her distress. But her real undoing had occurred years earlier when she'd put herself at risk by meeting the charismatic Jihadi bride recruiter, Zinah al-Rashid. She'd been sixteen. Tessa had renamed herself Amirah. She'd started wearing full Islamic dress and had spouted pro-ISIS propaganda to her schoolmates. Fortunately, her smart mother had raised the alarm with Karen Andersen. As a result, with Karen having intervened, Tessa Clark hadn't gone down the wrong road for too long. After a period when she'd gone back and forth between Amirah and Tessa, she'd returned to her senses.

Karen had promised Tessa Clark anonymity and a clean break from the past if she'd help her infiltrate the brides' circle. Three years on and a Twitter stream had inexplicably erupted. Self-imposed.

'I'm so, so scared. It was so long back. Why?'

It was now apt for Karen to adopt a softer tone. 'It's unfortunate someone at your graphics job saw the posts on Twitter.'

'I know who it was at the art studio,' she said to Karen. 'I can work that out easily enough.'

But then several nasty girls from her class at school could have done it too. The likelihood was an Islamophobic troll had chanced across the Myspace account. It was rich pickings to come across a white girl wearing the full Muslim garb and flying the black flag. People displayed less tolerance than they did in 2016. There'd been too many accounts of atrocities at the hands of ISIS.

'Whoever's done it has taken the selfie you put up years ago. Don't blame them or me. Take responsibility for yourself.' When she hung up, Karen slumped onto the sofa. A light cloud of dust rose. She let her head fall back with the sheer relief. She closed her eyes. Her job was secure. Andersen's agency reputation was still intact.

They'd all played the blame game. Quacker'd blamed Karen, who'd blamed Tessa, who blamed the girls at school. Not one of them was bringing up the real source of the problem. The woman who'd radicalised them. Thankfully, she was safely locked-up.

The bullying would stop soon. This nastiness would die down. But it prompted her to tidy her paperwork.

She looked around the room, her home, her office. The familiar clutter. Motorbike gear. Books. Paperwork. There were photos of herself with Haruto Fraser. Still. Prints of London streets. The wall was a display worthy of a Royal Academy exhibition. Pictures of company sites. Print outs on cyber-crime. Terror suspects. Newspaper stories. A news clipping about Karen Andersen, address undisclosed. A story about Jihadi brides. Hundreds of printed Google maps. Black stabbings. White-collar crime. Another, 'How I conned my boss,' article.

It'd been tempting to be angry with Quacker over the Tessa Clark affair. She'd wanted to battle on the spot. Who did he think he'd accused of being slapdash? But she'd controlled it. Start afresh. The buck stops here. Let's return to work with hurricane force. Yes, it was time to get efficient. The place needed cleaning up. Cut the clutter. This affair may have been a false alarm and she could now put it behind her.

But first things first. Call Quacker. It would be a help for him to know the outcome. Quacker always answered her. Without fail. He offered that repeatedly when she was working for him just in case it was urgent. Even if he was out and about, or crawling through London traffic, he would speak briefly.

But this time it was different. Karen's call went straight to voicemail.

She continued with the spruce-up. There was an envelope lying under some files. Inside was a set of A4 photographs. She slid one out. It was a close-up of an ISIS execution. Horrifying. How long had they been there? Could she remember them from before? Or had someone been inside her flat?

CHAPTER SIX

CAREFUL, NOW. BIDE your time. Make sure she's alone. Give her the leaflet.

It was five past six in the evening. Glen Gibb watched the young woman return home. She'd not a clue someone was studying her every move on that Wednesday evening. Waiting to present her with a nice little flyer. Show her some pretty photos. Want to see what you were a part of? Happy to show you.

The house was a semi-detached in a road next to Gunnersbury Cemetery. The Jihadi bride lived near a burial ground. Ha. But at least she was near to the graveyard. Not in it. Unlike Greg. He was six foot under. He'd spent his final moments talking to someone like her. She was British, like you!

Finally, it was now a chance to carry on the conversation.

She didn't look too bright. Or too old. Maybe only twenty-one, a petite, pretty girl. Slim as a reed with a neat dinky headscarf.

She didn't have a clue about *him*. How Also Ran, the loser, had smartened up his lousy little act. Done well. He'd schooled up on her plenty. He could only imagine her face if she knew just how much!

How Fatima Ahmed once made a tiny little bomb with a mobile. Where was it you met up with Zinah al-Rashid? Harrods? How smart. What a shame you didn't get to wed an Islamic fighter before they caught her.

And how is it that Mr and Mrs Ahmed know absolutely nothing about all this? Not one teeny weeny scrap of what their daughter was up to back then.

What'll the owners of Acton Food And Phones do with that little gem of knowledge when they get to read about it?

It was time to find out.

'Do you need a bag with that?' *How often did she ask that?*

Fatima got back to the house she shared with her parents expecting her brother to be home from school. It was past six.

She was thinking, what a boring day it had been at the shop. Dire. How'd she get stuck working there for so long? How to get out of it? There had to be a way. If only she could find another job. She hated sitting at the till. She often felt cross with herself for leaving education early. Not getting into university. Right now she could look at something more academic, perhaps with computers. And move away. It'd spice up her crushingly predictable life.

The same thing, day after day after day? The shop, the mosque, the family. Keep off the subject of an arranged marriage. Did they not realise she needed more excitement? A distraction that awakened her spirit? Energising and amazing. Come on!

What was on the agenda instead? Her Mum and Dad were planning to visit the warehouse area for lamb shawarma after they closed. She'd suggested she'd look after Mahmoud when he came back from football practice. Anything to duck the dinner.

She wanted to get her duties done to watch TV on her laptop in her room. But she was being watched herself. She hadn't noticed the red car drive past her house three times and then pull up down the street.

Fatima Ahmed was a good cook. Even of chips. Or as she would say, 'Even of chips—yeah? They ain't easy.' She'd never ever used the oven-heated variety. That was just for lazy arseholes.

Her brother, as per usual, was late home again. And seeing as the only pulse-pounding activity on her agenda was making chips, she'd do it right. They weren't the easiest to do well.

She knew all the varieties of potatoes. She'd tried them all in her quest to get the crispiness like in the restaurants. Duke of York, Maris Piper. You name them. So long as they were floury. You couldn't make chips with bakers. No way. She peeled four King Edwards. She rinsed them under the cold tap and then soaked them in salty water. Preparation was key. Then she patted each one with a paper towel.

The only way to cook them was as hot as hell. For five or six minutes. It required 185 degrees. Smoking. Fatima Ahmed was lost in what she was doing. The gas burnt blue. She almost forgot what time it was. The oil was bubbling. Maybe she should have been a chef like the girl who won the cooking show on TV. It was an idea, wasn't it? There was a shrill ring on the doorbell. Several times. Who could it be? It broke her concentration. Her brother? He always used the back door. But this evening he'd rung the sodding bell. Great timing!

The oil was now scorching. She moved flat out to answer the door. Added to that, Mahmoud was playing games. Because when she flung it open, there was no one there. But as she was about to shut it again, a man stepped out of the bushes.

He was clutching a phone, which he'd just used to snap a shot of her. Some canvasser, she imagined.

'Fatima Ahmed? I'm writing a special on why women want to go to the Islamic State and betray Britain,' the man said, somewhat politely.

The reporter wore a smart suit, white shirt and tie. He looked like someone from the papers. What? Why her? How'd he learnt about my past? Fatima thought to herself. Who'd told him?

'I don't know what you're talking about,' Fatima blurted out. 'I didn't go anywhere. What are you doing at my house?'

'One question. And one question only. You will deny it, no doubt. Your lot always do. But girls like you are responsible for the deaths of so many innocent people. How d'you feel about that? Did your parents know about your plans to travel to the Islamic State?'

She froze. Her parents didn't know. If they did, they'd bloody kill her. 'Smart immigrants respect Britain,' her Dad had said. Several times they'd spoken of it when he'd been reading a newspaper. How disobedient girls had defied their families. Flitted off to join the fighting in Syria rather than marrying someone from back home in Pakistan. There had been too much debate on it recently.

She slammed the door in his face, so hard it kept shuddering. The first sounds she heard were a whooshing. Smoke poured out into the hall. Their kitchen was on fire. She'd not been able to get back to the chip pan in time.

'What have you fucking done?' she screamed, as she saw how the blaze spread. Her brother had come through the back, seen the flames and thrown water on the pan. 'Get out and call 999!'

Glen Gibb felt a sense of achievement. He'd confronted the girl, for Greg's sake. She'd slammed the door in his face. But there was fear in her eyes. He'd asserted himself.

There was screaming still coming from inside. Good. Midnight would be proud of Also Ran. He'd won. Seconds stood still on the crumbling porch of the Acton house. Victory. But he'd planned to hand her one of the English Concern Group pamphlets. Six pages jam-packed with grisly images. Beheadings. Stonings. A poor sod burnt alive. The Far Right slamming off against Jihadi brides wanting to slide back into Britain. So, not a hundred per cent success.

He doubled over the flyer, crouched down and stuffed it through the tiny letterbox.

And so perhaps he'd not have too many more of these calls to make. Tessa Clark, tick. Fatima Ahmed, tick. The word would now fly around. It was a satisfying experience to hound these women out of hiding. He'd made a mark. You've lost someone to those bastards? You may be content to turn the other cheek. Not me. Well, fine for you, he thought. But he couldn't do that. Not anymore. He owed it to the family. But had he done enough? Maybe. The GG boys were peace-loving. Perhaps Greg would let him off doing more.

He left the doorway, retraced his steps to his car and drove away. It was just past six-thirty in the evening. The raging fire at the rear of the Ahmed house wasn't of any concern to him. Not at all.

The reason for this was he knew nothing about it.

CHAPTER SEVEN

AT A QUARTER to seven that evening, Karen Andersen poured herself a mammoth glass of wine. Quacker hadn't yet returned her call, and she was weighing up telling him about the pictures. Alcohol helped. Why had they appeared in her flat? Had someone sent them to her? Her concern was she couldn't remember whether she'd come across them way back. And absent-mindedness wasn't a great fit for an agent.

She heard canned laughter coming from her neighbour's TV. Would the night ahead be fun? Regine Mendoza had pleaded for her to go to The Ritz Casino to check out the Russian, and there was just a slim chance she'd see Haruto again. Could he really have been there? Or was it someone else? She'd not known her ex-boyfriend to be a high-stakes gambler, but what did she know about him, anyway?

She hadn't expected him to drift out of her life. What was that all about? All she needed was to learn where she'd messed up, because she knew she had, somehow. There was a stirring in her stomach.

What if he was at the casino that night? How would he react? Would he be alone? She had to stop fantasising about seeing him. In case it didn't happen. Chances were, it was mistaken identity.

There was even the possibility Regine had invented the whole story as bait. She was as crafty as a cartload of monkeys. But, then again, it could have been Haruto at the Ritz. His business ventures may have taken off. He had a hundred crazy ideas. One could have developed into a winner. There was ever that probability.

Karen let the shower run as she breathed in the sweetly scented shampoo. She allowed herself to think happy thoughts. They might see each other again. Then what would happen? Haruto Fraser had a Japanese mother and Scottish diplomat father, now divorced. When she'd met him, he'd been a photographer specialising in architecture. They'd been inseparable for eighteen months. He helped solve two of her cases. They'd become lovers. Haruto took her to Tokyo where he owned some gaming machines, his 'small fry' business.

She let the water break over her in the shower. The wine glass on the shelf was empty. She should get out and refill it. But she couldn't stop herself drowning in sentimental memories.

What had happened? And why? How can you just drift apart? There was no specific time or place for the breakup. But it was after a trip to the Rhine Franconian region of Germany.

Yes, everything had been perfect until Mainz. Haruto had grown distant from her over a matter of days. Afterwards, she'd come back to London, and he'd gone off on his own to Sri Lanka. Something had got to him.

She'd followed his Far East travels on his Facebook page, but the updates were brief. And Karen never called. It wasn't her style to chase him. As much as she'd wanted to. And no photos of them together on his social media was the clue he'd put her into the past.

There'd been nothing to change that. Nothing on her, nor returning to London. Or gambling. The Ritz didn't fit with this at all. So how come Regine had seen him there?

Karen decided, for the hundredth time, she must get over him.

It'd been such a miserable period since they broke up. But just hearing that morning Regine could have spotted him, had given her an adrenalin rush. She was desperate to talk to him. Look into his eyes. Then, if he didn't respond, she could put the whole love affair behind her, once and for all.

Anyway, she was on a job that evening. Surveillance. She had to keep that in mind. Being an investigator these days was all about keeping a low profile and having a credible alias, if required.

For this assignment, Karen was posing as a potential flatmate who was meeting up to talk rental stuff. Ms Mendoza had invited her to the Ritz to prove she had the cash. Regine's idea. She had to play the part, however ludicrous it was.

The hot spray relaxed her muscles and settled her nerves. But stepping out and finding still no message from Quacker troubled her. He'd not called back.

She hid the offensive pictures in a drawer. They were serving no purpose, except feeding her paranoia that someone was out to get her.

CHAPTER EIGHT

IT WAS JUST past nine-fifteen in the evening when Karen Andersen arrived at the Ritz Casino.

She'd travelled to Piccadilly by London Underground, which took the best part of an hour. She had no phone signal on the Tube, but Quacker had still had plenty of time to call back before. So, she was edgy on several accounts when she got there.

Regine's reprimand didn't help. She'd changed roles and was now playing Pussy Galore from Goldfinger. She wore a slinky blue cheongsam, flirtatiously slit to the upper thigh. 'Why you not wearing a long dress?' were her first words.

'I'm supposed to have come from a late office meeting,' Karen reminded her. 'We are playing parts. And we don't know each other, remember? So I can ask the questions.'

The guy she was dating was muscle-bound, blonde, with bland good looks, around thirty-four. He'd perched himself at a roulette table. Regine led her by the arm to meet him. He seemed unimpressed at the extra company. He nodded hello, then continued to play with his tower of chips, waiting for his turn. He'd bargained on a quiet hour to study the rotating disk and the small ball. Win money.

'Hi,' said Karen. She took the pew to the left of him. 'You're Ivan—?' He had a Russian look, though Karen suspected he was anything but Eastern European.

She could just make out his mumblings, 'Who is this?'

Regine fondled the base of his neck. He was not happy.

'I wanted her to meet you. My flatmate,' Regine cooed. She ran her palm over the back of his bright green shirt and blew in his ear to make it right. 'And maybe she would see her friend again. The man I saw yesterday?'

Karen knew after this break from the script their game plan was unravelling fast. Ivan removed her hand. He twisted his head first to face Karen, seated on his left, and then to Regine on his right, and sighed deeply. He crossed his heavily tattooed arms. The chips stayed put. He was on strike.

'Why you like this?' asked Regine. 'Play, play.'

Ivan rubbed his chin and started blinking. He stonewalled both of them. An awkward silence.

'You silly man,' Karen heard Regine say. Her eyes bright and glossy, staring into his. She tapped him on the leg. The teasing was irritating. 'She wants to learn more about you?'

The place was by now half full. Gamblers filled the tables, watching the curious spectacle. Karen's cover with Ivan was blown. Ivan raised his wrist to check his gleaming gold watch. He cupped the bright orange chips with both hands and swept them over to Regine. He fumbled for his phone. He had to make an urgent call from outside. Don't worry, he'd be back. Carry on without him. He slid off the stool and hurried out.

'You see what he's like?' Regine beamed, with pride. 'He gives me so many of his chips.'

Regine bet with the Koslov chips. One by one, taking her time, she placed them on either red or black. An hour passed. Then another. Despite her constant searching the room, by twenty past eleven, there was no sign of Ivan.

Soon only six chips remained. 'We keep them. Three for you and three for me,' Regine said, moving three of the chips towards Karen. The remaining chips still cashed up as a small fortune. 'Gambling is bad. You can lose all your money.'

'I don't want to take these,' said Karen, moving the chips back in front of Regine. 'You keep them for yourself.'

Karen was eager to get back to Devonshire Road. It was clear Haruto was unlikely to show his face. Nor Ivan whoever-he-was would return before midnight. It'd been a lengthy day. Regine didn't want to stay on at the casino alone and asserted she had nowhere to go at that late hour. They ordered a taxi back to Karen's flat.

Within fifteen minutes of returning to Chiswick and learning from Regine how Ivan had boasted about stunt driving, Karen confirmed what she'd suspected all along. A check on the website of a casting agency for models established it. Ivan Koslov was, in fact, Ivan Caves from Kent. He'd likely picked up a few words of Russian to compliment his East European looks. He was not a billionaire, but a bouncer, chauffeur, and TV extra.

'Just because this actor looks the same, does not mean it is him,' argued Regine, whilst eating out-of-date ice cream from Karen's freezer.

Ivan was not replying to her messages. Nor Quacker to Karen's. It seemed no one was taking calls from Devonshire Road that night.

The flat was tidier, but still a mess. And further, it'd now gained an extra person.

By midnight, Regine was tucked into the divan in the spare office space, crying her eyes out. Karen was hoping after Regine moved on from her place the following morning, it'd be the end of all the business about Russian imposters.

CHAPTER NINE

KAREN SLEPT HEAVILY and woke at twenty past eight on the Thursday morning to find a voice message from Quacker.

Her boss needed to see her again, as soon as possible. Same as before. If she could. Quacker told her not to drop what she was doing specifically. It seemed she was back and forth to Piccadilly day and night.

She caught her reflection in a shop window as she belted down Turnham Green Terrace. White as a sheet. She'd calculated getting there around ten, earliest. But she was expecting a better session this time. It was worth the sprint.

'You get my voicemail about Tessa Clark?' she opened with, as she burst into the meeting room.

'Yes, I did. I also got a call from her mother. Apparently, you've been bullying her daughter,' Quacker said sternly.

'She'd overlooked a picture she'd put up during her ISIS phase. But I made her take it down. That'll blow over now.'

He looked down at the desk. 'You reckon? Maybe. Maybe not. But I'll speak about that later, if I may.'

'Sure.' Speak about what later if you may?

'How are you on money laundering?' He leant back in his chair. She could tell he still wasn't his old relaxed self.

'Never had enough to worry about,' Karen joked.

46

He was always the first to appreciate a little irony. But not today. He kept his eyes pinned on her. He truly had lost his sense of humour. 'Someone said they saw you leaving the Ritz late last night.'

Instantly Karen recalled Partridge Security placed cameras and door staff in a range of casinos across the city. They'd caught her on tape. Filmed her departing after the time-wasting exercise, propping up a pissed Filipino and piling her into the back of a four-door white Toyota.

'Just wondered if you were on a job, or what? Looked for a second like you were abducting one of their female customers.' Phew. Quacker was making funnies again.

'It was only an identity check.'

'Interested in casino work, are you?'

'Not particularly. Why do you ask?'

'Know about it, do you?'

'Not much,' she said. Only how lots of PIs snapped it up the minute it was available, she thought. Gambling tables are a known gathering point for crooks to steal cash. All this led to greater demand for detectives to monitor them.

'In recent years there've been several occasions where wealthy individuals have sued the establishments when they've lost money. Exploiting the addiction loophole. It's such a hot potato. Billionaires are right on to it. "I've got a gambling problem" is a great excuse to use if you drop an extra million. "You should have stopped me!" More jobs for us.'

'If sitting at a blackjack table all night is your type of thing,' replied Karen. 'I suppose it is.'

'Most of the high-profile cases have been won by the casinos. Were you aware of that? All because of investigators. Might be a good line of work for you.' Quacker looked up and then down at his cuff, waiting for her response. His striped shirt was a Goa job, which his wife Chris had probably brought back.

'I'll think about it. But thanks.' Karen said, eager to end the conversation. 'Chris got home from her trip all right, did she?'

'Yes,' he said, then trailed off. 'This laundering. As we all know London keeps itself afloat on washed money. Big retailers don't care where it comes from.'

'Maybe they don't know.'

'You're right there,' said Quacker. 'Not everyone's a crook! Someone comes into your shop to buy a string of pearls or a fur jacket and pulls out their wallet. You don't ask where the cash has come from, do you? Crazy if you did. Happy to flog the goods any way they can. Especially diamonds and those costly clothes.' There was a brief lull in their conversation before he said, 'Yes, and the reason I asked what you were doing there? We've been tracking a few people.'

We?

'One of these charming characters is a Russian oligarch type who goes by the name of Koslov, Quacker continued. 'Like so many others, he's found a way of getting around the rules. And he's not a bloke you'd bump into in the pub, though you could I guess, if you knew where he went to drink. So, when you showed up on the security camera, I wondered whether you'd had any personal contact with him at the Ritz.'

It was a leading question. He'd seen the tape.

'Only someone who's been putting himself about as Koslov.' There was no escaping it. Karen now filled Quacker in on the full background to her being there. How Regine had pitched up at her flat, cajoled her into going to the casino.

Quacker remembered her. 'Yes, she helped us on the Alesha Downes case, didn't she? Touch of blackmail, then!'

'Let's just say I got talked into doing it,' said Karen. She wasn't about to tell him the bit about Haruto. Her love life was none of Quacker's business.

He tapped his pen on the counter. 'So that was why you were at the roulette table with her?'

Blimey.

'Why did the boyfriend storm out, do you reckon? Looked like he was doing pretty well up until then.'

'She blew my cover straight away. So, it was over,' Karen answered bluntly. 'She'd bought into the idea he was a loaded Russian businessman –'

'When he is, in fact, the—'

'Chauffeur and bodyguard,' Karen cut across.

'Life is full of disappointments.' Quacker was ahead of her. 'Ivan Caves. I know him. When I saw him on camera, I recognised the lad straightaway. Once worked for me on an estate in Brixton doing patrol work. BNP supporter. Yobs used to spray-paint graffiti. Then police discovered one of them unconscious. I suspected Ivan had taken the law into his own hands. Had to let him go. Anyway, it seems like he's found himself a far more lucrative position looking after this Mr Koslov.'

'Is he up to anything wrong?'

'Not at all. His licence is up to date. Just thought I should advise you he can get rather emotional. He has a short fuse. Have you informed the Filipino lady about his real work status?'

'I've pointed it out, shall we say?'

'Good luck with that, then. Well, think about this casino activity. Might suit you better than chasing around after terrorists in headscarves.'

'Can I be the judge of that?'

'Of course. As you say, not everyone wants to sit at a blackjack table all night. But I could do with more investigators there. I've had to resort to having temporaries fill in for me—' Quacker pointed out, rising from his chair to bring the conversation to a close.

'You said you would speak about Tessa Clark. What did you mean it hasn't blown over?'

Quacker was about to wave it off, but he saw Karen wasn't leaving the room without hearing what he had to say.

'I need to know,' she insisted.

He sat down again with a sigh. 'I had a call from a local shop owner in Acton. His daughter was home alone early evening. Someone came to their front door and accused her of being involved in a bride circle. He denies she ever was. Yet I suspect the opposite. Does this name mean anything to you?'

He'd scrawled 'Fatima Ahmed' on a piece of paper and slid it across the desk for Karen to read. She looked at it.

'She was the girl Tessa Clark put me on to. Who got me to meet up with Zinah al-Rashid. You know that.'

'I thought as much. Not that I let on to him about it. I recall the parents weren't fully aware of their daughter's activities, were they? Anyway, this guy set their house alight. Fire brigade called. Apparently, the son sustained facial injuries. English Concern leaflet through the letterbox. It's a Far Right group.'

Karen was aware of an emptiness in her stomach. Two girls in the same Jihadi bridal circle targeted within weeks was more serious and might have a pattern to it. 'I'll get on to that—'

At that point, there was a firm knock on the door.

'There's no need,' Quacker interjected.

No need?

'I've dealt with it myself,' he continued. 'But do let me know if you want this casino work. It's cushy as a number. You just can't drink on the job, which is unfortunate. Otherwise, I'd be doing it myself.' Quacker leant on the table in front to end the meeting.

He was taking her off her own case. Showing her the door.

CHAPTER TEN

QUACKER OPENED THE meeting room door. 'I'll be five minutes.' His quarter to eleven was waiting outside. 'I'm just finishing up. Can you wait? Many thanks.'

Finishing up? Karen was thinking of the philosopher Sun Tzu. In particular, his views on agents. 'Of all matters, none is more confidential than those relating to secret operations,' was a quote from The Art of War. Something serious was unfolding which involved her in a trust issue. To walk out now would be an admission she'd divulged classified information.

'I need to find out what is going on with these girls,' Karen insisted. 'Two from the same circle is no coincidence. You know that. I know that.'

An embarrassing silence lasted about five seconds. Quacker wasn't budging. But nor was she.

'I'm not afraid to go undercover again. I'm masterful at it,' Karen started again.

'The problem is there are a few extra provisos. I'm only thinking about you.'

Karen knew it was useless appealing to Quacker. Begging never works to change someone's mind once it's set. He'd only keep her on out of self-interest. 'If you need someone to look into the Acton attack, go behind the scenes, you know I'm the best one for the job. I understand these people. How they operate.'

'We're talking the Far Right here. And— '

'And I brought this work in. I'm the one who knows who the girls are.'

He shot her a look that suggested he was weakening. 'Yes, you did.'

'I want to do this,' she affirmed. 'Any proviso.' It was a move she would regret.

'You might as well stay on in this meeting, in that case. Hear what Lawrence has got to say.'

Quacker opened the door and ushered in a man in his early thirties with a beard that covered his collar.

'Karen, this is Lawrence Hughes-Lewis. He's from the anti-terror group, Stop Hate. You may have heard of them?'

'Stop Hate Soon Not Late,' Lawrence corrected. Super polite, he bowed his head in greeting. He was also wearing a suit, but this was only because of the dress code of the club. A tee-shirt was just visible under his crumpled shirt.

'Karen Andersen works for me on the cyber front. We've been having a meeting about various matters. She could have an 'in' with someone from the Far Right. And we think they're responsible for the attacks on these Muslim girls we spoke about on the phone.'

They shook hands and took their seats. Lawrence from Stop Hate flipped open his briefcase. He dug around and pulled out a report the thickness of an old phone directory.

Karen was about to get the complete lowdown. Fascism was on the up and up. The Far Right was on the rise. They brainstormed how they could deter them.

'It's no longer hooligans jostling police at football. They're organised groups, most of which MI5 monitor,' Lawrence said.

'Since the assassination of Jo Cox in 2016, the risk from them has increased,' added Quacker.

'Which is why some work filters through to trusted security companies like Partridge,' Lawrence continued. He looked from Karen to Quacker and back again. 'The Far Right is on the move. It's an even greater threat than ISIS. The government has proscribed one neo-Nazi group as a terrorist organisation. More will follow. We're sure of that.'

Karen flicked through the report. It would take some absorbing. 'You can take that,' said Lawrence. 'It's all yours.'

'So— '

'Women who've changed faith to Islam are one of their principal targets. We've had reports from several. Hijab pulling mostly. But rape threats, nasty messages on Twitter.'

'Tessa Clark,' said Quacker. 'And we've had a house attack in Acton that we think's connected.'

'But how?' asked Karen. She was still smarting from his insinuation she'd caused the trouble. This was obviously a wider problem.

Quacker wasn't letting her off just yet. 'As Karen and I were discussing, there's been a breach in data from somewhere.'

'Well, whoever it is, it's only a matter of time before we have a death on our hands.' Lawrence emphasised the point by raising his eyebrows. Assassination was what he was suggesting. 'And seeing as you have a link—'

'With Ivan Koslov for starters.' Quacker had sealed her fate.

'Well, I don't have—'

He'd warned her. You want this case? You take it all. He eased it now with, 'Well, if not, you could help research the online stuff.'

'Exactly. What used to be "Death to traitors, freedom for Britain" is no longer their style. They're more so-*phist*-icated now,' said Lawrence.

Quacker smoothed down the front of his new shirt. He addressed both of them, 'How I see it, the modus operandi of this strange crowd is to stir up the politicos. If you won't deal with the Muslim problem, we will.'

'Yes, yes, yes,' Lawrence added.

Karen shifted in her seat. 'Shouldn't we be more worried about Islamic terrorists coming back from Syria?'

'It's not unrelated, Karen. The Jihadis love all this Far Right activity,' Lawrence answered. 'It takes the heat off them and gives the perfect excuse to rearm.'

'Karen undercovered to get information on a circle of Jihadi brides. In particular, the recruiter Zinah al-Rashid,' Quacker informed Lawrence.

'Oh, well done,' Lawrence said. 'Marvellous.'

'Baz—?' Quacker had forgotten again.

'Basilah. I got Zinah al-Rashid locked up in Bronzefield,' Karen added proudly.

Quacker looked away. 'Yes, well. Erm—'

'She posed as a political candidate and slit the throat of an innocent fellow activist who'd discovered her in her abaya,' Karen reported. 'She then planned a suicide bombing at the Tory Party Conference. She wrote to me the other day saying she didn't kill him, but back then said she did, as well as making other delusional demands. Now calls herself Tammy Bishop.'

There was another pause as the two men looked to one another, then back to Karen. Quacker was first to speak.

'The autopsy confirmed he *could* have killed himself,' he said. 'And other things have happened. There's been a change in her status. Time we brought you up to date.'

'What change?' Karen asked, bemused.

'She's being released.' It was like a silent explosion. *Released?*

'She's agreed to help MI5 with the deradicalisation of fighters and wives coming back from Syria.' Quacker fixed Karen with his gaze. 'As you know we have a huge problem with that. We've already had several hundred return from the Caliphate and they still pose some risk. So, we would need you to meet with her.'

'And she'll be a magnet for the Far Right or whoever is targeting these women.' Lawrence was beaming. 'Unless we find out who - is - behind - these - attacks!'

Karen had showed up at the RAF Club to clear her name over any mishandling of information. It had been vital to prove to Quacker she was trustworthy, diligent and up for any commission. But having to work side by side with someone who'd once tried to kill her was a step too far. Too late.

Quacker's parting shot didn't help. 'Are you back with Haruto yet?' he asked. 'He was at The Ritz the other night. My first thought was that was why you'd gone in there.'

CHAPTER ELEVEN

IT WAS DEFINITELY crazy time!

Karen had landed herself in it well and good. Between a former female Jihadi bride network and the Far Right. She should have stuck to security checks. Her nemesis, Tammy Bishop, a onetime terrorist, had turned model prisoner and was shortly being released from Bronzefield. It had to be an act, thought Karen. She'd written in her two letters about her wish to discover more about her dead mother's past. Karen had conveniently ignored the request. Now she'd be compelled to answer.

Under suspicion of leaking security data to a Far Right extremist group, Quacker had coerced her into investigating Ivan Caves. She had access to him, didn't she? His Filipino girlfriend had overnighted in Karen's spare room. But it was now half-past twelve, and she'd most likely be gone. And Karen had left her key.

She rang her own bell, just in case. Regine hadn't taken off, and all was well. Her not leaving was a mixed blessing. It appeared in the interim she'd taken full possession, had been back and forth to the High Road and was now cooking herself something to eat.

She was sporting Karen's scarlet kimono, having run the water cold in the shower. A mobile on speakers blasted out discordant jazz. There was half a ton of cooked rice on the sideboard. Tangy vinegar was wafting off some freshly chopped carrots and there were two eggs frying.

Making herself at home.

'Where did you go?' Regine asked, taking control. 'I looked for you.'

'I had a meeting.'

'You left your key,' she said. It was clear Regine had used it. That was worrying. The inference she was capable of security breaches still stung. Mostly because it was the truth. The place was a tip. Files and folders were all around for anyone to read. She shouldn't take in overnights and lodgers. Devonshire Road wasn't the average doss house. It was where she worked on occasional high-profile cases.

'You have so much Japanese food in your cupboards.' Regine pinched her nose as a sign that most of it was time-expired.

'I used to go out with a guy from Tokyo. Remember? The one you claimed you saw at The Ritz the other night.' The most unlikely suspect to have been there. An eco-warrior who was supposed to be in Kilimanjaro. Who both Regine and Quacker claimed to have seen at the craps table.

'Old food can make you sick.'

'Regine, how did you meet this man you were with last night?'

'Why. What's it to you?'

'I may need to ask him something.'

'You can't.'

'Why not?'

'I don't want to talk about him to you. He shit. You say so yourself.'

'Have you ever met the real Mr Koslov?'

'Why you think he is not the real Mr Koslov?'

'No, the guy you are seeing is not Ivan Koslov. He's Ivan Caves. We went through all this last night.'

'How do I know you know what you are talking about?'

'You wanted me to find out about him. Remember? I did. He's not who you thought he was. He only works for Koslov.'

Regine was livid. Or at least she pretended to be, closing her eyes and huffing. 'I don't want you on this job anymore.' She threw the tea towel into the sink and crashed her plate on the sideboard. It then occurred to Karen she'd probably known it all along. 'Has he actually ever called himself Ivan Koslov?'

Regine looked at her with incredulity. 'Why would he do that? He just calls himself Ivan. You expect him to call himself Mr? Why would he use the other name?'

'When you first met him, was he alone?'

'No. He was with other men. He came into the Blue Fox when I was singing. Why? Why do you want to know these things?'

'As I said, I might need to speak to him.'

'No. You don't like him.'

'It has nothing to do with me liking him. I merely suggested he was not the real Ivan Koslov.'

'Then why does he have a credit card with this name on it?'

'Possibly because he can put work expenses on his account. Even gambling.'

Regine shrugged her shoulders. Karen could tell by the look in her eye she bloody well knew the truth.

'As Mr Koslov's chauffeur, they would pay him lots of money. He's a bodyguard,' Karen clarified.

'But he's not the billionaire.'

'So what's wrong with that?'

'I am too trusting. I need to trust him. And he is now history.'

Karen's mind was now on separate subjects at once. She had to look into the assaults. Urgently. Two girls being harassed from the same WhatsApp group was not a coincidence. Tammy Bishop aka Zinah al Rashid, who'd set it up, would be a target too if that was so. The government needed her protected. None of the others mattered that much. But morality didn't come into it. Karen was on a case and she had to prove herself, and quickly. But how? How to get back in with the 'Jihadi girls', as Quacker had referred to them?

At the same time, she had to find out whether this Far Right guy with a grudge was a member of English Concern or a lone wolf just using them as a cover. And for this, she had to somehow forge a meeting with the elusive Ivan Koslov. His bodyguard, Regine's ex-lover, was her easiest way in.

'Hist-or-ee,' sing-songed Regine several times, aware she was being highly provocative.

'You shouldn't be too hasty,' Karen said. She didn't want Regine to break ties before she had time to exploit the opportunity. 'He looked like he really cared for you.'

There was a silence between them as they both worked out the best next move in the mind games. Regine broke it first with an explosion of passion.

'Don't you mess with me!' she yelled. Her voice cracked as she cranked up the emotion. 'You said he was a liar. You said bad things about him.'

Oh, don't go down that route, Karen thought. Don't start crying and carrying on. I can't handle it. 'Ok. Calm down and stop shouting. You will bring my neighbour in and I don't want that.'

'Your neighbour much nicer than you.'

'Don't say things like that. Who brought you home here last night? Gave you a place to stay?'

'You only brought me here so you can say bad things about the man who loves me. Because you don't have one of your own. Maybe you want him for yourself?'

With this, Regine disappeared into the bedroom for ten minutes. Karen could hear her on the phone. She returned reeking of perfume and dressed in the high-collared evening dress she'd worn the night before. It seemed inappropriate and out of place for that time of day. Then out of her giant bag, she produced a stretchy belt, which hitched the whole outfit up knee-length. She was going straight back to the Ritz. Ivan whoever-he-was had a room there, and the two of them had made up. The affair was on again.

That suited Karen fine. She could now infiltrate the Koslov circle to learn who was pulling the strings of the Far Right extremist crowd. But before she could arrange anything, Regine stormed out and slammed the door behind her.

CHAPTER TWELVE

WHAT GLEN LIKED about rental cars was you could trade them in for a new model at a moment's notice. He needed to do so now. It was time to stop hassling these girls. It hadn't been a big deal talking to Fatima Ahmed. But he'd heard her screaming. Just in case a neighbour reported his vehicle, he'd changed it.

His master plan was complete. He'd scrap the other girls. He had all their details. But he'd move on. Quit while you're ahead. Forfeit the rest. The visit had restored GG's dignity. Preserved his sanity. By confronting the ex-Jihadi, he'd completed the course. Also Ran, the horse which usually came in last, was at least a finisher.

Speaking in a whisper, he repeated the words, 'Sleep in peace, Greg.'

The Audi then pulled off at Junction 38 at a service station and parked up. He got out, removed his jacket and folded it neatly. It was a warm morning. Being well-dressed and clean-shaven knocked years off. He could still pass for thirty-five, easy.

It had been part of the firm's former success. Their hands-on, but formal approach to business. Look business-like. Even when business meant an inspection of an abandoned building plot. A construction site near Luton. Another one lying empty. Gibbs was a firm that had started out small in the

Home Counties, grown big, and now was going bust. They were in liquidation.

Glen walked towards the restaurant area. There was a rumble of engines and the rattle and stutter of a truck starting up. It reeked of diesel. He smiled at the guy he passed who was walking in a circle to stretch his stiff legs. Remembered the days he'd driven an HGV himself.

The place he'd pulled in at was a known coach and lorry stop. He liked those. At one of the shiny tables, a trucker was poring over a copy of the Racing Post. Truckers were companions and friends.

He managed a friendly smile. 'Picking the winners?'

GG lined up at the cafeteria. He ordered a flat white and a Danish. The barista sprang into action, tapping out used grounds from the filter to produce the goods. He took his tray to the area where there were bistro tables, casting around for a stray copy of The Sun. That morning he was in luck.

The pit stop and the paper were also the start of a chain reaction he couldn't control, from a feeling of calm to one of boiling outrage.

Glen Gibb's visit to Fatima Ahmed's house had made the papers. But only because the facts were lies. The truth spun like a bottle. The headline read: THE TORCHING OF MUSLIM HOUSEHOLD PROVES THAT ENGLISH CONCERN GROUP USE SICKENING VIOLENCE AND SHOULD BE OUTLAWED.

The seconds stretched into minutes. Torched? He barely touched his coffee. He stared over and over at the article. It was definitely Fatima Ahmed. Who else could it be? They used the surname but there was no mention of the former schoolgirl traitor. Nothing about her being on a Jihadi marriage list.

The arson attack baffled him. Arson? How could it have happened? He'd only spoken to her. The coverage was crap. What was going on?

As a responsible citizen, he had to fight back against the lies she spun!

CHAPTER THIRTEEN

REGINE HAD SPAT out her dummy, and it seemed crazy to follow her to the Ritz. Plus, there was too much other work to do on the Jihadi bride circle.

Karen dug out the old burner phones and spread them on the bed. Which one had she used? She identified it from her records. It was as dead as a dodo. The charging was painstaking. Eventually, the phone burst into life. It was like watching paint dry waiting for it fully power up. It took until ten to two in the afternoon to get it operational.

It was nearly three years since Karen had inveigled her way into a WhatsApp channel. Social media was fuelling a Hijrah movement, or Muslim emigration involving young British women. It'd taken a while, but finally she'd got accepted. She'd been working undercover to track Tessa Clark. The private group was for potential Jihadi brides and fundraisers recruited by Zinah al-Rashid. Burly bearded soldiers dominated their chat.

It had been a highly risky operation. Once in it, she'd swayed eighteen-year-old Fatima Ahmed to introduce her to Zinah al-Rashid. She'd been the instigator of the network. The WhatsApp group access had been pivotal to Karen. It helped her flush out the secret ring. Now someone had accessed data from it. How had they done so? Was Karen to blame for it? Had she left the phone somewhere?

It could be fatal for the girls on it. For Tessa Clark, the ISIS bride period had been a fad. So too for many of the others. The gloss was off Daesh. They believed their Jihadi episode was behind them. Forgotten. Their secret. But their past was still ahead of them waiting to catch up.

Now Tessa Clark was watching everyone who entered the lingerie store with an interest. Her safety. The Far Right had torched Fatima Ahmed's parents' freshly decorated home. And Zinah al-Rashid, who had caused all the mayhem in the first place, was the one the authorities wanted to protect. She was about to swan out of prison to re-join British society as Tammy Bishop. Was there no justice?

With the phone charged enough to read, she flicked through the familiar names. Fatima. Amirah. Mia. Yasmin. Zinah. Malika. Her own. At fifteen per cent battery charge, she could post a message on the group as Basilah. 'Hi.' It was still low on battery and plugged in when she set out.

She needed to talk to Fatima Ahmed herself. Find out about the fire. What had happened?

Karen drove to the Chiswick High Road, turning left on to Birkbeck and Churchfield Road towards Acton Central. She knew from Quacker that the former beauty therapist was now working in a 'convenience store'. It was a minute's walk from Acton Central Station, between an op-shop and a computer repairs. Fortunately, there was parking out front.

Karen parked up and entered just as the last of the lunchtime sandwich crowd had left. Fatima had aged five years in the three since she'd last seen her. Both her and a woman who appeared to be her mother were wearing hijabs. They were behind the counter. Karen loitered around the shop waiting to get Fatima on her own. It didn't take too long.

Five minutes later, when Fatima was crouched down stocking a bottom shelf, Karen picked up a box of Weetabix and walked over and stood alongside her.

Fatima looked up at her immediately. Her skin smelt faintly of smoke. Friendly recognition spread across her face. She then turned concerned eyes towards her mother, who was still behind the till, and then back to Karen clutching the cereal.

'I sometimes have it for breakfast,' Karen said.

'You're not covered,' was the first thing Fatima came back with.

'Long story.' Karen recalled the last time they'd met, Karen was wearing Islamic dress.

'You want anything else?'

'That's probably all I need for the moment. You got a moment?' Karen asked softly as Fatima made her way to the till.

At that point, a man appeared from an office at the back of the shop. He was small and thin, but there was an air of menace about him. Fatima slid the cereal under a pile of newspapers. She then intimated she wanted Karen to leave.

Karen picked up it was a charade. And when she was outside in the street, starting up her bike, wondering what would happen next, Fatima emerged. She was holding the yellow and blue packet. Her father had followed her and was watching everything she was doing.

'You left this,' she said to Karen, so her dad could hear.

'Thanks.'

Karen saw a message scrawled on the side. 'Feltham Bowling Alley. 4pm.'

CHAPTER FOURTEEN

FATIMA AHMED PITCHED up late. She didn't arrive at the bowling alley until ten past four. Karen was beginning to think she wouldn't show.

'Basilah?' Her high-pitched voice stood out above the noise of balls dropping and rolling. 'Sorry I'm late. Shall we get on?'

She was a keen and wicked bowler. She'd even played in a team. They could still talk about what was going on in between turns. And that way if anyone was watching her it would look like they were legit. 'I've only got an hour,' she said, punching in her name on a computerised screen.

There came a loud crash and two people in the lane next door high fived. Fatima was motivated into stride. She smoothly swung the next ball and it flew down the lane like a pro. Her hijab bounced around as she sent eight pins flying. She turned back to address Karen, 'I need to know what's going on.'

'Who was it who set your house on fire? How did that happen?'

'That was me. Well, my brother. I left the chip pan on. He just made it worse. But it was all their fault. There was a guy from the Far Right. Listen to me.'

'I'm listening.'

'It's not like I went to Southend or anything?' This was shorthand to mean Syria. 'So why me?' Fatima picked up her second ball and rolled it so it took out

70

one of the two pins left standing. Clonk. When she returned, she then said, 'Don't you see? Someone must have told them about us.'

Karen seized her own ball, which was much too heavy for her. She arced it with determination towards the centre pin and watched as it went straight into the gutter three metres down the lane.

'You should copy what I do. I can see you're no good at this.'

They were not being watched. But Fatima thought they were. She looked round constantly.

Her parents had put two and two together, she told Karen. Learned she'd been up for going to the Caliphate. They'd been livid. But they didn't want anyone else to hear about it. It was so humiliating for them to have their daughter connected with ISIS. It might ruin the marriage they were arranging. They couldn't care a stuff about the chip fire. Her father made it out to be worse to fiddle insurance. Then he'd phoned a detective who lived close by and fed him a load of lies about the Far Right starting it. They'd told the local paper the same thing and given them the extremist leaflet.

She ended her tirade with, 'But how did that guy know about me? He said he was from the Mirror.'

'Do you think he was a proper reporter?' Karen asked, taking her second go.

'How did I know what he was? At first, I thought so. But he knew about Syria. And the government promised no one would know about us. Maybe they lied. That's what they're like, aren't they?'

A third of the way through the game, Fatima had several strikes in a row.

'Yes, we were guaranteed that.' Karen was lagging far behind with the bowling.

'Do you think it was Zinah al-Rashid? She's still in the nick, isn't she?' Fatima turned back to Karen. 'Who do you think it is, Basilah? Has to be someone. Who else would know about the group? I hate Zinah. I hope she stays in there for years. I think it was her who shafted us and told the Far Right who to go for, don't you?'

'Why would she tell them about the girls who wanted to travel to the Caliphate? To Syria? What would be her motive?'

'Because she's crazy, isn't she? And she wrote me a letter the other day. She sent it to the shop. Saying she had renounced Islam and was sorry for what she had done. All about my bomb and that. I hid the letter in my room. What if you-know-who had seen it? She's insane, isn't she? Have you had a letter, Basilah?'

'She doesn't have my address.' This was a lie.

'There was a sister called Amirah who was in the group. She lost her job, didn't she? But you know what?' Fatima confided in Karen. 'She had it coming to her. She renounced her faith. And there was this girl who went to Southend but didn't cross. She moved to the Midlands because her mum found out where she'd been. She's on the group too, isn't she? So, if we still want to serve Allah and marry a fighter we must move quickly. Yeah?'

'And you still want to marry a fighter?'

'Now I do, more than ever.' Fatima stiffened her spine and held up her next ball. 'Unless I do, my parents will force me to wed this utter creep next month. They've been threatening it. They'll kill me if I don't. They're like that.'

They talked through who all the girls were who were left on the WhatsApp group. Amirah—who'd gone back to calling herself Tessa—was history. She was a right loser. Leaving a photo up of herself with the flag. It was all her own fault she'd been trolled.

Fatima plopped down next to Karen. She was wearing all the proper bowling gear. 'I'm far too good for this place, don't you think?' She took a swig of her water. 'And if you can work out who it was who's given our details out, you will let me know, yeah?'

Fatima left on the hour of five to return to the shop. The kitchen wasn't that big of a deal. Her brother's scar was from a bicycle crash when he was five. But it had been useful to name the English Concern Group. Her father was a total asshole and her mother just went along with him. Fatima poured out a stream of her regrets. Not running away. Her fights at home. Defiance and bitterness over an arranged marriage. Her renewed support for Jihad ever since the Far Right bloke had called. It was all out there for Karen to digest.

It was obvious Fatima still bought into Karen's story. Believed in her alias, her false story from years back. She was acting as if she hadn't a clue Karen was working undercover.

CHAPTER FIFTEEN

AT TWENTY PAST four that afternoon, rather than drive north to a property auction, Glen Gibb turned his hire car around. He'd bought a length of hosepipe at the nearby builders' supply store. Suicide was his only way out. It wasn't what he'd planned, but there was no other option.

He knew the area well. An hour away was the perfect place. A side road, badly potted and densely overgrown, led to a building site. The plot belonged to the GG network, which had gone bankrupt. It was all now overgrown bushes and thorny scrub.

Glen Gibb drove the car to where it couldn't be seen from the main road. He turned off the engine. This way it would be over soon. To kill yourself because of business worries was an everyday event. It was a copout, yes. But who would care?

They wouldn't even attribute it to ISIS. Just a guy who'd gone bust. They'd not blame it on the brutal regime. On the crowd who'd butchered his brother. Decent guys like Greg could rot in the desert and the so-called authorities did bugger all. While quislings like Jihadi sympathisers lived high on the hog in the UK.

God, his whole brain ached as if someone had hit it with a sledgehammer. It built to a bone-crushing agony.

He wished he'd torched the Acton house. It was what Fatima Ahmed deserved. But he wasn't responsible. They'd lied through their teeth.

May as well be hung for a sheep as a lamb. If he had his time around, he'd burn the bloody street down. But why take the rap for something you've not done?

And if he killed himself now, they'd think he had done it. They'd believe Ahmed.

Scrap that. He couldn't bring that shame on the family.

His clothes were sweaty. No one had heard him screaming out in rage. Banging the steering wheel. The radio at one hundred and twenty decibels. The isolation had been perfect to bring him out of his crisis.

He finally turned on the ignition and drove away from the empty lot. It was a quarter to six in the evening.

But all of a sudden, he was turbocharged. His mojo was back.

So, this is how these young women showed their true colours. They lied and made up stories that got in the media. Want to play that game? *Let's go.*

The Ashpark Motel was a four-star with parking outside. It was six miles from Cherrywood but situated in a quiet street with no passing traffic.

At six o'clock in the afternoon, Glen Gibb checked into his room. It was ideal for his requirements. All purple and beige, no florals, with a TV, mini-bar, Wi-Fi, and room service. He'd lock himself away for a while. He blamed Fatima Ahmed for not allowing him to die. It was her fault. She'd framed him for the fire. Or was it because he was a coward? A fraidy cat. Someone with the nickname Also Ran would have to be, wouldn't they? He was gutless. He'd chickened out.

Glen's father Garth created the problem. A racehorse fanatic and former journalist he'd given each of his boys first names beginning with G. Nicknamed them his gee gees.

It was always Greg out ahead so Garth called him Midnight. Midnight was a winner. But Glen was the dodger in his father's eyes. He never pushed to the front. He called him Also Ran. When ISIS captured and murdered Midnight, Glen was once again not around. So, the names suited them.

Sweet Mary, his mother, should have stopped Garth's bullying. But she was his doormat. When she'd drowned herself in three feet of water, he'd taken up boozing. He couldn't wipe his feet on his wife anymore.

Glen Gibb idolised Greg. He could have got over the nightmare, he often thought to himself. He'd almost made it. All he needed was to keep the GG firm alive after his brother's death. Become senior GG's replacement. And he'd fought hard. But grief weakened him.

It had hit them all hard. First, they'd blown a fortune on the search. Consumed with regret at having allowed his favourite son to pursue contracts in the Middle East, Garth upped his drinking. He consumed a bottle before breakfast. The old man had wasted away on whiskey and milk first, and shortly after dropped dead of heart failure.

His investments in Aberdeen had crashed in value with the decline in the price of oil. Crippled by debts, he'd made poor decisions. Offloaded good houses and been left with duds. Loaded up with a factory site not fit for a recycling centre. The GG network laid off staff. It was running out of steam. And creditors were baying for blood.

Glen took out his laptop and fired it up. He flicked through the folder of pictures marked 'execution'. Then he opened up the next marked 'Women who love ISIS fighters'. He scrolled through the names and aliases he'd picked up on to see what they'd been up to since. Some had made the trip from the UK to Syria. Others had just been silly girls toying with the idea and craving the status.

He tossed his car keys across the room. What got into their heads? What made girls reject nice guys and get turned on by terrorists?

He imagined stripping Fatima naked and making her crawl on all fours. He'd heard that was how ISIS treated Yazidi girls. Flogged their women and forced them to cover up in black so you couldn't see the bruises.

He'd hunt them down and humiliate them. So Tessa Clark called herself by her English name these days? How convenient! Look what he'd done to her? She deserved it. Glen had found the picture she'd put up and reposted it. Not much really. But White Supremacists and trolls had piled in and shared it on the dark web. They'd done the work for him. Had she learnt her lesson now?

But perhaps he hadn't gone far enough. These women loved bastards. Maybe that's how he should be. A coward dies a thousand deaths, a brave man just one.

Time to man up.
Time to be brave.
Ratchet up the pressure.

CHAPTER SIXTEEN

IT WAS RUSH hour so Karen didn't get back to Devonshire Road until after six. There was no sign of Regine. But she'd called Karen's landline and left a marathon voicemail updating her situation.

Regine and Ivan were out on the town. They'd made up after their scrap. Everything was fine. The limo, the expense account and the occasional room at the Ritz came with working for the actual Ivan Koslov. It was his boss who had big, big money. But Regine didn't care about that anymore.

All you need is love! They were making plans, which included him getting a substantial deposit for a house out of Ivan Koslov. But, despite listening to various messages, which added up to fifteen minutes, there was no mention of Regine having fixed for Karen to meet him.

A call to Quacker after that alerted her boss to the fact Mr Ahmed had spun him a line about the arson attack. Yes, the English Concern Group had called at the door. Fatima had described him as a tall weirdo with mad eyes.

'What's the connection with the WhatsApp group?'

Karen reflected on the link. There could have been some data gone missing. And maybe Tammy Bishop was guilty as Fatima had suggested? If she was about to be released from prison and had turned against the Islamic regime, then that was a possibility.

Quacker dismissed it. Axed the idea straight away. What would be her motive? Anyway, the immediate task was to track down whoever it was who'd knocked at the door.

'I think when it comes to English Concern, they would probably want to know about this activity.'

'I'm doing my best,' Karen said.

'It might be nothing to do with them. And it's giving them a bad name. Most likely a lone wolf.'

'On their website, the group purport to be non-violent.'

'Suggest you move in that direction as quickly as possible,' Quacker retorted, ending the conversation.

CHAPTER SEVENTEEN

TWITTER. FACEBOOK. INSTAGRAM. Look at them. Nine o'clock at night and it's all they're doing.

Tweet. Like. Smiley face.

Glen Gibb chewed on a leathery pizza. He'd decided on a noisy local Italian rather than stay in his room that evening. It was walking distance to the joint, and he'd taken his laptop for a distraction.

He'd ended up stalking for more news on Tessa Clark. MySpace had removed the account. The photo in full Islamic dress with the ISIS flag had vanished. Or she'd taken it down herself. She'd had her fair share of trolling. But he'd shared it plenty and so had others. The mob on the web had gone ballistic.

He checked on her Facebook. She'd set up a new one. He almost laughed out loud when he saw her new picture. An English rose? Hardly. What happened to Amirah, sweetheart?

Glen Gibb kept going over the fire story. These girls were all the same. Jamillah now called herself Beth Lane again. He'd stalked her, watched her activity on Twitter. Learnt how she'd moved up to Cherrywood to live with her aunt. Miss Lane had forgotten all about her little interlude during school term when she'd been right up for travelling to the Caliphate.

He'd seen so many of her type when he was out there searching for his brother. Girls pouring out of Europe. Spoilt teenagers with too little to worry about.

Madness. They trooped out of the West to marry some show-off brandishing a weapon. They posted it as their avatar on WhatsApp.

There was a blog piece to write and post. He'd begun it.

'Young women, wooed by the promise of adventure and Mills and Boon romance in a far distant land evade concerned parents to travel to meet their future murderous spouses. Terrorists. I don't buy it that these privileged adolescents are being groomed. Grooming is what you do to a horse.'

He called for the bill and prepared to leave. His phone buzzed with several texts chasing money. Who in their right fucking mind expected him to answer those at this time of night, he was thinking to himself. Following the social media feed averted his mind. Fun, fun, fun.

He belched some beer gas. It was like tunnel vision. A shot of anger passed through his body. None of this would have happened if it hadn't been for girls like Beth Lane.

Out in the fresh air was a relief. The doughy-laden air of the restaurant had bene oppressive. His failed suicide attempt hadn't been wasted. It was a recce. The perfect location for what he now had in mind.

He jogged all the way back to his room.

CHAPTER EIGHTEEN

HUW THOMAS, MP for Cherrywood, was invariably late. So much so his initials, HT, were shorthand for the fact he often showed up at meetings at Half Time, if at all. He never wore a watch. But on Friday, 12 April, he arrived at his Labour Party constituency office early. At least a quarter past nine was early for him. Birds chirped. A cracking spring day.

He clutched a take-away coffee in hand. To be there fresh and well before ten to do the press interview they'd organised for him, meant he'd be able to scoot off to London where he much preferred to spend most of his life. Huw was looking forward to his Friday evening. Living part-time with Bea Harrington, Baroness Harrington, at her flat in Dolphin Square was convenient for him. Despite their poles-apart politics, she was great fun to be with after a few drinks.

Huw and Bea were the perfect odd couple. Him the Etonian-educated Labour MP waiting for his second divorce, and her, the girl from the council estate who'd 'done good'. Their shared history went as far back as the late 1980s when she'd been an aspiring model after a rich bloke and he'd been the manager of a pop group after making a quick mint.

The Thomas team were already hard at it when he turned up. 'Morning HT. How are you today?' Blinds drawn down blocked the cheerless, cherryless view. Fluorescent lights lit up the large room with its four desks facing the window. At one of them sat Mustafa al-Sayed, his election agent of Pakistani origin, at another, Nigel Harris, the accountant, and the third belonged to a female intern permanently on the phone.

'Do we still need that on?' Huw peeked through the blind before raising it. Instantly the sun shone through. It was clear someone had been there since the crack of dawn when the office would have been in darkness.

'We can turn the overheads off now for sure,' said Mustafa. 'No point wasting power.'

The morning interview would fit in nicely. The sunny forecast gave it twenty-four degrees for later. The topic was internet abuse. How parents were demanding tighter government controls. So, Huw was dressed smart-ish. Suit, red tie, white shirt. Only hint to his flamboyance was his steel-grey hair, which he knotted in a ponytail.

This place is a shithole, let's be honest, he'd often say to his staff about the state of their office. But it was also important to have the Labour banner in place when he was on the local news.

The building needed bulldozing completely. But a company that had quoted a refurbishment had gone bust before they started. Then this was the story throughout Cherrywood. Firms going under. Unemployment. Cutbacks were all to blame.

Huw sat at his cleared desk and tapped his fingers on the surface. What next? Salma got up to make him some instant coffee, which he knew would taste like mud. He raised his take-away coffee cup to her and smiled, 'No need!'

Already he couldn't wait to return to civilisation.

First things first. A text on his mobile from the forty-something Deputy Chair of Cherry Green ward from West Bromwich he'd slept with after a leafleting session. When could she see him next? Married. Obsessive. Fifth message that day. He texted back, 'Let's do dinner week after next.' By then he'd think of another excuse to avoid her.

At Mustafa's side was the hired caseworker who'd moved up from London and had already adopted the Brummie accent when she answered telephone calls. They'd allocated her most of the casework focusing on the female issues such as child allowance. Whispering together as they stuffed envelopes in a small room off to the side were two sixth formers in hijabs on work experience.

'They were both here bright and early too.' Mustafa was stressing a point. 'Listening to that rap stuff through their headphones.' He grinned at Huw, who understood he was poking fun at the teenagers. They were far from the type to play the local drill music with its dark, violent, gangster beats.

'Don't tease them,' said Huw. 'Or they'll be off out the place in no time.'

The girls beamed and continued folding leaflets.

'No, we can't have that. They're doing excellent work here.'

'Well, I'd better brief myself for the paper.' Huw picked up the A4 page that Mustafa had run out on the printer and left on his desk. Everything he needed to say. How social media was having a detrimental impact on the constituents. Cyberbullying was rife.

'And you've put here we've had two suicide attempts because of bullying?'

'Racist bullying,' said Mustafa.

'Can't live without the 'net any more. Got some of the fastest speeds in the country now.' There was no pleasing some people, Huw thought. He crossed his arms and gave Mustafa a cheeky grin.

'I don't agree. The internet does nobody any good.' Nigel Harris was on his usual anti-tech rant. He expounded the merits of the Labour philosophy. 'Equality. Society. Opportunity for all. And a better life for ordinary folk. Where does the worldwide bloody web come into that?'

'You're living in the past, Nigel, my old fruit.'

'And there's this other business, like kids cutting themselves. And where are they getting it from? The sodding 'net. Never heard of it back in my day.' Harris was off.

'Or falling in front of a train to get a selfie,' the intern had found a subject she could contribute to.

'When are they coming, Mustafa? Remind me.' Huw was by now doodling a car. They'd told him ten o'clock when he'd last been in touch so there was plenty of time.

'I re-scheduled for eleven outside the mosque. You've got an hour yet. So, we could go through some post.'

'Mosque? I'm not going to the mosque. Why would I be going there? Tell them to come over here as they always do.'

'We've fixed it for the mosque and they've agreed. Did you not get my message?' Mustafa gave him a sardonic look.

'I was driving. I don't do messages when I'm driving. What was it?' He flicked open his phone and trolled through the inbox.

'I sent a WhatsApp to you, but it was several days ago now.'

'Aha. Found it.' It was a great long thing. 'They've vandalised the mosque again,' Huw started to read. 'Didn't hear that go off, did I?'

'It was forty-eight hours back, Huw. More, maybe. I could see you hadn't got it.' Added to abusive graffiti, which had been happening for months, and a broken window, there'd been two recent attempts to ram the door with shopping trolleys. 'My thought was you could cover that issue too. It'd give them a scoop. This Islamophobia has to stop.'

'I suppose I could,' Huw sighed, already factoring in the extra delay.

'It shouldn't take too long to drive over there. But that's why I changed the time. To allow you the opportunity to make it without being late.'

After thirty minutes of signing letters and reading through the new briefing on the seriousness of the Islamophobic outrage, Huw gathered up his things and drove off. He didn't expect to be returning, so he'd made his farewells. And read his brief.

Instead of the pitch on cyberbullying, the headlines were to be how the Far Right was stirring up trouble. Fair enough.

A camera crew were waiting for him when he arrived at the mosque. They filmed him beside the broken window. The piece to film took all of seven minutes. 'And just one more question–' asked the journalist, pointing the microphone in Huw's direction.

'Internet bullying?' Huw Thomas cut across the question with a practised response. 'Yes, we've had a lot of that. There's more than an argument for banning smartphones in class.'

'No. Something else. Can I ask you, Mr Thomas, is there any truth in the rumour that your constituency is attempting to deselect you?'

Even before he got back to Cherrywood Labour Headquarters, the broadcast bulletins were full of the gossip that the often-absentee MP was on his way out. Unprepared, he'd done a good job. Dismissed it as a tall story put out by the opposition trying to gain a head start in the next election.

'What the fuck is going on?' Huw blasted Mustafa as soon as he was only halfway through the door.

CHAPTER NINETEEN

HUW THOMAS HAD just been humiliated on local television. Made to look like a complete arse. Someone had told the press he was on the list for deselection. The first time he'd heard of it. Who'd rigged it? He rolled up his sleeves and bounced back into the wonky swivel chair. He wanted answers. Someone had engineered the whole thing. Cooked up a story. His muscles tensed as anger engulfed him.

'Can we have some privacy? Go, go.' Mustafa al-Sayed shooed the intern out of the office. He slid his seat to face opposite the MP's desk.

'What the fuck is going on? Who has been briefing these people?' At that moment the MP could have thrown the files in front of him across the room. 'What's this about deselection?'

'Huw, I didn't know about that. I had no idea the interviewer would ask you that.'

'Ask me what exactly?' Huw could tell Mustafa was lying because his voice was higher than usual.

'OK. I will come straight with you.' Mustafa sat forward in the squeaky chair. 'So, I knew that the matter may raise its ugly head at some point. But, not this morning. I didn't expect the press would outsmart us on this issue.'

'What issue?'

'There are some evil forces gathering,' said his election agent. 'They are the ones behind what the press had to ask you. There is absolutely no doubt about that.'

'I don't have a clue about what is going on.'

'Then if you calm down, Huw, I will tell you.'

One of the work experience girls opened the door. 'Can you take a hike for a bit?' said Mustafa, in his Paki-British vernacular. She was waiting for further instruction. 'Go for a walk around the block. Or maybe go for an early lunch.'

'Okay. Cool,' she said, shutting herself out.

'Huw,' Mustafa continued. 'The local constituents, on the whole, are super thrilled with you being their MP. But there are some who are not. They have had their ears bashed. Obviously, they have. And you are aware of how these ideas take root.'

Huw Thomas felt the reddening in his cheeks fade as he took control. Outbursts like this were not his usual behaviour. Also, he needed facts. To know what had led up to the press interview. Why had he not heard about it before? What had the graffiti-plastered Mosque got to do with his deselection?

'So why not fill me in? I'm listening.'

'We need to stem the tide of discontent.' Mustafa passed Huw a full-colour flyer that would explain all. A bunch of people staring into the camera. Beneath it read:

Hundreds of asylum seekers are being tortured in this country. They left Syria to find a better life. But what do they get instead? The Nazis of Britain. Won't anyone listen to us? We are the doctors, teachers, scientists and engineers the community needs, but we are treated like second-class citizens!

90

'Some members are unhappy that you spend so little time here in the constituency. That you are always in the Big Smoke. I have explained how you do good things for us down there–'

'So, the members are missing me? How touching,' Huw said bitterly.

Huw was trying not to be sarcastic. But that was his usual tone when he was caught off guard. He didn't, in fact, care what the members felt about his private life, not one bit. But he couldn't admit that. Nor could he fess up it suited him perfectly for Mustafa to run the office as he wanted to.

Mustafa's son, Ali al-Sayed, worked at the local hospital as a psychiatrist. And it was fine by Huw Thomas for him and his wife, Chadia, to stay in his constituency house when Huw was down in London. Which was why when a sinkhole had opened up outside Ali's front door three months earlier, he'd offered it. But now he was furious. Was that all the thanks you got for helping people out? He flipped out.

'How's Ali?' he said, wanting to rile him. 'Haven't seen him in a while.'

'He's in London I believe today. Then he visits these prisons around the capital.'

'And the renovation work? How's that coming along?' Huw queried.

'Four construction companies have gone under which has put a right cat amongst the pigeons.'

'So, the work is still unfinished? After all this time?'

'If this is about them staying with you?' Mustafa picked up on Huw's sarcasm. 'They can always use our box room. It's cramped, but it will suffice. Obviously, they prefer it at yours. They finished asphalting their road. But the jolly ceiling needs plastering. Hope they are no burden on you. When I know you'll be up in Cherrywood, I make damn well sure they are out long before you arrive.'

'None at all. They're no trouble. Hardly know there's been anyone in the house.' All this was true, but his point had been taken.

He was stinging over the deselection news. Not hearing about it before.

It was hard to hide the fact that Huw Thomas would use any excuse to pursue politics from London if possible. The constituents often saw him out and about in curry houses in Soho and Westminster. With the best Indian food on offer in the UK in downtown Cherrywood, they considered him dining at The Cinnamon Club and Veeraswamy's in Regent Street twice in two days a bit rich.

'It doesn't sit well you always being on Facebook, socialising, with all this going on up here,' said Mustafa, with just enough lack of deference for Huw to question whether he'd handed him too much authority.

'Everyone is talking about what's happening in the town. Last week two girls on their way to school had their hijabs pulled off by two Cherrywood racists and the police did nothing about it. Then there have been these feral youths. As our MP they think maybe you should raise the matter in Parliament.

They well knew there had been an upsurge of Islamophobia right across the UK. The head of the Muslim Council had raised it in the House of Commons. Women in Islamic dress made an easy target. They blamed it on Brexit.

It was perfect timing when Nigel Harris entered the office to scratch around in the drawer for some receipts. The girls were still chatting in the sunshine outside.

'Nigel?' asked Huw. 'Anti-Muslim feeling? On the rise? What d'you think?'

Mustafa looked down to the desk. As if Harris would know.

There was an awkwardness in the room. Nigel Harris was one of those old-fashioned lefties who loved Corbyn and everything he stood for. He hated the rich, all of them. Black or white. Along with big corporations. It always surprised Huw that he was an accountant in the first place with his anti-business views on wealth.

'There are thirty-six thousand households in this constituency and not all of them are Muslim.'

'Quite,' said Huw Thomas, in agreement.

'Me? I've been a Labour voter all my life. Worked my bloody socks off for the party. We've always been for the working man and for the working woman, too. And, mind, some Asians around these parts work hard and are now very well off.' He was studying a receipt like it was a fragment from the Dead Sea Scrolls.

'I think you should read this,' said Mustafa. He handed Huw a letter. It was all about how the MP was not from there in the first place, was white and privileged and didn't represent the people any more. Plus, he'd defected from the Tories, hadn't he?

Deselection? It was there in print. But who was leading it?

'Is there are anything you suggest?' Huw was one of the most colourful MPs in the region, so him being voted out by the constituency was preposterous. But he had to take it seriously.

'They could hold an election at any time,' said Mustafa. 'And this latest conference proposal to cut the threshold to a third hasn't helped.'

He was referring to a trigger ballot whereby, until recently, fifty per cent of local branches and affiliated unions were needed to deselect an MP. 'They've already gone and dumped two jolly players since then.'

'So, you think the association wants to get rid of me?'

Is this for real?

CHAPTER TWENTY

AT NINE-THIRTY on Friday, 11 April, Baroness Harrington of West Lingford emerged from the power shower of the Italian bathroom in her London flat. Her towelling robe was the perfect get-up for a brief scan of the mail first thing.

The recent remake of her living room was a great success. It'd removed the heavy browns of the former decor and replaced them with sunnier colours. Yellows and golds. The communal gardens were in deep purple bloom and they'd forecast temperatures in the early twenties. It couldn't have been a lovelier start to her day. Bloody hot for spring.

Bea Harrington was pretty, spritely and a formidable defender of women's rights. Two, in particular. Pension entitlements for women over sixty and rehabilitation of female prisoners. People wrote her constant emails and letters about these issues. So that morning, when there was a handwritten envelope from HMP Bronzefield, addressed to her, she ripped it open without alarm. It contained:

Dear Bea,

I remember our friendship when I was on the Conservative Party candidate's list. We became close, didn't we? It must have come as a big shock to you that James, the husband you so admired, once abused me as a child.

However, I am very sorry for his suicide. I know that my actions in blackmailing him were not laudable. But neither were they responsible for how he died. It is obvious from what I read in the newspapers that several other women accused him of sexual impropriety. Also, how he was in debt and had a gambling addiction. Addiction is something I have learned much about since I have been in prison. So many of the girls in here should not be serving time for what is, in effect, an illness.

I have now renounced support for radical Islam. As I have explained to the authorities, my birth father converted me when I re-met him later in life. Having never known him as a youngster, I was vulnerable at the age we met when I was twenty-seven, unmarried because of what happened to me, and very confused about people. The American and British Coalition killed him in a drone strike the following year while he was fighting in Syria for what he believed in.

But would I have ever sought him out if my mum was still alive? If she'd not drowned when I was six? Absolutely not. Nor would someone have left me in the care of my stepfather and your husband, which was when the abuse went on. So many of these things would never have happened. Do you see how analytical I have become?

Receiving the letter was like being hit by a freight train. She read it several times to take in the full horror. Petrifying. Maybe fifteen minutes passed while she was pawing at the velour of the sofa, then scratching it. Next minute she was up pacing the room. Her palms were clammy. What to do?

It stunned her. This woman was being released from prison? Was there no justice?

She had to stop marching up and down, wearing the carpet out. There was other mail to deal with. An address to prepare. But she was giddy with fear. She stumbled into the kitchen and steadied herself against the cabinets.

She needed a second shower. It was the only way to slow her heartbeat. She rubbed and scoured until her skin stung. Despite deluging herself with water, the anxiety was still there. Was she paranoid? She had to focus, make a plan. Battle on. And fast. She had to get into some clothes.

She reread the last paragraphs. Their significance.

My mother, who was called Miriam Bishop, is now the fixation of my every waking thought. There was so little I knew about her except she never took her eyes off me from morning till night. They have told me it will assist my mental health to learn more about her, and therefore I intend to commission the Private Investigator, Karen Andersen, to find out further about what happened at the time of her death.

I am getting out of prison on licence to help authorities with their deradicalisation programme. And I hope we, too, will work together again. Are there some committees I can join on my release?

Tammy Bishop.

Husband James and all guilt Bea Harrington felt about his suicide had all but faded until this very moment. But then it all came rushing back. It had been a wretched few years. And Tammy Bishop had been at the centre of the problem. Or at least that was what Bea kept telling herself.

James Harrington, now deceased, had slept with heaps. All social climbers. He'd bloody banged for Britain, it had surfaced. Women came out of the woodwork constantly after he'd killed himself, claiming abuse. Or how he had deceived them!

But a child of seven? He would have had to be in his early thirties when he'd done it. If he had. Tammy Bishop was the creature who'd accused him of it. She'd turned up in his life two decades later as a hopeful Tory candidate. Was he supposed to recognise her? Know who she was? But he hadn't a clue. It'd angered the girl beyond belief. She'd blackmailed him over it.

But for sexual abuse to be the catalyst that drove her to join bloody ISIS was something else. And for her to then want to blow them all sky-high at the Conservative Party Conference. Tammy Bishop, which was what she called herself as of today, was a sodding psycho then, and equally deranged now. She was demented.

She fired up the hissy espresso machine, inhaling the aroma of South America and wishing she was there. A thousand miles away. Brazilian coffee had been James's favourite and somehow, she'd stuck to it in his memory. Maybe time to switch to French.

Bea Harrington had completely turned her life around since James's death. There had been loads of bullshit claims about why he'd leapt from the Bromsgrove Highway footbridge. Out to destroy his reputation. And she was proud of how she'd kept her head held high. It'd been hell. She didn't want to go through that again.

The Tories had rewarded her for it. A peerage for her unpaid work for them for a damn age and a half. Bloody sacrifices. Keeping husband's secrets. No children of her own. Putting to the back of her mind what he could have been up to when he wasn't home. Pretending he was faithful. Covering up for how he'd forced himself on her one night. Remained all-there when Dear Husband had drained the joint accounts dry with his gambling.

She took a stale Austrian pastry out of the fridge. It was rock solid and tasted of nothing. Only good for the food waste bin.

Was she fretting about nothing? Memories of the 'Tammy Kell period' freshly haunted her. How there'd been a full-on terrorist attack at the Tory Conference outside the hall. But how Tammy's lightweight suicide belt had cocked-up. Or she would have killed half the conference. But James had missed it all, having dived from the bridge into the speeding traffic four hours earlier.

Bea was now sharing the flat she and James once jointly owned with a labour MP called Huw Thomas. He had the back room and the second bathroom and was only there half the week. The arrangement was supposed to be temporary, except it'd been close to a year since he'd moved in, and they'd started an apology of an affair. But now they were more mates than lovers. So, she picked up the phone and rang him.

'The bloody woman is deluded,' she said, recounting most of what Tammy had covered in the letter. But not all. Some bits she kept to herself. 'I think I need a second opinion on this.'

'How did she get your address?' he'd asked.

'She used to pester James here with her extortion letters. She's had it all along. I should have sold the damn place, shouldn't I? Got out when I could.'

At one o'clock that day, Bea Harrington had to be in Harley Street. She'd ordered a cab to get her there. Just as well she had an appointment with her psychiatrist. It'd be an excuse to escape the choking apartment. She'd done nothing else all morning but panic about the letter. Sat there for bloody hours. She'd not even renewed the foul-smelling water in her lily bowl. A job for later. It was time to sprint. She threw on a coat, pulled the door behind her and double-locked it.

Then she charged off into the Westminster streets to meet the cab. She refused to let herself reflect too much more on things. Not until she'd spoken to Huw. Her rock. But she was still freaking out. After everything life had dished her out, she'd only ever had her husband's suicide on her conscience and one other matter. And that was the death of Miriam Bishop.

CHAPTER TWENTY-ONE

GLEN GIBB FINALLY found a place to park at the multi-storey in the centre of town. It meant driving round and round because it was Friday afternoon. Crazy busy.

The car park was close to the Cherrywood Library where Beth Lane worked. His plan was to stalk her from behind the bookshelves. He'd monitor her every move. Perhaps he'd overhear something. He needed an excuse, any excuse to get into a conversation with her. Get her chatting.

But where was she? While he was poking around the shelves of non-fiction, he'd ended up thinking about what came next. Did he have a plan? What was he going to say to her? Would she have any clue who he was? For a whole half hour he went through this anguish, flicking pages, glancing over at the front desk. Staking the place out.

Finally, he caught sight of her. Could he believe it? She was still wearing the headscarf! What was that about? If he kept his head in a book, he could spy on her with one eye. He followed her around the huge building with his head down. He felt as if he was sleepwalking. It was mesmerising.

She began talking to another library worker, and he closed in. They were discussing a poetry reading later. She was going to the event. He felt the adrenalin kick in. Don't get too excited. You've done nothing yet. Listen and learn.

There was something library-wise going on. Several of the staff chipped into the conversation with suggestions. They were talking numbers. It was a public gathering. There would be ample opportunity to move in on her then. He knew it in his bones.

He lost himself in *Top 100 Racehorses of All Time*. Began dreaming up what would happen. When he checked again, she'd disappeared.

Was that her leaving through the door?

He pretended to scan the book through the scanner next to the exit and followed her out.

CHAPTER TWENTY-TWO

AT FIVE TO twelve Bea was in the back of a white Toyota Camry Hybrid, cruising along Belgrave Road through Grosvenor Place. She'd finally done something with her Friday morning other than sitting there and moping. She was en route to her psychiatrist.

Bea liked Ali al-Sayed. Also, the fact that he was a Muslim. Didn't that give her a liberal outlook? For a conservative politician that was a good thing, wasn't it? Anyway, it made her feel modern. She was not Islamophobic. She couldn't care a shit about the burka, whether they wanted Halal in East London, or spoke Arabic incessantly on the bus at the top of their voices.

It was Huw Thomas who had first suggested him. Ali was one of his constituents, the son of his election agent and only in Harley Street a few days a month. The rest of the time he practised at Cherrywood Hospital.

Because Ali came from an opposite background, she felt less inhibited with him. She could open up more, which was why she'd gone along with the recommendation.

Bea marvelled at the capital as the cab sped up Park Lane. London now had this horrible knife crime reputation. But it was a great city, the people understated and modest. Maybe fire up a campaign to have Shaftesbury Avenue renamed Shakespeare Avenue. Before the gangs called it Shanksbury Avenue.

And that morning as the car lurched right onto Wigmore Street and left into Wimpole, her phone slipped out of her hand and under the seat in front. Serves her right. She'd been swiping it all through the journey. Huw had cut her short on her call and hadn't got back to her. So what? She could unburden to Ali. There'd been the hideous TV debate two days before. She could cover that fiasco with him too.

They'd been a tricky bunch of shits on the panel. Why'd she gone on the damn programme? The topic was the rise in false rape claims. Sextortion. How women were sleeping with married men and threatening to post it online unless they got a pay-out. Bea had put the star of the show offside with her view that girls should then not play the victim card. Victims, victims, victims.

The host had then sprung her with, 'Your husband, James Harrington–who tragically ended his own life–several women accused him of sexual abuse. How must that have been for you? Dreadful I should think?'

Bea had come back quick as a flash. 'Yes, when these allegations are complete lies.' It'd been the tack Bea had taken all along. Deny all. Stuff them if it wasn't true.

'But as a woman's campaigner, doesn't that put you at odds with feminism?'

'Not at all. I still support women's right to have a safe abortion, get ahead in the workplace. Not be biffed about like a punching bag at home.'

The car dropped her outside the impressive Edwardian building and someone buzzed her in.

Inside was all coral coloured and dim lighting. The door to Ali al-Sayed's consulting room was half open, and he stood beckoning her straight through.

'Good morning Lady Harrington!' greeted the psychiatrist, as he invariably did, at the start of the session. After that, he referred to her by her first name, Bea.

'Your secretary's not here today' Bea said, as she plonked herself onto a firm chair. Hard as concrete. The appointments were always bloody difficult to start.

'She's on a short break. And how has your mood been?' He put his gold-tipped fountain pen down on the table in front and hopped back in his pivot armchair. Taking in how she was 'presenting to him'.

It had been damn awful since she'd got the letter from Tammy Bishop. But no doubt they'd get to that later.

As part of building a rapport, Ali was attuned to her. He now knew a fair bit about her personal life. So, he picked up on the slack. 'How have your thoughts on James been this week?' he continued.

'The same.'

'You are not to blame.' He said the same thing over and over. She was a textbook case. Believed her husband's suicide was her fault, and she should have seen the signs and been able to stop him.

Usually, she welcomed the assurance that being filled with remorse was normal. But doubt clouded her mind. What was it? Did I say something wrong? Did he say something wrong? She couldn't put her finger on it.

'I can't accept how I didn't know what he was up to,' she said, to keep the flow. 'We were married for twenty years. He wanted to leave politics, but I wasn't happy with that. What would he have done after that, was what troubled me?'

But what came out after his death was a shock. He'd told her a pack of lies.

'Making me the liar now,' Bea added.

'Why does what James did make you out to be a liar?' Ali asked.

'He had affairs with other women. And I told the media it was all hocus when it wasn't. That's why. I've just done that again on television.'

Nothing.

It was always slightly irritating the damn silence.

'How is your alcohol intake?'

'I drink too much. I know.'

Bea knew the psychiatrist was devout and prayed five times a day. And didn't touch a drop. It hadn't bothered her before. Why now?

'So, there were other women? You can tell me whatever you like,' said Ali al-Sayed. He was staring into her face. 'You never mentioned that before when we spoke about him.'

Nor the assault. She knew that some Muslim men considered it fair game to rape a wife.

'I don't want to talk about that at the moment.'

Should she show him the letter she received? It was in her bag. Sexual abuse of a seven year old. She had her fingers on it ready to take it out.

She was backing away from that idea fast. But what about the underage bit? She'd heard Muslims believed in girls marrying young.

The silence between them was growing. 'Let's have a heart-to-heart, shall we? When we first met you spoke about your years as a model. When you were in your early thirties. That the death of your husband brought on flashbacks from then.'

She froze. A jolt of fear. That was it. His heart-to-heart. They'd had several of these before. The source of her doubts. What had she told him exactly? She cleared her throat. 'Did I?' Let's go way back, he'd suggested at an earlier meeting.

The smell of new upholstery was overpowering, she leant forward and took a handful of tissues from a box on Ali's desk.

A jumble of mixed memories rushed in. What were they again? Her anxiety issues even before James. The wish to avoid boats. Her constant scrubbing in the shower.

She played it back in her head. 'Something I can't get over. It was years ago. I talked this other model into doing a shoot aboard a boat. It was a band video. There were drugs and stuff. Things happened. She wouldn't have done it without me. And she died. It seems I'm only capable of betraying people, aren't I?'

That was it! She'd told him about St. Tropez. This morning the letter from Bishop had arrived. Had it been a coincidence? How had Tammy Bishop got her information? Bea needed time to think all this through.

So, she said she didn't choose to go over the bad past today. Just the good past. Often, she missed her husband, the decent side of him, their partnership. The outings together. They were of one mind on so many matters. She was lonely and out of medication.

Could Ali al-Sayed have somehow contacted Tammy Bishop? Or was it all in her mind?

'What type of outings?'

She plucked at her cardigan. 'Lovely holidays. We'd go to the rugby. You don't tend to do those things alone.'

'My wife used to play rugby,' he said. 'But for me? I've never as much as held one of those silly shaped balls.'

It caught her unawares. Mrs Ali al-Sayed must be white, she reckoned. But it changed the subject. She would ask Huw later what he knew about Ali. Where else he worked?

Muffled sounds outside the room signalled the secretary was back from her break and the next patient waiting. A convenient excuse to leave. She rose from her seat.

'We've plenty more time,' he assured her.

'I've realised something I need to do urgently.'

What more had she said? Could she trust him? Was he solid? What was wrong?

Perhaps nothing. But she'd check him out all the same.

CHAPTER TWENTY-THREE

GLEN GIBB DIDN'T much care for fast food. But that's where he found himself at five that afternoon. Hanging by the front counter of a downmarket chippie bar in Cherrywood.

His target wore skinny blue jeans and a fashionable leather jacket. And a headdress. He'd taken in all her movements from a distance. Firstly, her working in the library. Clicking on the computer, stacking books. Then the Food Bar. Giving her order. The fryers and ovens beeping. The salt being shaken over her chips.

Glen had expected her to leave with it. She'd picked up her plastic cutlery and thin sticks for stirring crap coffee. But instead, she'd slid to the end of a table. Jamillah, or Beth Lane, as madam now called herself, was tucking into her take-away just inches from him.

The self-obsessed fake female would never pick Glen Gibb as someone she'd been chatting to online on a poetry forum. He'd replied to her on Facebook. Just to get into her head. Actually, he'd become bored with it. But the idea of doing something really wicked excited him suddenly.

He made his way over to where the part-time librarian was eating her greasy chicken and studying her poem. He didn't take his eyes off her until he was in position. And when his coffee spilt, and narrowly missed the poetry, it was on purpose. Clever trick.

'You write that? 'He sat opposite, drinking some hot foamy milk they tried to pass off as a flat white.

The girl looked up and said she did.

'Are you going to the verse reading at the library later?' Deliberate mistake.

She felt compelled to correct him. There was a poetry gathering. But it wasn't at the library. It was another building. Somewhere else.

'There was a poster in the window. I must have read it wrong.'

'Just assumed it was in the library because the one-page advert was on the billboard? Easily done. Sorry about that.'

'I didn't read it carefully enough.'

She apologised. It was confusing, obviously. Where it was being held was only a bus ride away.

Within a few minutes, they were in easy conversation. She had helped organise the small event. She'd even posted it on a poetry forum online.

It's me who responded! You have become so involved with your fake friends on the internet, you wouldn't know if one was in front of you.

'Just as well I ran into you,' he said, introducing himself as GG. He explained that although he wasn't great, he'd written some lines at school.

The car was a problem. He'd poked it in the multi-storey and would have to get it out to go to where the talk was being held. Get there on time. But, seeing as he was going, could he give her a lift?

He could see the thought of being driven was tempting.

'No thanks.' She was looking down at the table. Meet someone and go in his car? No way.

But when he pulled up outside the bus stop when she was out on the street, he knew she'd jump at the lift. By then, the librarian was almost a friend. He presented as respectable in a suit, older. They'd had fifteen minutes in the grotty canteen after all. The black hire car was all shiny with a new upholstery smell. He removed the clutter from the front seat. She jumped in and clicked the belt across her chest.

Plus, he didn't know the way and she could show him. It was an act of pure goodwill. But by now Glen Gibb wasn't in the mood for kindness. And he felt invisible, a nobody, an irrelevance to all.

So much had happened in the last two years to destroy his life. And he held her responsible. The wind rushed in from the open window as he pulled away.

By the time they had navigated the clogged traffic for five minutes, she'd begun to twig it. When she turned and saw the book from the library on the back seat. The question mark look on her face. She recognised the battered, plastic cover.

'You were in the library earlier? You a member?'

'I borrowed a friend's card. Very naughty.' She nearly caught him out. At last! He wasn't entirely invisible to everyone after all. The six-foot-something booted and spurred clean-shaven decent guy was still alive. Functioning.

'I work there.'

'I know.' That shocked her.

'What are you reading?'

He never responded, but gave a slow smile.

But then instead of heading according to her directions, he took a turn away and started hunting with his right hand for something.

For a second, she thought he would produce a knife, a spray, something to immobilise her.

Instead, he thrust an envelope in her face.

'Look at those.'

By now she was shaking. She knew things were taking a bad turn.

Inside the magazine were pictures of gruesome beheadings and white children wielding knives. The title, 'How the ISIS dream turned sour.'

'That's what happened to you, didn't it? Your little fantasy to run away into the sunset? Any help? Now do you know who I am?'

Who was the guy and what did he want?

'I don't know what you mean,' she claimed, with panic in her voice.

Glen knew all these girls were scared of the backlash. Far Right thugs who would make their lives hell if they knew they'd once backed the murderous Islamic State. The right wing extremists were everywhere now, spreading their anti-Muslim hate. Glen could expose them without doing too much to incriminate himself if he was careful. Look at what had happened to Tessa Clark and Fatima Ahmed.

He said, 'I'm with the English Concern Group.'

CHAPTER TWENTY-FOUR

'NO, NO, NO. They hold you in the highest regard.' It was twenty past five on Friday afternoon and Mustafa was pulling out all the stops to convince Huw Thomas, MP for Cherrywood, that his constituents liked him. They'd been in discussion over it most of the day. 'You still have the respect and confidence of the local party.'

'But you just told me I didn't.'

'I also said we need to keep it, Huw,' said Mustafa. 'We don't want these other blighters to blot your copybook, do we?'

Huw threw his hands up in the air. 'Look, what does the region need? Jobs. I'm down in bloody Westminster arguing for investment 24/7.'

'Before that, what Cherrywood has to attract, Huw, is more development. The big stuff.'

'This town does not have quite as much to offer as central Birmingham. Or Nottingham.' He examined his nails. How often they'd gone through all this before.

'What is the problem with Cherrywood becoming the next Wigan?'

'Aside from daily factory closures in favour of overseas manufacturing. Online shopping. Robots doing what people once did? Talent.'

'So, you don't think the folk round here have that? And couldn't be an asset to the great British society?'

'Course I think we have talent. That they're a credit.'

'Well, it doesn't sound it. What I mean is, I know you think they are all good stuff round here, but others don't think you think they are all good stuff round here.'

'Well obviously not,' said Huw, wondering where all this was going.

'I know personally of business people who are looking to put money in here. Cherrywood. Big time. You would get the credit for it, Huw.'

'These things take time.'

'But they are ready to go, man. Go cat go. They have money. The dosh.'

'It's immigration which puts people off.' Nigel Harris clipped a bunch of invoices together to stress his point.

'No, no, no. These individuals I know are not worried by the immigrants. What they concern themselves with is anti-social behaviour in the town. Kids in hoodies. Knife crime. The places of worship being defaced. Huw, you went on TV today, stood in front of the mosque and said you want to do something about it. Now is the chance.'

'I went on TV today because you set it up that way,' Huw Thomas reminded him. But Mustafa was correct. The centre of Cherrywood was rapidly becoming a no-go area after dark. 'There'll be extra money once the UK leaves the EU to replace the slush funds. I'll make sure we qualify for our share. Youth opportunities. Clubs.'

'How's that going to bloody well help? What you need are curfews to take hoodlums off the streets. Get rid. What is the Labour position? A social policy that affects the many, not the few. And you have to ask yourself what do the many want in Cherrywood?'

He was touching on the demographics. The constituency was now on the upside of fifty per cent Muslim.

'This crowd has been buying in Birmingham big time. But they can get far more bang for their buck here. These people could kill two birds with one stone. Revive the community and keep their popular MP in post.'

Crawler, thought Huw.

'What we need is a strong campaign to show them how much you care about them. That you are not just looking at this as a 'job for life'. Hit the nail on the head!'

Huw and Nigel listened as Mustafa outlined his scheme. His 'crowd' had a radical plan for the region with a capital R. They'd set eyes on a block which was all betting shops and an old public house losing money. A bad area. The source of several brawls. Who needed an off licence? Only the winos.

'Nobody wants to visit this part of town anymore. You know that, Huw. It should be actioned.'

Then the argument flared big time. Harris was against the plan. The pub in question had been his local for forty years. 'Pandering to Muslim demands to close pubs is a bad call,' he added.

'There you go again,' shouted Mustafa. His hands were flying around. And he'd heard it all before. How getting rid of The Kings Arms would send the CAMRA crowd into a fit. They were a good Labour lot. Yes, the tavern was a four-hundred-year-old landmark. But, so bloody what?

Nigel Harris also pointed out, as he tapped his fingers on the desk, that, along with the great alehouse and gaming outlets there was a kosher store.

'They can move someplace else,' said Mustafa. 'It's all boarded up anyway, Nige.'

'It's boarded up at night because they smash the windows, that's why.'

'Exactly. So, they'd be better off moving across town.'

'And what are you going to do with the Jewish primary? Shift that too?' Harris was now on his feet, shaking with rage. 'I'm a Labour man through and through, as you know. Bring back the mining community spirit and yours truly is the happiest alive. And don't take this the wrong way, but what Cherrywood doesn't need is another bloody mosque.'

There was a heavy silence. Then Mustafa stormed out.

'I'm going to The Arms,' Nigel said to Huw, after the door slammed shut. 'While it's still open, that is.'

'I'll drop you off,' offered Huw. 'But I won't join you.'

Spend Friday night wallowing in the past? No thanks, he thought.

They left the office together. Huw gave the accountant a lift. He watched from the car as Nigel disappeared inside along with a gaggle of female staff from a nearby shop.

Back home, he took a shower and changed into a clean shirt. The thought of deselection had made him reflect on his own situation seriously. Out of a job? End of a lifestyle? Would the Party follow through with it?

Huw Thomas had served three parliamentary terms since he'd been elected for Cherrywood. He'd joined the Labour party in 2000 as a disillusioned Tory hopeful going nowhere. His selection had been a cakewalk. He'd been the shoe-in over an ethnic candidate. But times had changed. Labour had become more radical.

Despite his sacrifice at having to live forty miles north of Jermyn Street, representing Cherrywood constituency was simple. It was an easy job, and the spec fitted. After all, Huw Thomas was a renegade. He thrived on the challenge.

The unexpected had introduced itself. He wasn't radical enough. Someone at Labour HQ was complicit. He was about to be kicked out for pussyfooting on Muslim issues.

It was ridiculous. Huw Thomas was a hundred per cent the opposite. So much so he'd received a death threat that very morning from some racist nutter. What more did they need?

But Mustafa was right. Huw Thomas needed something to raise his profile in the community.

He called Bea Harrington. 'I'm not going to make it back to Dolphin Square tonight.'

She wasn't too happy. 'You could have let me know earlier.'

'I'm letting you know now.'

He was trying to be humorous. He didn't care if she reacted negatively. Events were out of his control. She sounded on edge. There were three bottles of Polish beer in the fridge that needed drinking. Drowsing under the influence he nodded off on the grey fabric couch.

A call at midnight on his mobile woke him. It was Mustafa. Nigel Harris was in hospital. He'd been in an altercation at the pub. He'd been stabbed four times.

CHAPTER TWENTY-FIVE

IN BRONZEFIELD WOMEN'S Prison, Ashford, Tammy Bishop was conveying her good news to her psychiatrist Ali al-Sayed. It was late Friday afternoon, 12 April. She'd been baring her soul to him for months.

He travelled all the way from Cherrywood on a fortnightly basis to listen. And he followed everything about her past, picked up on everything instantly. Her work for ISIS. What went on with the prisoners. The bullying and backstabbing. He'd absorbed every small detail. They'd even become rather buddy-buddy. And he wore well-tailored suits, très hot.

She knew the moment she saw his face drop he'd not taken the announcement of her early release well. So why had she told him? Because she thought he was an ally, that's why. Hadn't he helped to get her freed?

The officers advised the inmates not to let on to anyone if they were given an early release. Prisoners had a nose for news. It travelled to the wrong people quickly. But she'd never thought that would apply to him. His reaction to it had been unexpected. He was being a bloody pain.

Now her stomach was in knots. There was a clattering from outside the room and a jangling of keys. But inside all was silent. She hated that.

'I want you to tell me exactly what you will do with yourself when you leave here.' There was a tightness in his eyes.

'I'm bursting to talk about it. I've got loads and loads of ideas.' While locked up in Bronzefield, she'd taken on a poker face. It kept her out of trouble. But with Ali al-Sayed, she could be herself again. She could smile!

'Do you think you will miss the place?' His brown eyes were glassy and moist. He was not smiling. 'So many prisoners feel rather uncomfortable when they leave.'

'I won't miss the noise. They slam the doors. And the bloody intercom. The keys always turning. Drives me up the wall.'

'And are you praying?' Since Tammy had been inside, she'd done a lot of that. At first, five times daily to Allah. But towards the end of her term, just once, and to a different God.

'Yes,' she said. 'I pray to speak with Robin Miller's father. Convince him I'm telling the truth. I've written to him, but he doesn't believe me. Why doesn't he accept my story?'

'But is that the truth? Didn't you stab the boy because he was a non-believer? You did it because it was the right thing to do. Come on. Heart-to-heart.'

He was testing her. She got it!

'That's what they are suggesting. But it's not what happened. They refuse to listen to me.'

'How many other letters have you written? And what are you saying in them?' He wanted to know the exact number. Who were they to? And had any replied?

'There is a girl, Fatima Ahmed, who I radicalised. She is still in denial and wants to engage in jihad. She called me an apostate and said I deserved to die.'

'Don't you think an apostate deserves a punishment? You are a good Muslim and you wish to serve Allah. You want to make God's Law supreme on earth.'

She smiled. Another test. 'You're testing me.'

'When you get out of here, you will be ready to perform again. You will study the Koran. You will support the Jihadist cause once more.'

She shook her head and gave a broad grin. 'You have helped me learn about myself. I have forgiven James Harrington who sexually abused me.'

He fixed her with a hard stare. 'You have not forgiven him.'

'Children who've been through abuse often change their dress to cover up their bodies. You told me that. I listened. Maybe that's why I wore the burka, don't you think?'

'You wore it because it was the right thing to wear,' he said. 'And you will seek to take revenge on the West for what Harrington did to you.'

'If you don't forgive, you can never move forward. After what you found out, I wrote to his wife and said all this. I'm hoping she will see me when I get out.'

He was watching her closely. He had his hands locked together in front of him. He'd convinced her she wasn't a bad daughter because of what happened to her. She was free to be herself. But he was acting strangely. Perhaps he was worried ISIS would tempt her back.

'And where will you live when they let you out? Have you thought about that small matter?'

She took out a picture of the Victorian Terrace in Acton Vale her grandmother had left to her. The house with the basement, which had formerly been her operational headquarters.

'How lucky I am, don't you think?' For several months she'd been clipping pictures out of any magazine. Home furnishings. Fancy curtains. She would smarten up the decor throughout. And then put it to good use.

She immediately regretted that too. Hadn't he earlier told her they'd found a sinkhole outside his property. And he and his wife had been 'camping' at his local MP's place when he was out of town. It sounded miserable. Worse than this place.

Perhaps that was why he was in such a foul mood.

CHAPTER TWENTY-SIX

CALM IT, JUST think about what you are doing, Also Ran. Don't lose the plot.

Glen Gibb watched the girl out of the corner of his eye. It was twenty past six in the evening. They were parked at the empty lot. Click! He locked her door from his side of the car. Twenty-four hours ago, he'd come here to kill himself. He hadn't been planning to be back so soon.

He'd watched Beth Lane change. From bubbly to broken. She squirmed in her seat. He'd been planning to kidnap a Jihadi bride for months. But for months he'd dismissed the idea as too fanciful. The idea as something to think about if the visits to the library were unsuccessful. But now he'd done it. The opportunity had presented, and he'd grabbed it.

They sat in silence while she stared at the photographs.

Nothing. The pictures of slaughtered men slipped between her bony legs. She showed no emotion. Unmoved. She didn't care one way or the other about those poor buggers. Also Ran thought she looked like one of those contestants on The Apprentice who sits back and lets the others get into trouble.

'I'm sorry to have to do this,' he said. The crux was she'd brought it on herself, and he told her that. He wasn't born a violent person, nor did he ever want to be one.

'Why am I here?' Her skin was clammy.

'Just look at the pictures.' She was an ignoramus who'd fallen for all the Islamic shit. They punished the innocent. Couldn't she see that? Her chin trembled a little. Would she apologise?

'I don't know what this is.'

'You went to the Islamic State. In 2016.'

'No, I didn't.'

'So, what are you doing back, Jamillah?' It was the name she'd given herself when she first converted to Islam. 'Why didn't you stay out there?'

'I've never been to Syria.' She kept whispering the same thing, her voice cracking. 'Are you a journalist?'

'But you were hoping to, weren't you? Don't lie to me, Jamillah.'

'How do you know that?'

She didn't have a clue why Glen had abducted her. Even though she and all of her other sisters in arms had been well up for viewing the odd stoning. Lynching. Watching men like Greg being slaughtered like a pig. So much for the 'deeply regret involvement' crap in the media. No wonder he'd been fucking driven to this.

It was hot in the car. So why was he shivering uncontrollably? He had, at last, turned the tables. He had the power. He could do whatever he wanted with this girl. She was fully under his control. Just like Greg had been under ISIS. He'd done the same. Driven her to a remote spot just like they'd done with Midnight. So she couldn't escape.

Glen Gibb removed his tie and undid his top button. It was stifling. He got out of the car, shut his side, then crossed over and unlocked her door. She was curling up in the seat.

'Ma'am?' He wanted her out. He had his phone in his hand. It would be dark at ten to eight that night, so time was moving on. 'It's warm, isn't it? But not as warm as the desert.'

She protested.

'Out!' he yelled. He didn't recognise his own voice. Also Ran never shouted. Never raised his voice.

She crumpled with the shock and he caught her by the arm. Pulled her upright. He bound her hands behind her back using his tie.

His deep-seated resentment. Listen, you fake Muslim. Don't you know what you and your lot have done to my family? Destroyed it. Look around at this place. Enjoy!

He yanked off the hijab. Without it, she had the silkiest, softest hair. She even had blue and red streaks. Jamillah was quite a looker. 'Whoa! Very trendy. What's the point of the hair if you can't show it off?'

He pushed her toward the woods. The heavy stench of rotting garbage filled the air. She was scared stiff and hyperventilating.

'Thought you would recite the Koran for me.'

His fury. I paid Tessa Clark back. Posted her picture on Facebook. It was the ISIS supporters who gleefully rejoiced at the death threats that followed. She got fame all right. But at least she's learnt her lesson.

His rage. Everything went ok until Fatima Ahmed. I never torched her house. But her lies spread.

That's the crafty bullshit that got Greg killed.

She squealed in panic. Glen's top pocket square was too small for a gag, but the hijab worked. She turned and fixed her gaze on him, her eyes full and moist as if she was about to cry.

Welling up wasn't good enough. Now he wanted to see her bawl her eyes out. Say sorry.

'You just walk ahead of me. Go!' he bellowed.

The woods were even denser now, and the branches scratched at her leather jacket. He wondered what was going through her head. He hoped it was shame and remorse. Did she see him in the library? Was she filled with regret? But how didn't she recognise him?

He was thinking about what he would do to her in the woods. He must control his emotions. Restrain himself from going too far. He was not a psychopath. He'd been stalking these women for ages. This moment proved it had been worth every dreary minute.

She stopped dead and turned towards him. It was now or never. They were at a trashy patch. Junkies had dropped needles. Shit and condoms. A filthy, dirty place.

'You want to stop here, do you? Well, that might work. But you cannot speak to me. And if we stop here, who knows what I might do to you.'

She struggled to speak to him, but only muffled sounds came through.

'Can't understand that. Arabic is it?' He had flipped. He knew it. 'Here? Really?' He kicked her feet from under her and she fell down hard into the undergrowth. 'Let's get it over with here, shall we?'

'Noooo!' she screamed into the gag, which covered her mouth. Her eyes widened in terror. He must be some kind of crazy psycho. What was he going to do?

He untied her wrists. Took one hand and raised it. A proposal. 'Jamillah, will you marry me?'

Was this a sick joke, she was thinking.

'Don't you recognise me?'

She shook her head, but her mind was racing. He could tell she was thinking hard. Bookshelves? Or the dating site on the 'net? Facebook? Where? Tears streamed down her cheeks. She couldn't help it. He was crazy.

'Now strip completely. You're going to be the star of a show. If you don't do what I say, I'll kill you.'

CHAPTER TWENTY-SEVEN

BETH LANE COULDN'T believe she was still alive. What she had just been through was beyond terrifying. It was freaky. He hadn't raped her at least. Nor beaten her. What she'd just had happen was a million times worse than she'd imagined being kidnapped could be. And it wasn't over yet.

It was growing dark, probably about eight. Maybe after that. The pervert had led her by the hand back to his car. He'd made her put on her headscarf. Forced her to put her clothes back on. What would happen next?

She must make a getaway somehow, she told herself. She had to. But how? The blackness would hide her if she could run fast enough. She would survive somehow and get this dirty old man caught and jailed. Forever. But it seemed impossible. Her legs were jelly already. They wouldn't work at all if she had to use them to run for her life.

He unlocked the passenger door and pushed her in. He circled the front of the vehicle and clambered into the driving seat.

He started the car, switching on the headlights.

Too late now to run, she thought.

'Okay, Jam?' he asked. He'd been using this shortened form of Jamillah. Now all smiles.

It thrilled him the way things had turned out. He kept muttering to himself. Congratulating himself.

But Jam sat there good as gold. What else could she do? She'd expected the full treatment. Rape. Or even to have her throat sliced. So, she gave a half-smile. Form a connection. Maybe he won't kill you. Pretend you like him.

'Oh, you said you wanted to be famous. Don't you remember? When I asked what would make your dreams come true at the chicken place? You said money and fame. Want to see how you could do it? If you want to.'

He took out his phone to show her the film. She turned to the window.

'I feel sick.'

The short videos showed a range of different shots of her uncovered, stripped off, nude. Sprawled legs apart and feigning pleasure.

'Please take me to the main road,' she whispered, as he began to drive. They bumped off down the pot-holed drive and turned back towards the busy junction. 'You can drop me there. I won't say anything.'

'I wouldn't leave you here. Why would I do that? Who do you think I am? All sorts come down here. The council approved it for offices and warehousing.'

'What are you going to do with me?' Her mouth felt like she had swallowed cotton wool.

'Just talk. But you now have the option of when. Right away or tomorrow. It's up to you. I'd like a chat. You could explain things from your side. Maybe we'll get to an apology, eventually.'

'About what things?' She was desperate for water.

'Well, there's only one, really. I understand you don't want to. But you must. So, I can get to figure out why women like you do what you do. And I can stop doing this and get back to my life. Are all of you girls so stupid to want to join a regime that treats you like half a person? I need to know. So, what we will do is sit together and have something to drink or to eat, just you and me.'

'I'm so tired. I want to go home. Please let me go home.'

'We don't have to do it this evening.'

'I have to work at the library tomorrow.'

'After you finish then.'

'No, please don't make me.'

'I shouldn't have to make you. I'm quite decent, really. We will spend more time, just the two of us, talking. Maybe two or three dates. We might get on well. Who knows? Anyway, think it through. I'll come by your work tomorrow.'

'I don't want you to.'

'You're tired right now. Next time we'll go somewhere nice. Not like that shit hole of a place today.'

'Which place?' She looked at him. The guy was totally barking mad. She could smell strong body odour and his breath was stale.

'The chicken shop. You chose that. Not me.'

They drove down Ashington Road towards the town in silence. It was as if time stood still. The indicator clacked as they turned into the main shopping area. He pulled up halfway down the High Street where he'd picked her up earlier and leant over as if to open the door with his left hand. It made her jerk.

'Don't be jumpy.'

As soon as he'd let her, she'd make a bolt for it.

'Can I go?'

'If you do something silly?' He held up his phone with the right one.

'What?' she whispered, tears streaming more than before. The relief of almost being free. A second more and she could be away from him and the nightmare would end.

'This film goes straight up to YouTube. It doesn't have to. You know that, don't you, Jam? It's your call. We just have to hang out for a bit. Talk. Nothing more. Otherwise—a former ISIS bride doing a raunchy movie will get a million hits.'

CHAPTER TWENTY-EIGHT

THE ROYAL OAK at nine o'clock that Friday night was full. Karen Andersen had gone there because Regine was now ignoring her phone calls. She needed to infiltrate the English Concern Group. And upstairs a small meeting of the Camden branch had gathered for a pint and politics.

The organiser was waiting at the top of the stairs for any newcomers. He had a huge beer gut. And the location was always the opening topic. The Far Right had enemies everywhere, so it didn't pay to advertise. 'Find it all right?'

Karen explained she was meeting a friend there who needed to hear what they had to say. The organiser seemed to buy it.

Rubbing his stomach, he ushered her in. The room stank of yeast and hamburger meat. 'Couldn't hold it at the Red Lion, could we? And you can't meet at the White Hart or you're called racist. Rose and Crown. The Plough. The Bulldog. They're ok as names. But they've also got to be near the station. And run by landlords who support us. It's what we have done to ourselves, not being main stream. I'm Kev. And your friend is–?'

'Harry Fraser?' At that moment she wished more than ever he was with her.

'Fraser? Real name or otherwise?' Kev said, he knew that prospective new members often used an assumed one to protect their families. 'Harry Fraser, you say? No, don't know him. Get you a drink while you're waiting?'

'Glass of Chardonnay please, if you're offering,' she said, keeping up the bravado.

Kev moved to the polished wood bar. He placed a hand on a craft tap.

'Nice pub, anyway.' she said. 'I'm Karen.'

Someone passed a beer along the counter. 'Cheers, John,' Kev said.

Karen stepped back to put space between her and the organiser. She had a drink, she was in, standing in the midst of it all.

What was Harry Fraser's interest in the organisation, Kev wanted to know?

At this point, a fresh crowd surged in. One of them was saying, 'Them politicos have to listen. There was this geezer in his robes down the market the other day sounding off about Allah and nobody stopping him. And look how they've taken over Cherrywood.'

'Time to group up, mate. Do some graffiti. Don't you think?' said a thick set member, his arms covered in tattoos. There was a demo coming up the following weekend.

'This is mad, isn't it?' said Kev, as he broke away from Karen to greet them. He offered them a copy of the manifesto, but it seemed they knew it backwards.

'You can't trust the government,' she heard.

Karen picked up the three-page document. It began: 'We will not surrender Europe to our enemies. We oppose political Islam, extreme Islamic regimes and their collaborators.'

A blonde girl joined the group, giving Karen the eye, taking in the wine. 'Well, you're all right then,' she said, with instant hostility.

Kev was already making his way back to them after delivering a quick pep talk to some bikers.

'I'm his other half,' she continued, nodding in his direction. 'So, what brings you and Harry here to join us then?'

Kev lent on the bar to order more drinks. He seemed to be going broke for the cause. His girlfriend pushed her empty glass to the fore.

'Terrible what's happening, isn't it? The Great Caliphate of Britain. Or will be soon.' She fixed Karen for the second time with a sceptical look. 'I'm Lynn.'

Kev joined in. 'Fight fire with fire.' At this, the place erupted in noisy approval. Voices grew louder as the small room filled up.

'No, no, no,' said Lynn. 'That's just playing into their hands, isn't it, Karen?'

'Whose hands?' asked Karen.

'Whose hands? Are you serious? Whose hands do you bloody think? The extremists' hands. The Allahu Akbar lot. They then are well happy, aren't they? Paint us as the bad boys.' She downed the wine.

'What do you make of the ISIS brides and them wanting to come back to the UK?' Karen asked, as casually as she could.

'They're bloody stupid, don't you think? You saw the one on the 'net?' Karen reckoned Lynn had to be talking about Tessa Clark. At last, she was getting somewhere. 'Did you see that?'

'I did.'

'Who d'you reckon gave her the worst time? The Muslims. That's who did.'

'But someone posted it using her Western name. Any ideas who could have done that?'

'Not them.' Lynn nodded towards two young brothers in jackboots with shaven heads. 'They're pussycats, but they don't bleedin' help, do they? Look like ruffians. Get us a bad reputation. Because arseholes from the press set out to do just that. Stitch us up, don't they, Karen?'

'So, what's planned next? I heard about a demo in the week?' The bar was getting raucous. It was hard to make herself heard above the din now. 'Is there anything else organised?'

Lynn spoke into Kev's ear, which prompted him to point Karen towards the stairs. Maybe it would be quieter down there. But the girlfriend looked too pleased with herself. Something had to be up.

When they were alone, Kevin said, 'Like we've got to put up with these Jihadis coming back from Syria and wanting to blow us all up, but we can't say much with the likes of you here.'

It was obvious Lynn had told him Karen was a journalist.

'And you're dying to catch our lot just being rowdy. Or plotting a massacre or direct action. Which is not what we are about.'

'I'm not a journalist,' Karen said bluntly.

She wanted to tell him she was on the target list for a lone wolf Far Right extremist who'd come across names of a group of past British Jihadi brides. Their social media accounts. Women like Basilah. Amirah. Fatima. And she was on it because she worked

135

undercover for Partridge Security who in turn were used by the Home Office to investigate extremism. But that wouldn't fly. And anyway, by that time they'd physically bundled her out the door.

CHAPTER TWENTY-NINE

IT WAS THE PERFECT fill in! A meeting of the English Concern Group was taking place in North London. He could just make it for nine if he put his foot down.

So Glen Gibb did not return to the motel, but drove straight away to Camden. He'd see what it was like. Maybe to atone for her sins he would one day bring Beth Lane along to one. Who knows? It depended on how they got along on Saturday.

It was a smart move. Listen and learn. He might pick up more news on the Acton fire. The Ahmeds had blamed him for causing the blaze. Falsely accused. They'd named the English Concern Group because Glen had left behind one of their handouts. But at the right wing meet up, there was not a peep about it. That's thanks for you! Just a crowd of half pissed pansies boasting about having kicked out some unauthorised journalist and a load of waffle about the demo coming up the following week.

The whole notion of marching down a street holding a banner didn't excite him. On the other hand, nor did the Swedish activists; a mob of hooligans in balaclavas who attacked anyone who looked foreign.

GG ordered a glass of Merlot and stood at the back of the bar. What was the point of these meetings? They were maddening. The swaggering annoyed him. Just a bunch of dills downing pints and acting tough.

He watched the organiser's girlfriend sweet-talking to get signatures. He'd seen her before. Completely clueless. She was along for the fun, nothing more.

This lot were all piss and wind, he thought. They were the 'coming on the march?' sort. So why was he there? Restocking with more of their leaflets? Why bother? He'd plenty of his own material now. Evil deeds do not go unpunished! The bastards who had killed Greg deserved to be taken down. The women who helped them play out their macabre fantasies. They were as much to blame, if not more. The ISIS bride who laughed when she found a human head in her dustbin.

GG had been against physical retaliation all his life. Until this point. The boy his father called Also Ran had always been the one at the tail end, a nonstarter, behind the fight. Nonviolent, love-thy-neighbour type. And a damn sissy. Where was he when Midnight needed him? Bloody nowhere. Turn the other cheek? Not anymore.

A commotion at the head of the stairs signalled an infiltration by an opposing group. Three Islamic lads had come up to provoke. They were standing together, arms crossed. Kev was on to them straight away.

'Look, mate,' he told the guy ordering crisps. 'This is a private meetup to organise a peaceful demo. We want no trouble.'

GG squeezed through the drinkers, holding in his tie, past the dartboard on the wall, and down the narrow stairs. He exited the pub. The Muslims had left a brother outside. One of the young pups, head in his phone, checking his status.

Beside the front door where the smokers went to light up, were two empty beer bottles. Sitting on the sill. GG picked one up and smashed it behind his back against the bricks. The shards fell to the ground around him. He held it tight against his upper right thigh. The lad looked up at the noise. He gave a friendly nod.

GG had a charge of energy. He'd half seen it in his mind. Pulling the Muslim towards him, smashing the rim into his face. Disfiguring him, like he'd been accused of.

He could have got away with it. Maybe slashing out would stop him going insane with bitterness. Perhaps Glen could have then sent him flying into the downstairs revellers. It would have taken them an age to work out who'd cut him. They would have once again pinned his actions on the ECG.

Instead, he walked from the scene. It was a quarter past ten in the evening. Character is a powerful defence in a world that would like to change you. At that moment Glen Gibb believed he had heaps of that. He'd never resorted to brutality. And he had to keep sharp.

He had a date with Beth Lane the next day.

CHAPTER THIRTY

BETH LANE HAD been at home for three hours. After the abuser had dropped her, she'd run all the way from the town centre via the back routes.

She'd let herself in, collapsed on the sofa. Drowned herself in the shower until the plug was blocked. Washed the scary memories away. Him watching her undress, filming her doing things. It was now just after eleven at night and she felt no better.

Beth Lane was living with her aunt who worked nights. They shared a small terraced house near the Cherrywood Bus Garage. The situation worked well because her mother's younger sister knew nothing of what happened back in 2016. How Beth had gone to Turkey. All she'd been told was Beth's mother disapproved of her daughter's conversion to Islam and had kicked her out.

The job was great. She'd been working at the library for six months now. She still wore the headscarf because so many young women did in Cherrywood. It was cool to do so. Everyone knew her as Beth. No one called her Jamillah.

So how long had he been stalking her? Where did he learn the things he knew which were secret? He'd asked her about Zinah al-Rashid who'd recruited her to the Islamic cause. Why? She was in prison.

And what about tomorrow? Was he serious? He'd crowed about having exposed a girl as a former Jihadi sympathiser before. Was that true?

Beth knew she should have gone straight to the police. But the idea terrified her. The past was the past. And if she told them about the abduction, it would all come out. Turkey would no longer be a secret. And then the creep would have won. And what if they didn't believe her? Maybe they'd die laughing. What then? The shame she felt was mortifying. But she had to tell someone about it. The other girls on the WhatsApp group who'd put themselves forward for Syria would be sympathetic.

What had happened to them? It was more than a year since she'd been on it.

She took out her phone and scrolled through twenty or more groups until it came up under Zinah London. She was still under the name of Jamillah. There were a thousand messages to catch up on. Some new people.

The group was still mega-active. The latest message was a selfie of Basilah at a bowling alley with Fatima.

Jamillah: Hi. Anyone from here give out my address?

A few seconds later, a reply.

Mia: Not me, mate. How's you?

Jamillah: A guy just kidnapped me. The English Concern Group. He came to where I work at the library.

Yasmin: What did he look like?

Jamillah: Tall guy. I was crazy scared

141

Malika: OMG. Fatima's house got torched.

Yasmin: How d'you know that?

Malika: Read it in the paper. And Tessa Clark who was Amirah was abused online. He posted stuff on her.

Jamillah: He'll do that to me.

Malika: That was all over. Why did you not see it?

Jamillah: She ok? Was it the same guy?

Fatima: Yeah. I'm fine. Just the kitchen got burnt. My Dad told the police it was the Far Right. But a guy like that came to my house. Tall bloke.

Jamillah: Wearing a suit?

Mia: Someone's posted shit on my Twitter. Zinah's in prison. She can't have her phone in there. So, it wasn't her.

Fatima: Someone knows who we are.

Mia: You been to the cops?

Jamillah: No. He's got naked pictures of me. He wants to meet me!!!

Yasmin: What you gonna do?

Jamillah: He's coming back tomorrow.

Fatima: How many in your office, Jam?

Jamillah: It's the library.

Malika: You posted you got the library job in Cherrywood last year.

Fatima: Basilah came by my Dad's shop. We went bowling. She didn't know about the guy who's been doing this.

Jamillah: I don't want to go to work.

Fatima: When do you have to go in?

Jamillah: Tomorrow. I'll say I'm sick.

Yasmin: Go into work.

Fatima: Yeah. You gotta tell them, sis.

Jamillah: I'll lose my job if they find out. I feel like I'm being watched by him.

Malika: You need to get away, sis. You should get a train to London.

Jamillah: I can't go home. I don't get on with my mum.

Malika: Can anyone put you up from here?

Fatima: You can't come to my home. My parents are acting up. Want me to marry. And Mia's been stalked by him. I can give you Basilah's address.

Jamillah: How?

Basilah: Basilah here. Don't post too much on this WhatsApp group. Someone may have hacked it.

CHAPTER THIRTY-ONE

ANOTHER VICTIM. AN abduction. What next? The news was a catalyst. It stirred Karen Andersen into action. It was vital to find the guy who was fronting up to the onetime Jihadi girls.

A late-night trip to the Ritz had located Regine who was still off with her, and Ivan Caves refused to leave the roulette table. But she couldn't stay around waiting forever. She returned to Devonshire Road. At half-past one on Saturday morning, Regine sent a message to say she'd 'sorted something'.

So, the following day, a black motorcycle with Karen Andersen bent over the controls sped out of Chiswick at a quarter to ten. She took the A4 via the Hogarth Roundabout, tore through Fulham and down Wandsworth Bridge Road en route to Battersea.

Her style of dress was black jeans, a leather biking jacket and engineering boots. She was expecting to find Caves waiting for her. But nothing was for certain. What had Regine told him to get her an introduction to the brains behind the English Concern Group? Why Battersea Heliport?

Everything remained a mystery. It only deepened when she was welcomed into the hush-hush circle by a guy in navy-blue uniform and Tom Cruise shades with, 'My name is Alex. You have a meeting with Mr Koslov? Follow me. Let's go!'

He led the way to a small helicopter. Alex had perfect stubble and close-cropped hair. 'Hope you're not afraid of heights?' he said, as they boarded.

The rotor blades sprung into life and lifted the chopper clear of the deck. At 300 feet it banked hard left to pick up the cleared track south-west. Karen looked down on the Thames and felt airsick.

Where were they going? Why the secrecy? But it seemed this was one way the enigmatic Russian billionaire travelled to and from his office. It was no big deal.

Karen was hopeful by the texts she'd sent last minute that Quacker at least would track her. But then a strange possibility occurred to her. That maybe Koslov thought she was delving into his money laundering. And that made her feel instantly on-edge. But if so, why wouldn't the pilot have taken her phone?

'Where are we going exactly?' she shouted to him over the din.

'They ordered me to deliver you. That's all. No questions.'

CHAPTER THIRTY-TWO

AT 2,000 FEET, with a pale blue sky above and the twisty Thames below, Karen Andersen assessed the situation. It was just eleven-thirty and she had no idea what the pilot had planned. She shivered. How had she got herself into this position?

She choked back her fear and suddenly needed Haruto. Regine had used him as bait to get Karen to take on her ridiculous case. Without the strong urge to see him again, she would not have gone to the casino. And not involved herself with Ivan Caves. Not be here right now.

He'd been at the Ritz because Quacker had confirmed that. Why? Where was he? Why had he not got back in touch? What was love? Women fall in love with love itself, the story, the fairy tale. For example, Fatima Ahmed lusted after a warrior, a macho and fearless fighter, any fighter. It was clear as the air around that love drove women to do mad things.

Or women fall in love with what the man can provide for them, the implicit security. Take Regine. Was that her motive? Was she in love with Caves or just flattered because he was spending money on her?

Or they fall in love with the validation. 'If I am with someone, then I must have moved up the food chain.' Or the man himself? Surely that's how it should be.

She used the interphone this time to get through to the pilot. 'Perhaps you could give me a clue where are we headed exactly?' The helicopter was en route out of London. But what was the destination?

'We're going to where Mr Koslov has one of his places of residence. That's all I can tell you.' Alex was saying nothing.

As a distraction, Karen resumed her musing. Women can just fall in love because someone makes them feel protected. Haruto had made her feel safe.
Fear of God. Why was she trembling? She could cope ok. But not seeing Haruto again scared the hell out of her.

Attraction isn't an option. It's instant. Unavoidable. It's not something you can switch on and off. And that's how she'd felt the first time they'd met. But after that, what? She'd become too emotionally dependent on him.

'Love is a choice, isn't it?' she said to Pilot Alex, who seemed to chuckle. It was a one-way conversation.
And Karen Andersen had allowed herself to fall in love with Haruto Fraser. And right then she had an uncontrollable urge to communicate with him.

She'd shoot him a text. A goodbye message, just in case. She tapped out the words, 'I love you. I have always loved you. For whatever reason you broke off with me, I understand. Karen.'

So, she spent the next ten minutes staring not out at the view, but down at the phone. Should she press send? She had the shakes.

Just wait a while longer. When she got back, if she got back, she would call and speak to him in person.

The helicopter landed on a lawn the size of a football pitch, behind a massive Palladian-style pile. The smell of freshly mowed lawn swept through the cockpit.

Karen was expecting the pilot to wait to fly her back to the city. But before he could shut down the engines a woman, neatly dressed in black, ran up to the helicopter and shouted over the blade noise, 'You can go now. Mr Koslov will handle it from here.'

And without further ado, the pilot applied take-off power and departed in the direction of London.

CHAPTER THIRTY-THREE

GLEN GIBB HATED mirrors. He would walk a hundred miles out of his way to avoid them. They upset him. But that Saturday morning he felt different. He snuck a look.

You're not that bad! What's the problem? Pull yourself together.

He straightened his hair, checked his profile and raised his chin. He was tall, tick. Dark-haired, tick. Handsome?

Speaking in a hushed voice he said, 'Greg. Why can't I be like you?'

He'd had no trouble accepting his twin brother physically looked like him. They were peas in a pod. Same build, same facial features. But Greg Gibb was a super guy. Women flocked to him. He was witty and wise. A babe magnet and a brilliant friend. When Glen compared the two of them, he didn't come anywhere close. Greg Gibb had more in his little finger than Glen in his whole body. Greg outshone Glen a hundred to one.

He'd had one fantasy all his life. He'd dreamt it up when he was twelve years old. It was about turning into his brother. Waking up and being someone so so different. Going to bed as Also Ran and getting up in the morning as Midnight. A story he told himself over and over to try and better himself. He made up stories in his head to stop going insane with self-loathing.

Glen Gibb had committed everything about his beloved brother to memory. Just as well, because he was dead, wasn't he? He would go over and over all the details about him in the hope that one day Glen himself would become a stronger person like his brother. Maybe he would start the transformation today.

At eleven-thirty in the morning on Saturday, 13 April he found his mind wandering again. He could visualise every detail of Cherrywood Library. How would Greg handle this? What would he do in Glen's place? He'd been consumed with 'what would Greg do?' ever since he was first locked in the stinking stable. The first time for being late. But after that for just being behind. Being a failure. Being Glen Gibb.

'You're a completely useless piece of shit, Also Ran. How can you not be more like your brother? You should be. You're a bloody twin, after all.'

He knew more than anyone alive about looking the same but feeling different. He'd even been part of a trial on twins for a German researcher. They'd found it boiled down to 'non-shared environmental and stored experiences.'

No one understood it. Not his father. Not his mother. Only Greg. The brother who would find him in the horse box or the outhouse and let him out.

Glen went over his action plan. If he could act more like Greg, maybe Beth Lane would fall in love with him.

CHAPTER THIRTY-FOUR

'TAMMY BISHOP GETS out next Wednesday,' Quacker addressed a Stop Hate gathering. They'd convened around his kitchen table. 'And we've got a lone wolf activist it seems with a fetish for female Western converts. We heard of another girl he's had dealings with. My investigator is working on leads as we speak.'

They had all agreed on keeping it from the press as much as possible. Which meant no blogs, no comments, no social media. Since Bishop had been inside, there'd been the Manchester arena bombing where women and children had been targets.

'Not a lot of sympathy for reformed terrorists.' The campaign leader wasn't interested in rocking the boat.

Quacker watched with interest a bug crawling across his brief before swatting it flat. The unexpected high temperatures for the season had brought out the pests early. 'London Bridge.' Whack! 'Westminster Bridge.' Thud!

The Stop Hate boss leapt up to join in. 'I'm coming to get you, little bastard!' he called out to the fly, following its progress with a rolled-up newspaper from the table to the ceiling and over to the food waste bin.

'It's the warm weather, brings them in,' said Quacker. He sat back in his chair. 'But back to Tammy Bishop. This woman doesn't help herself. She's been firing off letters all around the place, including to myself.'

He handed over a letter he'd received the day before. She had addressed it to him in person at the Met and they had passed it on to him.

She'd written: I've also sent letters to Karen Andersen, Bea Harrington, David Miller, Fatima Ahmed, Tessa Clark. I was hoping to get the addresses of some other women I radicalised. Could you assist? I believe a full apology and explanation of my deeds will help them recover from their ordeal.

'But Bishop is nothing special any more,' said Quacker. 'She's been silent as a mouse since her stint in Bronzefield. Very remorseful. And found a new interest I expect. But the public doesn't know that. Nor would they believe she's not a threat anymore.'

'They get mad. And the Far-Right loonies go on the offensive. Take it out on the innocent many.' The Stop Hate campaign leader referred to the attack on a crowd of Muslim worshippers where a grandfather had been killed.

Once it was over and everyone had left Quacker reread a psychiatric report on Tammy Bishop.

Miss Bishop (formerly Kell), a former sales person from Harrods, describes her struggle with insecurity in certain interpersonal interactions and social contexts when they involve competitive colleagues. In these situations, she shakes, loses cognitive flexibility, and cannot access words and expressions. She has been struggling with this since primary school and losing her mother at six, leaving her to be brought up by a stepfather, Archie Smythe, who punished her when she could not answer questions normally. In addition, she experienced sexual abuse at seven years when left one day with an employee of her stepfather's. On reporting the episode, her stepfather then labelled her a storyteller. He threatened to place her "in care" if she repeated the tale.

Despite her own feelings of inadequacy, Miss Bishop is perceived by her peers as a high-achieving, demanding personality who can make others feel insecure or even resentful. She claims never to have had any close friends. Her incarceration has allowed Miss Bishop the opportunity to seek treatment to address her drive to assume false identities. For many years she has hidden extreme mood swings and the need to exaggerate or create fictitious past endeavours. These mental adventures have helped her in the past to manage stress, insecurity, and the difficulty of intimate relationships. Tammy Bishop has never had a sexual encounter with another adult. She would now like to explore those options before she is in her mid-thirties.

It was signed off by Ali al-Sayed. He was an expert in Muslim mental health and had volunteered to study her case.

There was a vibration on the inside of his top pocket. A call. He expected it to be Karen Andersen with some inside information. But it was David Miller. He'd received his third Tammy Bishop letter.

'This is my son's killer. Why is she being released?'

As expected, Tammy had broken the code of silence herself.

David Miller was furious. He refused to acknowledge her as Tammy Bishop. She was still Zinah al-Rashid to him. And he believed she was a thousand per cent guilty of the murder of his twenty-one-year-old son, Robin. Why had she changed her story?

'She should be ashamed. You all should. I'm not buying into her lies.'

'Yes, it's upsetting.'

'She conveniently doesn't give the address of where she'll be living.'

'No, they have advised her against revealing where that'll be.'

'If she thinks she can hide away in a safe house she's mistaken.'

'Right.'

'Do you know where it is?'

'As a matter of fact, I don't.' It was a lie. Quacker knew where she'd be. But he sensed Miller was out to settle a personal score. It'd be wise to keep her address away from him. And anyway, a safe house wouldn't stay safe if everyone knew where it was. 'And there is just the chance her story stacks.'

'Why would Robin do that to himself? It makes little sense.' David Miller sounded close to tears. Quacker didn't want to elaborate on the throat injury. It was that which had killed him. 'And if he did take his own life, then someone's got to be answerable to have driven him to that point.'

Yes, Robin Miller had been sidelined, Quacker agreed.

Miller was correct. However, his son's bullying by some oaf in the Tory party, which had led to his suicide, was no big deal any more. Everything had moved on, hadn't it? Death threats through the mail were two a penny. Internet abuse: a rite of passage in political life. Intimidation was part of the Westminster culture. What could they do about it? The whole issue was passé.

CHAPTER THIRTY-FIVE

HUW THOMAS SEARCHED the cupboards for more coffee. He was rarely at his constituency home these days. He'd almost forgotten what was there. It was eleven-thirty on Saturday morning and he was in Cherrywood, when he'd expected to be back in London. It grated.

By good fortune, Ali al-Sayed, who'd stayed at the house the week before, had replenished stocks. Thank God Ali, a strict Muslim, considered caffeine *halal* and thus ok, unlike cigarettes and whiskey.

The news of his deselection rankled even more. It had kept him on the phone all night so he could head south first thing. But the assault on the accountant, Nigel Harris, was the final straw. His weekend was doomed.

Aggression on the streets was on the rise. Harris was just another number. A member of the public had spotted two young thugs hot-footing it from the pub where he'd been drinking. They were most likely the same ones who'd set fire to hedges at the school. It's how they got their kicks. Small fry, the police would have them in no time.

Just as the kettle came to the boil, the post arrived. Picking a letter up, he immediately recognised the scribbled scrawl. Huw felt his body temperature rise at the content. It accused him of being a 'Muslim lover who'd get what he deserved'. Unsigned. Another illiterate no doubt. Oh, the irony of it all, he thought.

He didn't want to waste precious life on crap like that. Even a report to the police meant clearing the diary again, focusing on nothing else. He would rather forget about it.

He chomped on the last of the biscuits and tried to collect his thoughts. Put on the agenda to do a shop locally. Priorities first. But the letter more annoyed than spooked, him. Didn't being abused by a bigot prove he was pro Muslim? So why did he have to go further? Where was all this coming from? Because it'd been on the news?

He heard the text tone sound and idly glanced down to read it. The crazy woman he'd slept with. 'Huw, I am in love with you. Do you remember how you asked if I was happy? I'll leave Fred. It's the only way.'

That got his attention. *Don't come up here to Cherrywood!* He replied immediately. 'This is not a great moment. I am very, very fond of you. But do not, do not move out. Someone from our office has been knifed. He's hanging in the balance. I need to spend time with him right now.'

Next, he put in a call to Mustafa who was organising flowers for the hospital.

'Looks like he's bloody discharged himself already,' Mustafa told him.

The situation was better than first reported. Far better, by the sounds of things.

'That pub is history,' Mustafa went on. 'Just brings trouble. But as I saw your car out front and as you are still around, you could probably manage a surgery, couldn't you? I have cancellation appointments in the diary I can reinstate. People will be so pleased to meet with you Huwie. They really will. And after that, you could whizz back up to the mosque and get some pictures with the imam. They were really disappointed not to see you yesterday.'

Huw Thomas didn't disagree for once. And when he told Mustafa about the abusive letter he'd received, he replied with, 'You know? That is a good thing, not a bad thing. Perhaps it would be great publicity. Sometimes you have to take what you can get.'

CHAPTER THIRTY-SIX

HALF AN HOUR later Huw Thomas strode into the Cherrywood Library. He felt empowered. The fact that Nigel Harris was on the mend boosted him. The sun shone brightly from the spring sky. It was the first surgery he'd attended in three months. He was looking forward to it.

'How was the poetry reading?' Huw Thomas pointed to the by now out-of-date poster on the wall. He was searching for clues about town activities to engage with the locals. Apply the charm, he told himself, but keep alert. He'd been threatened after all.

'It went very well. But there were several no-shows. Maybe the ad was misleading,' the library manager told him.

'And where's the nice young lady who usually helps me when I do a surgery?' Huw asked.

'Beth Lane? She normally works on a Saturday. But she called in sick. Very popular, isn't she? That man over there was just asking about her too.' The manager pointed at the exit.

Huw Thomas turned to see a tall, smartly dressed man leaving the library by the revolving glass door. He shrugged and strolled over to his allotted desk at the back as the public drifted in.

Mustafa had done wonders, he thought. He'd shifted the local councillor to the afternoon to make it possible to hold court. He greeted his constituents.

The Somalian family had benefits issues and he could pass that on. The head of Cherrywood Plumbing had anti-social behaviour issues with his neighbours. Everyone needed more money. And housing. And the streets to be rid of knife crime. They'd all heard of the attack on Nigel Harris. Opiodes had hit the streets lately with deadly effect. Standard stuff in general to get his caseworker to chase up.

An hour later Huw made his excuses and drove off to meet Mustafa at the mosque, who was waiting for him, beaming broadly.

'I have informed them about the death threat. This really is a police matter but let us keep it to ourselves for now.'

'Lead on McDuff,' said Huw.

Mustafa was in a brilliant mood. Huw Thomas did as he was told. He kicked off his shoes and placed them in an orderly row with several other pairs. They both padded barefoot across to meet the assembled reception committee.

'I wanted to learn more about these graffiti attacks. And the intimidation of Muslim girls.'

The Imam reacted with pleased surprise. Their MP was getting into the issues. Right on to it. Everyone was happy. 'We are most grateful for you speaking to the media from here yesterday. You don't know what that means to us,' he said, with a polite inclination of his head.

They both posed for a bevy of publicity photos taken by Mustafa. They would be perfect for Facebook presence, they assured him.

'I will be in Westminster next week, but when I'm back, I'd like to address a full meeting of the community,' said Huw. Mustafa gave a visible sigh of delight.

'We can put that out via our newsletter,' said the Imam. 'That way we are assured of a good crowd. It's time they got to know their MP better. And we will organise security.'

'That won't be necessary I assure you, sir,' said Huw. He was sure they were referring to the threatening letters.

'Any meeting where you give a talk to our Muslim community becomes a target for the EDL or any of the other groups. There are so many of them now. It will be very, very necessary.'

CHAPTER THIRTY-SEVEN

AN HOUR LATER Huw Thomas was back in his constituency office having a mug of tea with Mustafa and planning all the nitty-gritty for his new campaign. The one that would relaunch him. The personality offensive.

'Well, this has been a tremendous start. People are already saying, 'Thank God for our jolly MP!' Mustafa rubbed his hands together. 'We don't want to give these troublemakers the opportunity to divide our neighbourhood.'

'We're sure we know who is behind these graffiti smears?' Huw Thomas had heard that sometimes the Muslims did it themselves for their own agenda.

'Broken windows too. Don't forget that. We are getting too many. Smashed glass everywhere. Who would want to damage the mosque but the Far Right? Who would do that? These people are awful.'

'They are a bunch of thugs, most of them,' Huw agreed.

'You know we are all for free speech. Say what you like is great. But what are these people chanting everywhere they go? Every five minutes that Muslims are terrorists and they go to the mosque to learn how to blow us all up. We must make sure we can say Cherrywood is one place that does not tolerate this abuse. And all thanks to our wonderful MP.'

'I'll do what I can,' Huw Thomas mumbled in a doubtful tone. He knew he was being soft-soaped. 'But when they hear the word "Sharia", it scares not just the Far Right.'

'If you could just explain what it means. People do not understand Sharia at all. An endorsement coming from yourself would be an amazing thing.'

At that moment, the door swung open and in marched Nigel Harris, all bandages and plasters, white as a ghost, but otherwise in high spirits.

'Hello, hello. They'll not get the better of me that easily. Any chance of a coffee?'

Huw Thomas leapt up from his seat. 'Come in and make yourself useful, Nigel. You had us all worried about you.'

'Little sod took a swipe. Got me here, here and here.' Harris was straight into it. Nosing into drawers after receipts using his good arm. He still had booze breath.

But Mustafa's expression was one of displeasure. He was like a man who'd got rid of unwanted callers at the front gate only to have them return at the back. 'What are you jolly well doing here in the office so soon?'

'Thought you were down in London today, Huw.'

'Will you bugger off back home if you're feeling so lively?' said Mustafa. 'Someone has stabbed you all over the place and here you are checking in like an intern on their first morning.'

'Not at all. Good idea to spend a few hours at the sharp end of the business. Can do some of that photocopying now. I'm not completely disabled, you know.'

The three of them looked towards the rear of the office where the door to the upper stockroom and printing facilities was unlocked and ajar; unusual for a Saturday.

'What's up top these days, anyway?' Huw Thomas hadn't been there for ages. But if he was to embark on a campaign, he rationalised, he should refamiliarise himself with the resources available. Roll his sleeves up and get on with it. He started towards the door leading upstairs but Mustafa, moving even more quickly, blocked his path.

'The place is like a shit heap. And it's crawling in mice. I'll not have my MP up there until we have at least given it a good sweep and dust.'

A phone call for Huw resolved matters as Mustafa took the chance to close the door adding a chair in front for good measure.

'You should get some rest, Nigel,' he said.

'I've been doing that all night.'

'Huwie and I were just talking about the campaign. There is nothing to do here, really.'

Nigel capitulated. 'I might go for a sandwich down the road then.'

'Let's make sure that jolly website is up to date,' said Mustafa, after Nigel had left. 'You'll no doubt be down in Westminster next week. I've drafted some copy to take the rotten load off your back.'

Huw Thomas peered over his election agent's shoulder as he called up a page he'd been working on.

'Have to advertise to this crowd up here what you've been doing for them with your time all these years.'

What he'd drafted so far read well:

- *Answered 5,750 individual emails and thousands of letters from constituents.*
- *Taken up hundreds of cases on behalf of local families who have asked for help, often through regular Advice Surgeries at Cherrywood Library.*
- *Visited local schools, businesses and voluntary groups to listen to their views and concerns.*
- *Helped to secure action to deal with antisocial behaviour in the town and surrounding areas.*
- *Backed constituents in calling for more to be done to counter Islamophobia in Cherrywood.*

'Now let's get this speech written for the community meeting ahead of time, said Mustafa, 'So you can buzz off Tuesday.'

CHAPTER THIRTY-EIGHT

WENTWORTH IN VIRGINIA Water lay under gloomy, steely grey skies. It was ten past one on Saturday afternoon when most of the wealthy residents play a round of golf at the club.

The drive back to London had begun almost straightaway. Koslov had every detail organised from the trip down in the helicopter to the car out the front ready to return Karen Andersen to London. This was to be a very short visit.

Koslov lived in a sumptuous mansion with a vast expanse of grounds, typical of a location in an action movie. Security was all about. Karen was straight away marched through a gold tiled hall and out the front. A dark emerald Rolls Royce Wraith was waiting for her, engine purring. The aged tan leather interior felt soft and sank down gently beneath her weight.

The money man behind the English Concern Group greeted her with an insincere smile. He was in his late sixties and as bald as a North American eagle. Despite his huge wealth, Koslov looked thoroughly miserable. 'Did you enjoy the ride we organised?'

'I could have come by motorbike. It would have saved you the trouble. You just had to ask'

He asked, 'Pass me phone please.'

The text to Haruto declaring her love for him was still on it, unsent.

Koslov checked the mobile. 'Is anyone tracking you?' The inquisition had begun.

'Not that I know of.'

'Then they should be. Don't you have a bug on you?' It was clearly his attempt at humour, Russian style. He cracked up and started laughing. 'Take it,' he said handing the phone back.

The grilling was part of the gag. But it was pointless getting angry. She'd requested the meeting. It wasn't worth the cost of putting him offside.

'Ivan put in a good word for you. He pretends to be me sometimes. We have fun with that.' It was his form of a practical joke. 'But I'm better looking, don't you think?'

Koslov was not a scrap like Caves, half his height and at least double his BMI.

They passed the early part of the drive back in silence as the car negotiated its way out of the vast estate, past a security post manned by two uniformed guards.

She opened the conversation. 'Thank you for seeing me. Your cooperation is appreciated.'

Koslov turned towards Karen, his face hardening. 'What makes you think I will cooperate?' Like many Russians in the UK, he spoke almost perfect English. 'But first. Tell me, why do you want to probe into the running of an organisation like ECG?' He prodded the upholstery.

'We're searching for someone who says they're connected with you.'

He brushed that aside. 'How do I know what people say?'

'I'm a private investigator who helped identify a terrorist who recruited dozens of British women to become ISIS brides and leave the country.'

'Who is terrorist?' He didn't seem too impressed.

'But now it appears some girls who knew her are being targeted by a member of your organisation.'

'But you're not going to tell me the name of terrorist?'

'I'm afraid I'm not at liberty to reveal that. Does it matter? It's more important that you know there is a lone wolf operating within your organisation.'

'What makes you decide what is important and unimportant? What may be unimportant to you, may be important to me. Don't you think?

'But is it relevant to what we are talking about?'

'Exactly. Relevance is issue. It is essence of all politics. If I consider something relevant which you think is irrelevant, then we will disagree. Which leads me back to asking, who is terrorist we are talking about?'

'The terrorist is not the concern. That's why it's immaterial. What matters is the women she preyed on who are at threat. Not her.'

'And you make assumptions English Concern Group is my organisation. Where did you get this knowledge? It's what Mr Trump refers to as fake news. You create many hypotheses, Karen.'

She heard the suction sound of a car fridge door. Koslov found an oversized bar of Galaxy amongst the bottles.

'The security company I work for promised these women anonymity. In return, they helped out MI5.

Some of them were key to getting one Jihadi operation shut down.'

'Some of them?' Koslov was a quarter way through the chocolate. 'Some of them is the issue.'

'Most of them. And they've shed the veil.' It seemed pointless attempting to protect the women.

'You believe there is any importance at all in protection of wives of terrorists? Those who support mass murder?' His mouth was full of chocolate. 'And what is this 'shed the veil' nonsense? What do you mean by that crap? You sound like one of those girls off television.'

'If the English Concern Group is not directly behind these assaults, we thought you should know about it. That's all.'

'Why?'

'We were wondering if you knew about what's been going on within your group?'

'You wonder about a lot of things, Karen. Can you give us anything more? Like name of so-called ECG member? What has he done exactly?'

The car had cleared the Wentworth Estate and was off down the A3, towards the Egham Roundabout. The Indian chauffeur approached at high speed, braking at the last minute. Koslov broke off to swear at him in a mixture of Russian and English.

'There are violent groups who do carry out attacks on immigrants and Muslims in particular. But ECG is not among them. Most of assaults you read about are carried out by little people with big problems.' He tapped his head. 'Usually, they are white, and usually they are male.'

The mood of the in-car meeting became more agreeable. More and more groups like the ECG were forming. They were sceptical of the EU. The supporters thought social services should go first to the 'natives'. They weren't fascists. Nor vigilantes. Nor extremists. Violence was not condoned. They resented it when people labelled them the Far Right. That was the left-wing attitude to them.

Koslov turned unexpectedly charming. He called her Karen. He was open about the workings of the organisation. He wasn't alone in his political views that the UK was under threat of being Islamified. Britain had the greatest number of Far Right influencers. And despite Twitter shutting down a lot of accounts, new online platforms like Gab had reached out to supporters of Britain First. Under the new social network, Minds, there was a stream of sympathetic online users.

And in addition, there was a torrent of new alt-right groups forming daily like #GenerationReturn who vowed to set the clock back and restore countries to their former cultures.

The journey back to where she had come from such a short while before was over almost too soon. There was much more to find out.

'So, if you are sure this is nothing to do with your group, why does this individual claim he is with your organisation?'

'That is for you to find out. Not for me.'

'There has to be a connection.'

As was the nature of the beast, Koslov turned off the charisma. The pleasantries were over. He gave her a menacing look. 'But don't pry around too much. You could get yourself into hot water. What's happened to these women you go on about?'

'One lost her job. The other had her kitchen set on fire. Another kidnapped, filmed naked and blackmailed by threatening to post the clip on YouTube.' However bad it was, it didn't sound dramatic enough to lay Koslov in the aisles.

He shrugged. 'Few of our members would have much sympathy. A girl born here steals a passport and goes to a foreign country to learn to come back and kill you. We deem someone who takes action against girl who steals passport and wants to kill people in another country guilty of being member of terrorist cell. How can that be just? Can you answer me that?'

The car turned into Devonshire Road. It stopped right outside Karen's front door. Her temperature shot up.

She'd wasted the day with Ivan Koslov. He'd let on nothing. Her motorbike was now more than an hour away, which was a headache. But what chilled her was his hostility. And she'd never let on to him her address. So, how'd he known where she lived?

'I was hoping you'd support me,' she said, as she climbed out of the Rolls. 'But it's not going to be, is it?' Passers-by were suitably impressed by the limo.

'Try not to get yourself into too much trouble, Basilah. And give our best regards to Zinah al-Rashid if she contacts you from prison.'

The Rolls Royce purred off leaving her standing on the pavement, speechless.

CHAPTER THIRTY-NINE

IT WAS AROUND three in the afternoon when Karen got back through the door of her flat after her trip from Wentworth. The first thing that hit her was the pungent smell of disinfectant. A flush of adrenalin coursed through her veins.

The place had been deep-cleaned from top to bottom. She tiptoed across her front room, wary of what she might strike. Had she been robbed? It was the reverse of a ransack. Piled books, neatly organised papers. Carpet vacuumed; windows polished. The surface of the table and bar counter sparkled. In her bedroom, someone had sorted drawers, hung up clothes. The bathroom sink shone like a mirror. Who had done it?

Who had a spare key and could get access? Haruto?

The kitchen cupboard was ajar and all the old Japanese food had been binned. What was going on? An unlikely possibility entered her mind. Koslov had used her alias Basilah. Was this the extension of his private joke?

Or was it the same guy who'd kidnapped Jamillah?

Karen was au fait with how stalkers worked. They gained access to your life and left clues to let you know that they are around. One of them had targeted several of the Jihadi girls; Tessa Clark, Fatima, the librarian from Cherrywood. Maybe now it was her turn. If

Koslov knew her undercover name was Basilah, then perhaps the stalker did too.

She opened up the WhatsApp group.

> Basilah: How's everyone?
> Fatima: You said not to post on here.
> Basilah: True.
> Mia: I think I'm being followed.
> Basilah: Don't post. I'll call.

'I'm at work. Getting frightened about this,' said Mia. 'How did this bloke get my details?'

'I'll see if I can get over there. What time do you finish?'

They arranged to meet. Mia told Karen five-thirty. She brought her up on how she'd changed. She no longer wore the full-face veil. The jewellery shop where she worked in the Liberty Shopping Arcade in Romford had banned it after being targeted by thieves in burkas. She suggested they rendezvous at the outside entrance to the complex and find somewhere quiet to talk. Mia would wait out the front and give a wave when she saw Karen's motorbike.

Next, Karen called Quacker to update him on the flat invasion; that she was probably being stalked by a compulsive obsessive fanatic. 'I have to pick up my bike from Battersea.'

'Don't go anywhere until I get there.'

CHAPTER FORTY

'GET TO SEE inside the house, did you?' Quacker's face glowed. He'd either seen pictures of the sprawl online or knew someone who'd raided the joint.

'I was straight out the door. So not really,' she replied. 'It wasn't a social call.'

Quacker couldn't quite cover his disappointment. 'Shame that.' He looked around. 'So, this was not how you left it?' The kitchen tap dripped constantly. Quacker turned it off with an irritable twist of his hand.

'No.'

'Like someone's been through everything with a fine-tooth comb and then cleared their prints.'

She described in detail the conversation she'd had with Koslov. Also, how he'd delivered her to the front door like a parcel. How did he know her address?

'It's obvious the ECG knows your pseudonym. If this is their work, and we don't know that, then they got one of their characters in to do a spruce-up while you were down in Surrey. As you suggest, could be calculated on their part. A statement. We're watching what you're up to. We are well aware Ivan Koslov is paranoid. Nothing else odd at all before this?'

'Actually, yes, come to think of it. I found this set of prints which had been left. Of ISIS executions. As if someone had broken in and placed them deliberately. I can show you.'

Karen walked over to the drawer where she'd hidden them. They'd gone!

Her heart rate went into top gear. 'Whoever it is has taken the pictures too. Why?'

'Karen, how many keys do you have to this flat?'

'Elspeth holds a spare.' Quacker had met Karen's neighbour several times. 'But she's at her nephew's in the countryside at the moment. Haruto had one. But somehow I don't think he'd do this.'

Could it be him? Did she send the text after all? She checked her phone quickly. The message was still pending.

Quacker rustled a sandwich packet. 'Tell me about Haruto, can you? You did a trip to Japan together a while back, didn't you? Then what?'

He implied her former boyfriend was behind the exercise. 'Where did you two go after that?'

'We went on to Sydney for three weeks. Why?' She began searching around the clean cupboards for a plate to catch Quacker's crumbs. 'What does Haruto have to do with this? Someone's been in my flat. Are you still suggesting it was him?'

'You never told me about Mainz.' He took the plate. 'Thanks. That's where you broke up, I believe. Have you communicated with him at all this week?'

If Karen had thought it Quacker's business to know, she would have spoken about it. Yes, they'd met up there for a few days. It'd been after his travelling stint. But why was he asking?

'As a matter of fact, I haven't spoken to him for quite a while. Why?'

'But he still has a key to here, doesn't he? He's orderly, and he likes to work in a tidy environment. Which this now is,' he said, giving her a look of reproval. 'But it was you who introduced me to him, wasn't it? How trustworthy is he, Karen?'

'Why on earth would you ask something like that?' She didn't appreciate his tone. She'd quash that straightaway. 'Completely trustworthy,' she said firmly.

'Because he's been doing a few jobs for me.'

It was like a shot to the heart. It stung and Quacker noticed.

'Did you not know about it?'

'No, I didn't.'

How could he go behind her back? How could both of them? It was demeaning. Haruto was big-time into drone technology and tech inventions. Providing surveillance equipment for Quacker would be a welcome opportunity for both. But hearing it in this way seemed like a double-cross.

'I put him to use at the Ritz one night. Which, to be honest, is how I learned about the possibility that this crowd in Germany, where you stayed, may have got hold of your data.'

A voice over the intercom broke the tension.

'Delivery. Flowers for you.'

Karen ran down to pick up the delivery of fourteen red roses.

'Look Donald, beautiful!'

The pleasant aroma filled the flat. She read the message quickly. 'To My Queen. I'm sorry I've been out of your life for a while. What can I do to get you back?'

The hurt of a few minutes ago swept away and Karen gave into a new more powerful emotion. Switched off. She was consumed by a fantasy. It was creepy, but she didn't care. Haruto had sent the flowers. He'd been back home and cleared the place. Of course, he had. Why hadn't it occurred to her before? The thought was electrifying. She found herself on cloud nine. She couldn't hold the excitement back. She took two pictures on her phone of the bouquet to record the moment.

Quacker looked suitably impressed. 'I got the impression he was still pretty keen on you.'

She wanted to update him on Beth Lane and the WhatsApp posts but it was too late now.

'Sorry, I have to go. I have to meet up with Mia and I'm late already.'

'In that case I might stay on and do a sweep for bugs while you're gone,' said Quacker. 'You go about your duties. I'll be here for a couple of hours. Just in case you've picked up a proper stalker.'

The danger past, the rest of the afternoon flashed by. Taking the overground from Chiswick to Clapham Junction was an option. But that, plus the ten-minute walk to the heliport was likely to make her too late. So she ordered a cab.

She sat in the front passenger seat and took a deep breath. Everything was pulsating and singing. The world was full of possibilities once again. She and Haruto would be back together soon.

But right now she had a job to do. The man who may have bullied and exposed Tessa Clark on the net, had pitched up at Fatima's house and also abused Jamillah in Cherrywood, was still out there. He was becoming more audacious with each victim. If Mia was being followed, she was at risk.

It was twenty past four when she got to Battersea Heliport. From there to their meeting place was over an hour on her bike. She'd be pushed to make it in time for five-thirty. Deciding on the M25 option as the quickest she accelerated as soon as she joined the motorway of Junction 10.

She arrived in Romford a few minutes before the half-hour. But when she turned toward the centre of town, the traffic came to a halt. She braked the bike smoothly. Police had set up a diversion route. Karen sat idling in the stationery traffic. 'What's going on?'

The cabby alongside her knew it all. 'It appears a young woman who works in the jewellery shop ran into the crowd to flag down someone on a motorbike she thought she knew and got hit. Killed. So sad. So young. Called Me or Mia or something like that.'

Karen went cold as she told Quacker the news and broke down over the phone. 'It's all my fault.'

He empathised and was sympathetic. Remain calm. Regain composure. She'd been doing her job. That it had been central to the investigation to speak with Mia. It wasn't Karen's fault. He assured her that morality was complex. How duty is rarely easy, but it is important. He added that it was often the toughest choice.

Karen thanked him and he continued, 'There's a Filipino lady just arrived. Her name is Regine. She's the one you were with at the Ritz. And she's saying the

178

flowers sent to the flat are for her. They're from her husband.'

CHAPTER FORTY-ONE

OVER THE WEEKEND Karen Andersen barely slept. So she was groggy and out of it for thirty-six hours. Only her neighbour, Elspeth Cochrane, cared sufficiently to tell her to stop drinking and get to bed.

It had never occurred to Karen that Regine was married. She'd never mentioned a husband. It left a sour taste. No doubt Regine had spun him a line she had been living at Devonshire Road for the past few weeks.

More than that, Karen blamed herself for Mia's death. She self-recriminated. The girl had been outside the shopping centre early. She was waiting for Karen's bike to pass. Had Karen been at Romford by five twenty, Mia might still be alive. These thoughts drove her crazy. What if? She avoided going out and couldn't sit still. The guilt consumed her.

When she'd got back to the flat on Saturday night, it was empty. Quacker had left, but not before Regine had turned up and whisked her flowers away. After that there was no reason for him to hang about. They'd solved the mystery. Cleaning up the mess in the flat had been Regine's way of saying thank you to Karen for having let her stay overnight.

It should have been obvious. The former maid loved mopping and vacuuming. But learning it'd been Regine who had been inside the flat came as a bittersweet blow. It was not the stalker, nor one of

Koslov's cronies, which was a relief. But neither had it been Haruto arriving back into her life.

There'd been nothing from him, not a word. No explanation of what exactly he'd revealed to Quacker about what went on in Mainz. No rationale as to why he'd floated the unhelpful idea Karen could have leaked first-hand information on Jihadi brides while she was there. The whys and wherefores.

Okay, so I was wrong about you! What felt right back then, doesn't stand up anymore, does it? Falling in love had brought nothing but trouble. It didn't bear thinking about it. The short and long term implications for life made her sick in the stomach every time she thought about it.

Karen knew she ought to confront him and resolve it but couldn't summon up the strength. Struggling to pull herself out of it she cooked herself a hamburger, the first food in the last day and a half.

It had all begun with the trip to Japan. They'd holed up for five days in the city. Visits to the Miji Shrine, Senso-ji and even a day at Mount Fuji took up a whole week. But Haruto Fraser had a fascination with all things electronic. They were in his DNA and they spent a lot of time in the sprawling market at the Akhabara district.

Karen returned to London, but Haruto stayed on. She'd expected him back a few weeks later. But he had business arrangements to address. The drone technology field was taking off for him. A new extension to his photography line. Then a friend had pulled him in on doing the stills for a film. It'd been about the modernising way of life of Mongolian nomads. Daily messages weren't enough. They missed each other. So, he had proposed they meet up in Mainz after the shoot.

They'd been head over heels, hadn't they? It'd been his idea to go to Frankfurt and cross the Eiserner Steg. His suggestion to attach a padlock on a section of the bridge fence. The lock would be a lasting symbol of their love. It would remain there for all of eternity. But instead of hurling the key into the water, Haruto handed it to Karen. She'd kept it ever since, in her lucky box. Maybe her luck had timed-out.

Karen had the uneasy feeling she'd been betrayed without putting her finger on how exactly and it hurt like hell.

And something else was troubling her conscience. Beth Lane was a new victim. Karen had told Quacker she was in touch with her. But she'd lied to give herself more time to catch up with Beth. And now the girl who called herself Jamillah on the WhatsApp group was not answering her phone.

CHAPTER FORTY-TWO

THIS TIME SHE'LL be there.

At five-thirty on Saturday afternoon, Glen Gibb walked into the Cherrywood Library. It was his third visit that day. But on this one, he held tight to the horsey book he'd borrowed without scanning it only twenty hours earlier.

Glen's clothes were non-standard for him. On this occasion, he'd changed into jeans and a jacket. Cool gear. Greg style. Midnight would do things differently. He had a way with women. If Beth Lane got to see him dressed to impress, she'd take a fancy to him. They were going on a date. Maybe even a fairy-tale love affair would develop.

His mind boggled at what lay ahead. He'd planned where they would go and what they would do. His research had shortlisted two restaurants. Her choice. Asian or Italian? Perhaps starting off by chatting about poetry would give them something in common. It was her hobby horse. He was happy to learn more about her and what she enjoyed doing. Eventually, there'd be a thousand apologies on her part for having gone to Turkey, but not at first. Yes, she would say sorry to him. She had to. However, he wouldn't let her off the hook too quickly. Women admired strength.

He approached the front desk. The book was the ideal excuse to ask where she was.

'The assistant shouldn't have allowed you to take it out if you were not a member. Anyway, I will tell her you said thank you for it when I see her, but it won't be today. She's called in sick.'

The promise of tomorrow beckoned.

CHAPTER FORTY-THREE

GLEN GIBB DIDN'T get back to the motel room until past ten o'clock on Sunday evening. It was 14 April. His mind was spinning. It flipped between rage and excitement. He had to stop obsessing over Beth Lane.

He was fixated with her. She'd become a compulsion, occupying every waking second for the last two days. He had to get back control of himself and stop cycling between love and hate. One moment, hope against hope she'd fall for him, fancy him. The next, she was his victim, powerless against his hatred. The difference between Glen and other men turned on by a woman was that he could cut off his feelings. He'd done it before. Anyway, how could you go over the top for a girl who'd once been a Jihadi bride?

Glen Gibb had done his best. He'd put on his 'Greg hat'. Tried to copy him when he had the hots for someone. Been back and forth expecting to catch a glimpse of her.

On Saturday night he'd eaten at the Asian restaurant alone.

On Sunday, the library was closed. So, the day was spent driving around like a madman looking for her. He'd even returned to the construction site just in case she'd turned up there and was waiting to see him. But no. Where could she be? Now he was feeling slightly let down, but not too discouraged.

He knew she lived with her aunt, and so perhaps it had just been too hard to get away on her own. What would she tell her?

She can hardly tell her all about us? Not until we're truly in love.

Glen had to keep faith in the power of his positive mood over the weekend. He'd started to believe his own hype. Convinced himself he could be like his brother. If at first you don't succeed, be patient. It was a brilliant feeling. His self esteem had shot up like a rocket. On a scale from one to ten, it had reached twenty-five. Keep imagining it.

He heard the high-speed whir of a hand-held dryer through the walls of the motel. Recalled the dark silky hair that framed her face with the perfect pale skin. Beth Lane could have had a future with him. All she needed was to admit her mistake and that would be it. They'd make the perfect couple.

The fridge in the room had come in handy. He took out an ice-cold beer and ripped off the ring. The bottle of champagne was chilling nicely. If she was still into the Muslim stuff, she'd probably not touch a drop, he told himself. But he'd still pop a cork for her. Surely, she'd appreciate the gesture.

He fought hard to stem the images of Friday night. Her naked body. Full breasts. He mustn't allow the guilt to bring him down. It wouldn't have reached this point if he hadn't abducted her. Planning dates, life events. Girls liked tough guys. Not men like Also Ran who said sorry all the time. Greg had told him that. Powerful, not pathetic.

Stop thinking about her.

He fished his phone out of his pocket. He hadn't even looked at the film once through and he wouldn't. Not since she'd agreed to get together.

They had a date. He'd play the gentleman.

Maybe bring her back to the motel afterwards.

His watch read near midnight. So, Sunday was a write-off. But Monday would be better. Cherrywood Library was open. Beth Lane would be behind the counter expecting him. Their romance could begin tomorrow evening.

He picked up the phone and rang reception.

He said, 'I need my room for another night.'

On Tuesday morning at eleven o'clock, Glen Gibb walked out of Cherrywood Library. He caught his reflection in the glass swing door.

It wasn't Midnight he saw this time. Also Ran looked back at him. The suit and tie, and a clean white shirt. He burned with an intense inner pain. Why had he expected anything different? The outcome had been inevitable.

She'd smashed his hopes of a relationship. She regarded him as old and ugly. He was boring, was he? Well, he'd show her how dull he could be. The onetime Jihadi bride didn't respect him. Glen Gibb had done as much as he was prepared to do, chasing after her. Beth Lane had broken her word, as they all did, and gone into hiding.

Perhaps he needed to cool it. Why did he have the urge to drive his car down the pavement at sixty miles an hour? Surely that was insanity? He couldn't let himself go stark raving mad because some two-faced terrorist lover had dumped him.

He had to get over this snub and get after another of these fantasising lowlifes.

The safety of the public depended on him.

CHAPTER FORTY-FOUR

'ALLAHU AKBAR. GOD is greater.' At the end of the Friday session, Tammy Bishop's psychiatrist, Ali al-Sayed, had said those words to her. She hadn't responded. It was now Tuesday, 16 April. She'd not seen him since. But it was a day before her release from Bronzefield Prison and she sat motionless savouring the moment.

She'd not failed the test, had she? Not been fooled for a moment into his trap. Asking her about Jihad. Saying how she would serve Allah again. It was all a setup. Part of an experiment. An exam his clever student had passed with flying colours.

Otherwise, she would never have struck a deal.

Who else would have been able to rehabilitate her other than Ali? Everyone in prison had been out to mar her reputation. Get anything on her to turn the authorities against her. What they went on about inside was so small-time and of little use to both the world and mankind.

The waste bin was full of ripped envelopes and half-done puzzle books. What would come next? Out with the old and in with the new. Her self-improvement was astonishing. A dazzling new life waited less than twenty-four hours away.

How effective Ali was. He'd understood her from the moment she'd first spoken to him. How much she feared 'telling and not being believed'. They'd had real heart-to-heart sessions. The tests were all about that, weren't they?

And not everyone trusted her. The public were sceptical and saw her as an ongoing threat. Once a terrorist, always a terrorist. They expected her to lie to them. To seek the same path. Radicalise others. Don't deny it! That's what you're all about. Could you blame them? Maybe she'd never completely be above suspicion.

How could she display her commitment to debunk ISIS propaganda? Perhaps join an opposition group such as English Concern. Get serious, Tammy, she told herself. That'd be ridiculous. Anti-terrorism would be monitoring every move. Scrutinising. Sharp-eyed agents on her tail. But it was an idea.

The news had been full of returned Jihadi brides saying, 'I'm not the same silly little schoolgirl who ran away from Bethnal Green! But I don't regret coming here.'

I don't regret coming here? How does that work?

And, in an interview broadcast, Shamima Begum had been 'fine' about watching the odd beheading. It was Islamic law. No wonder decent people were so disgusted.

I have a job to do to help the British Government. I'm no longer Zinah al-Rashid. I'm Tammy Bishop.

She sat down and wrote her third letter to Karen Andersen. She told her she wanted to see her urgently, the minute she was out.

She would just have to convince them all that Tammy Bishop was from now on a force for good and a crusader against the evils of ISIS.

Unlike the others who were hemming and hawing about returning from Syria, she was at least back in wonderful London. And she had a plan to make it big. She owed it to herself.

Tammy laid out clothes for the next day. What to wear? It was hard to decide.

Ali al-Sayed was brilliant. But her thoughts about him also filled her with confusion. They could wreak havoc with her plans. It was time for them to part ways.

She could cope on her own.

CHAPTER FORTY-FIVE

AT ELEVEN FORTY on Tuesday morning, 16 April, Karen Andersen walked into the Costa on Gray's Inn Road. A phone call she'd long been expecting was just the jolt she needed. Beth Lane had turned up in London and wanted to talk.

Beth wore tight black trousers with a polka dot blouse and high-heeled boots. This somehow didn't fit with Karen's picture of her. Hardly the conventional image of someone who'd once contemplated joining the Jihadi cause in Syria. Her skin was breaking out and her nose dark pink from recent tears.

She appeared emotionally vulnerable. Possibly the after effects of being driven to a vacant lot and everything she went through there.

She allowed Karen to order her a brie and bacon panini. Karen got in the short queue and ordered the food and went back to Beth. 'Are you feeling okay?'

'Yeah, sort of.'

'Where have you been since Saturday?' Karen hassled her for more information. She was about to get it, everything. 'That was the last time you posted on the WhatsApp group?'

'Someone said not to put things on there. Did you read that? I only use Jamillah as a name on the group, anyway. Do you use Basilah much?'

'Not much. Only there.'

'Did Zinah al-Rashid give you that one?'

Beth Lane was loosening up. Karen had no intention of destroying the shaky relationship by revealing she was undercover. Not yet. 'No, I gave it to myself.'

'That's clever. Zinah said I needed one which had been 'praised by our Lord'. Bloody bullshit.' That 'Beth Lane' didn't sit well with Islamic principles and values. She needed something more pious sounding. 'I'd not been using the name Jamillah at the library, so how did the guy know about it? He used it several times. Jamillah means beautiful in Arabic. But I don't feel that any more. Not after what he did.' Beth paused. 'So, what's your real name?'

'It's Karen.'

The smell of cooked cheese wafted closer as the barista approached with the panini for Beth. She'd not been able to hold anything down since the assault, she told Karen.

'Can you tell me anything about the man who did it? You say he came into the library?'

'I could, but I don't want to. I just feel dirty after what he did to me. I'd rather forget about him.' Beth leaned over and unplugged her phone from the wall before starting on the food. 'How did he know the name, do you think? Nobody uses it. Only on that group.'

'I have no idea. But tell me what happened next. You went back to work or what?'

'I didn't know what to do. Several of the girls on WhatsApp said I should. But I couldn't bring myself to. What if he came in?'

'Who told you to go back?'

'Yasmin did and Mia did. A couple of others. Do you think I should have done?' Her eyes darted left and right as the coffee shop filled up.

'So, what did you do?'

'Stayed at home. Too scared.'

'What did he look like? And can you describe what happened exactly?'

Beth went through it stage by stage. Tall. Thirties. He'd met her at a takeaway place. Then she'd got into his car. He'd taken her out of town. Got her to strip. Filmed her. Then let her go on the condition they met the following day. He was a man who bore a hatred of ISIS. They'd killed his brother.

'Oh, and he made me look at these horrible pictures.'

'What pictures?' *Were they like the ones she'd received herself? It was a frightening thought.* 'Can you describe them to me?'

What she heard fed her growing sense of dread. The photos were definitely the same as the set she'd found in her flat. She was a jumble of emotions for the next few seconds. 'He's been inside my place too. I thought I imagined it.'

'I shouldn't have got in his car, should I? He seemed OK at first. He didn't rape me, though. That's at least a relief.'

'Beth, did he use a name at all?'

'Something like Orse or Orsa?'

'Orson?'

'Maybe. I can't remember. And there was some link up with horses. He was strange. The weirdest freak I have ever come across.'

'So, what did you do all over the weekend? Did he try to contact you?'

Beth had locked herself in her room at home. She'd been curled up in a ball watching Disney films to take her mind off the abduction. It'd all got too much by the Monday. So she took a bus to a nearby village and booked into a bed-and-breakfast. That's where she'd picked up the high-speed train south. Finally she returned Basilah's call.

'So who knows you've left Cherrywood?'

'I sent my aunt a text yesterday to say I'd be in London for a while. She's cool. She knows nothing about what he did though.'

Beth Lane finished eating and dusted the crumbs off her hands. It was the right moment for Karen to bring in Quacker. He could do an identikit. They needed a picture of this guy, and fast. But Beth was busy with her phone. 'Mia said I could stay and she might get me a job where she works. But I can't get hold of her right now.'

She was still tapping away when Karen told her Mia had been killed. Unsurprisingly, the news was crushing.

'What are you saying? It's impossible. Say it isn't true. No.' Beth blinked away the tears.

'It was an accident.' Karen went over the chain of events leading up to the tragedy.

'No, no, no. I don't believe it. Did Mia tell you I was coming to stay? That's maybe why he was following her. Why is he doing this?'

'He didn't do it. Couldn't have done.'

'He could have come down from Cherrywood.'

'Mia was killed outright as she stepped off the pavement. But it was by a bus. And she only thought she was being stalked. She wasn't sure of it.'

'What am I going to do? I'm so scared.' She gripped the table so tightly her knuckles turned white. 'He seemed to have found out all about me travelling to Syria. But that was years ago. I never crossed anyway. How would he know, Basilah? How? No one did. Where will I go now Mia's dead?'

If Karen had been feeling bad about things, she now felt even worse. 'It's cold in here, isn't it?' The air-conditioning duct directly above them spread a steady stream of refrigerated air on to their table. 'Why can't you go home? Your mum is in Hounslow.'

Beth became calmer weighing it all up, it could have been worse. 'I'm lucky he didn't kill me. Should I go back to Cherrywood and tell the police? But he filmed me. He said he'd let everyone know I was an ISIS bride. I only got as far as Turkey. I was being bullied at school at the time. That's why I left. I told my mum when I got home it was just a holiday. What'll that do to her?'

'Why didn't you go back to school after that?' It sounded more like an inquisition.

'Because it was worse there than when I left the country.' She stared at Karen. 'The rumours. My mum was acting like she was ashamed of me. You know, Hounslow is tiny. I've lived there all my life. I got the impression I was being watched wherever I went.'

'But you will have to go back there eventually.'

Beth said that frightened her to death, far more than Syria. 'I'd rather sleep rough than go home. I know where to go. And anyway, what if he knows my

Hounslow address? Fatima had her house torched, didn't she?' Her eyes widened with inner fears.

'No. He only turned up at her door. That was her dad's story.' The fake news had taken root. 'And it's likely this Orson man is just getting a kick out of frightening you.'

'Do you think so?' Her phone flashed with a text in from her aunt. Her mother wanted to know if she was ok. Beth brightened up immediately. 'Can you believe that?'

'See? Your mother's asking after you and she cares about you.' There was a light in the sky. Somewhere way out on the distant horizon. Beth Lane had been through a horrifying ordeal. But from that second she started looking forward again, open to a new set of plans. Maybe going back home after all was not out of the question. 'It's not as bad as all that,' said Karen. 'The likelihood is that this will all blow over and you'll be able to carry on as before.'

Then things changed. Beth's voice dropped to a whisper. 'Oh no. There's something on the net.' Then she clutched her throat. Covered her nose and mouth.

Karen leant forward. 'What is it? What's the matter?'

'Oh no. No, no, no.' She'd opened up Safari on her phone to find there was a film circulating showing her naked in the woods. It had been titled with the words 'Beth Lane from Hounslow.' On the next line, 'Alias Jamillah. Jihadi Brides Make the Best Porn Stars of All.'

Beth grabbed her bag. 'I'm going to be sick. I'll be right back. It's horrible.'

Karen waited anxiously. It was time to let her know she was a private investigator with Partridge Security and that she would help her. But Jamillah had shot through.

CHAPTER FORTY-SIX

TUESDAY, 16 APRIL. It was the day after the fire at Notre Dame in Paris. Bea Harrington's taxi from the House of Lords was a bright red, hardly an appropriate colour when so many were saddened at the destruction wrought on the great symbol of Christianity. But she took it all the same. It was essential to get back to Dolphin Square in a hurry.

Bea hated being set up and rushed. It made her feel sick to her stomach. In her mind, she urged her driver to go faster down the Embankment. Hurry! Tourists were everywhere, dodging across the road and slowing the traffic. It was a quarter past seven in the evening.

What was the rush? Huw Thomas showing up at short notice. Maddening bloody fool. She'd finally get to see him after four days of stewing. Every damn hour she'd read and reread the letter from Tammy Bishop going over and over again her counselling session with Huw's mate, Ali al-Sayed. She needed some advice and to share her thoughts and Huw was the only one who could help, who knew her way back in her thirties. He surely didn't want the rest of the world learning about what happened back then any more than she did.

That was exactly what filled her with panic. Dire. She could imagine it all. Just her luck to have a former terrorist who should be in prison or the nut house rake up the past. Bingo! It would all be history. Her position. The House of Lords. Her reputation. It was a depressing thought.

Huw had promised to talk it through and that he'd be in her corner. Then he'd cancelled the weekend on her. His damn deselection was all he cared about. If it existed. Never mind her needs. Or discussing their summer holiday plans, well down on his priorities.

What was he jabbering on about? Some trumped up campaign by the Leader of the Office, Mustafa al-Sayed, to 'realign him with the views of the constituency'. Some bullshit idea to win back the locals. A load of bollocks. What if Huw Thomas MP actually lost his seat? A disaster!

When she'd almost given up, Huw called. He was on his way down to London.

'I just got off the motorway and will be yours in twenty five minutes.'

But she knew his modus operandi. He was well aware she had an evening function. Likely he'd be in and off out again if she didn't make it back in time.

Huw Thomas was already in the kitchen when she rushed through the door. He picked up on her refusal of a hello kiss. The type which used to lead on to other things. Either before or after dinner. He could tell she was fuming about something or other as she threw her jacket to one side.

'How long have you been here, Huw?'

'Not more than ten minutes. Pretty good going. The traffic was light for a change.' He was standing by the refrigerator. 'You got back quick, didn't you? Thought you had a committee event?'

She saw the glass in his hand and the glint in his eye. Bemusement. He seemed pleased to have beaten her in through the door when only two hours ago he'd been north of Birmingham. Not apologetic about the Friday mess up.

'How're the Lords these days?' He took a swig of wine and raised an enquiring bottle in her direction.

'No thanks. Did you get my messages about this Tammy thing? You realise who she is, don't you? I didn't have a clue before I got the letter. I had no idea. Never connected her with Miriam Bishop. If I could stop her getting out of prison, I would. But I sense it's too late. I don't know what we will do.' It came out in a torrent.

'Why would you have wanted to do that? You of all people?' His biting sarcasm reflected the irony of the situation. Getting all women out of prison was her raison d'être. It had got her to where she was. What she stood for. Sticking up for injustices left, right and centre. He put the bottle back in the fridge.

'Are you just going to make a joke of everything?' It was a fact Bea was up to her neck with the Prisoner Listening Service. In on every campaign.

'You've always said they should release most of the female prisoners. How they're locked up for benefit fraud or because some guy had got them hooked on heroin.' His eyes were sparkling. He was playing his devil's advocate game. Enjoying tying her up in knots. Using her own words against her.

'That was when I was helping at Holloway. They were all petrified as hell of the twenty stoners who ran the place.'

'Thought Holloway closed down. That wasn't you, was it? And there was the other place. Downside or somewhere.'

He was being deliberately irritating. She'd organised selection and training for Downview. He was trying to dodge the subject. 'We really need to discuss this.'

'Well, I had one of my staff members stabbed twenty times over the weekend. I have had other things to think about other than your little dilemma.'

Little dilemma?

'A letter came for you this morning.' She grabbed her bag and pulled it out. 'I opened it in error. Sorry. Some woman from up North must have got this address.'

'You opened this deliberately.' His face reddened. 'Don't open my mail.'

'You are forgetting this is my flat. Most of what comes here is for me and addressed to me. It's not surprising I opened it by mistake.' Huw had once been a shoulder to cry on, a known entity from the distant past. They'd agreed never to talk about his ex-wife or politics. And it was assumed, at least by her, there'd be no other women while he was staying with her.

'So, this is what all this is about, is it?' He eyed the letter, not daring to open it while she was in this mood.

'You treat this place like a damn hotel.'

'Well, it is a hotel of sorts, is it not? Isn't it the arrangement we had? I thought it was what we agreed on. Help you with the rent. We don't have too much else in common, do we?'

'I thought we got on rather well. Once, when you fancied me enough to sleep with me.' Now she needed his help and wasn't getting it. 'We don't have to talk about politics. We never did before. I need some comfort over this issue.'

'Oh, I see. So, I can be useful to you, can I? What sort of comfort do you want?' He was annoyed about the hotel quip. Knowing she'd caught him out with the letter. 'So, I'm not the pro-Palestinian Corbyn loving communist anymore?'

'I never called you that. You know I didn't.' She threw open the fridge, took out the wine and splashed some in a glass.

'I have a feeling you did, once.' He looked at her with mounting anger. Not softening. 'It's no good blaming me for what's caught up with you. I can't do much about it.'

'Well, you can. It's your loathsome party behind accommodating these pro-ISIS supporters. Anyway, I think you are going totally overboard on this Islamic thing. Looked at your website. Sharia Law. What next? Think you are barking mad.'

'I think it was you who put forward the benefits of Sharia Law.' He tipped his wine down the sink, washed the glass and stacked it upside down on the drainer. 'So that women divorcing from an Islamic marriage living in the UK could claim a nice little share of assets, where previously they couldn't.'

She knew she'd touched a nerve. His own divorce was getting messy and expensive. 'Look, let's not fight.'

He crossed his arms. 'You have worked out that this Tammy Bishop's mother was the model who drowned off the boat. And the woman wants some answers. If it wasn't your fault, as you once told me, you have nothing to worry about, do you? You just have to explain to her all the circumstances and I am sure it will be fine. You don't need me to do that.'

'It was your boat. Your band. You've forgotten that.' It was odd. The conversation hadn't gone at all the way she'd expected it to. He was usually so placid. And helpful.

'Oh, no. You're not putting that one on me. I wasn't there, don't you remember? I don't have a clue what went on that night. How she drowned. How she ended up in the sea. I'd like to know myself.' He glowered at her.

She wanted to raise Ali al-Sayed. Find out more about him.

But it was far too late for that.

She trembled with rage.

'Get out!'

CHAPTER FORTY-SEVEN

HUW THOMAS WAS back on the M6 heading towards Cherrywood by a quarter past eight on Tuesday evening. So what if it was up and down the same road twice in a day? Perfectly fine! He'd told Mustafa he'd be in London all week so no one would expect him home. He needed time to himself, to organise his thoughts.

The drive up would give him the opportunity to mull things over. Bea Harrington's bitchy outburst had come out of nowhere. But the tension between them had been building for a while.

The Baroness of West Lingford was used to having her own way. She'd yelled 'Get out'. So that's what he'd done. The difference between him and all the other men she'd ordered around in her life was he could move on. These days he lived light. He would collect his shirts and suits from the cleaners the following week and find a serviced apartment somewhere close to Victoria at the same time.

It'd been a good idea to tip the wine down the sink. That way he wasn't over the limit. She would have loved to have got him on drink driving.

He was still smarting over her insults. It might have been tolerable if he'd been keen to keep the affair active. But he wasn't. So, he refused to let himself be drawn once again into her obsession. Her nagging memory. The drowning of the model. Huw and Bea had discussed it time and time again when they came across each other after so many years. 'Do you think I killed her,' she wallowed in self sympathy. 'If I hadn't insisted on her doing it, she would never have taken the job. I always felt bad about it.'

He'd comforted her more than once. A nice reply generally soothed her. 'If I hadn't owned the yacht and run the rock group, we'd have never made the film. She wouldn't have been on the boat. You can look at it in any way you want. But do I care? You worry too much.'

But it was never enough. 'Or maybe you don't worry enough,' she'd replied.

'Actions have consequences, but we are not always responsible. You need to see someone, Bea.' He'd put her on to Ali who only took on referrals for his London days via recommendations. Not that Huw got any thanks for it.

Huw pulled over at the first service station because now something she'd spat out at him in her anti-Muslim hissy fit bothered him. It needed checking.

He turned on his laptop. Mustafa had posted the photo of him and the Imam. The two elderly men from the mosque. What was so bad about a photo?

If it hadn't been for Mustafa, he'd throw his arms up in the air. Chuck it all in. And he didn't want the relationship between them screwed about by the likes of Bea Harrington.

His eyes ran over the section entitled: What I do for the community. Mustafa had done a good job.

Huw recalled how he'd watched him typing up the text on Saturday afternoon. They'd worked all over Sunday and into Monday.

But there were four extra entries.

- *Backed local residents in their development of the site of the Thirsty Farmer to include the provision of a new mosque.*
- *Joined local people to establish new faith schools.*
- *Agreed to bring in a curfew in Cherrywood to deal with rising antisocial behaviour in the Town Centre and, if necessary implement the banning of alcohol enforced by local community patrols.*
- *Campaigned to enforce standards of modesty in public to discourage prostitution, homosexual behaviour and immodest dress by underaged women.*

Huw Thomas read and reread the notice. He felt instant fury. He'd not approved those posts. The veins at the side of his head throbbed with anger. He took out his phone to call Mustafa to change the notices. Who gave you the right to put this bloody stuff up!?

But then he thought better of it. What a shit of a day! He needed a clear night to himself after all this domestic drama. He vowed to himself to leave it for now and tackle it first thing in the morning. Ring Nigel Harris. Take control of his own office affairs. Fix the site. Establish rules. Oversee his campaign. Schedule changes to the agenda.

He snapped the laptop shut, started the car and drove off flooring the pedal once on the M6. He was champing at the bit to get home. Longing for a can of soup and a hot shower.

At a little past ten-twenty he drove into his own road. The street, which was one of the most affluent in the area, was dark and quiet. So was the house. He parked in his drive, switched off the lights and slammed the car door shut behind him.

It wasn't until he approached the front door that he became aware of movement from within the house. He could have pulled his hair out. He'd forgotten about Mustafa's son Ali being there. How could he not have remembered when he'd been on his mind earlier? His coming home today was non-standard. So, what to do?

He would reassure them they were welcome to be there. It wasn't their fault he'd arrived home early. And the website was nothing to do with Ali, after all.

Ali al-Sayed and his wife were an unassuming couple. Bea Harrington had taken a couple of cracks at him and she'd been out of order. Her emotions were running wild.

They kept themselves to themselves. And you wouldn't know they were there except sometimes the coffee had to be replenished. They always kept any belongings packed away and out of sight when he was due back.

He unlocked the front door and called out, 'Hello.'

There was a lot of clattering from the kitchen area at the back of the house. He entered the lounge and flicked the switch. Two mugs and a couple of takeaway boxes stood on the coffee table. It reminded him he hadn't eaten for hours.

The door opened behind him and Ali wearing grey track pants and a tee-shirt came in looking very caught out.

'Huw. We weren't expecting you back. I'll clear the mess.' He raised a hand. 'Can you give me a minute?' He darted across to pick up the cups. 'I'm sorry, really.'

'No, not at all. It's all my doing. Change of plan.'

'So, what has brought you back?'

He didn't want to go into the personal fight between him and Bea. She was Ali's patient after all, wasn't she? And it was a trivial thing. 'I remembered a constituency issue which needed handling here tomorrow.'

'My father said you were in London this week.' Mustafa picked up the take-away boxes. 'When we know you will be around, we make ourselves scarce. Every time. You should have called or messaged. Advanced warning.'

Advanced warning? How would that work? He'd had no signs himself of being kicked out of Dolphin Square. 'You being here is fine with me. You can clear this in the morning. I'm going to make myself a quick coffee and get to bed.'

'Let me do it for you.'

'No, I'll do it myself.' He stretched and started towards the door.

'Please, I insist.'

'Really. I'd rather do it myself. I won't take long.'

'Well, that is not possible at the moment. Because my wife, Chadia, is in there. Ask me for whatever. I can get you anything, no problem.'

That was the problem. Someone he had allowed the use of his home was now standing in his way, blocking the door to his own fucking kitchen. Who needed it?

'We are just cooking up some food for tomorrow, nothing more. If you'd told us you were coming back.'

Huw couldn't smell a thing from the direction of the kitchen. They'd barely started. What was the big deal?

Huw knew some Muslims were uncomfortable with other men seeing their wives unveiled. As a

Labour MP for the constituency, he was sensitive to their needs. Muslim women's dress is not only a fashion statement. It's also an expression of their faith. He well knew that Ali's wife was ultra-religious. She covered her face, ears, and hair. He'd never seen what she actually looked like.

But this was Huw's house. And she was staying in it.

'We are busy cleaning up to leave. The place will be yours again in one hour. Less.'

'No worries. I'm off to bed.' It seemed a pointless debate. Leave the soup. He'd forgotten what else he intended to do. He'd deal with it later. Bea Harrington had booted him out of the flat in London. It seemed Ali and his wife were doing the same. Was there no justice in this world?

CHAPTER FORTY-EIGHT

IT WAS TUESDAY afternoon on a grey spring day and everybody with an interest was on the search for Beth Lane. Her abductor had released the film, and it was on every Far Right site from Europe to Australia and beyond.

It was a rough rerun of the Tessa Clark story, only worse. The humiliation and embarrassment had caused the girl to go into hiding, lose herself in the maze of London's labyrinth of back alleys and walkways. Hoping to find Beth before anyone else meant Karen Andersen had spent the entire afternoon looking for her.

Karen threw herself into the task. She wasted half the time taking the Central Line to Holborn, then back to Marble Arch. She walked the length of Park Lane and round to Piccadilly in a panic before focussing on locations where the odds of success were above zero, where the squatters and street people gathered, under the arches and underground passages connecting up London's ancient streets.

Karen kept Quacker informed on her progress, however ineffective. 'Beth said she'd rather sleep rough than go home. And she could be suicidal. I know I can work this out. Just give me some more time.'

Quacker called it mission impossible. But Karen couldn't go home, wouldn't go home, not without a result. She seethed with frustration. Another victim, another connection, another implication she'd fouled up somehow. 'I'm sure Tammy Bishop is behind this, Donald.'

But Quacker wasn't having it. 'There'd be little mileage in it for her. Any better ideas?'

'Beth said that once the guy used the name Orsa, something like that.' She puffed away near exhaustion point. 'Tall, creepy. The same as the one who called at Fatima's. Arms himself with photos of ISIS beheadings and a smartphone camera.'

From then on, they always referred to the perpetrator as Orson. It became Operation Orson.

Quacker was more concerned about Tammy Bishop. 'Orson's clear intention is to work through the women connected with the Jihadi bride list. Zinah al-Rashid might be a target too for him when she's released.'

Karen lost track of the number of Underground stations she checked out. She ran, and she ran and she ran.

At six o'clock, Quacker called her again. 'We should get someone round to Beth's house in Hounslow.'

'She won't be going there.'

'And there's always the media. But we don't want to go down that route more than we need,' said Quacker. 'These things have a habit of growing in the direction you don't want them to.'

'Growing badly in the direction you don't want them to? The film is already viral.'

'Look. I've rung some charity lines. People are concerned for her welfare other than yourself. We have her description out with the street crews.'

'She would not know who to go to or who to trust. Only me.'

'Karen. Why didn't you tell her you were undercover? Can't understand that,' Quacker challenged just before her phone died.

CHAPTER FORTY-NINE

'HAVE YOU SEEN this girl?'

Karen Andersen finally stopped from sheer exhaustion. It was past midnight, so technically Wednesday morning, 15 April. And she was in Westminster Underground Station.

'Well, maybe.' The rough sleeper had a neatly trimmed white beard and a friendly manner. Karen crouched down by his battered blue rucksack. 'A red head? I could help you if that is the case.'

She'd vowed to find Beth Lane. All she needed was to come across someone who had seen her. And she sensed she was getting close. 'But she doesn't have red hair.'

'You sure?'

'Long hair.'

'There was a woman here with jeans and boots last night but she had short hair to me. You got a picture?'

'My phone's dead. And she mentioned this place to me once.' The remnants of take-aways and beer cans were all about. A rat scurried across the rubbish. Karen jerked away in revulsion.

'If she's slept here before, she could very well come back. Most of us like to stick to the same routine. Are you here tonight?'

'No. But I hoped to find her by now.' Karen's breathing slowed, tired from the long and seemingly hopeless search. The acrid stench of urine was heavy in the air.

'There are some things you should know about it if you are. Sleeping rough is against the law. Section 4 of the Vagrancy Act. Four weeks ago, they told me to move on from this place. But here I am and it's the only home I know.' He held up a book of psalms. 'But our Lord will provide. Do you believe in the Lord?'

Karen sat down on a grubby mattress covered with an equally filthy bed sheet. It was as cold as a butcher's freezer and only April. She pulled a damp blanket over her shoulders ignoring the wreak of wet cigarette butts, shivering uncontrollably.

The passage was filled with the homeless, all wrapped up ready for the night. Beth Lane wasn't amongst them. Someone passed her a bottle and she drank deeply from it, filled with despair and slipping into unconsciousness.

A steady but insistent tapping on her shoulder woke her. 'Karen. Karen.' It was Haruto.

He slowly pulled her to her feet, whispering so as not to disturb anyone.

'How did you find me?' she said, when she realised who it was. 'I don't want to be found. Ever.'

'Quacker put a trace on your phone.'

Karen Andersen woke up from the most disturbed sleep she'd had in years. What day was it? Wednesday. For about ten minutes she floated in and out of post slumber. The most peaceful time for the human spirit. She was safe and amongst her familiar belongings. What had gone on in the last twenty-four hours?

She was in her own bed in her own flat. Alone. Everything was on silent alert. Who'd undressed her and got her under the covers? Haruto? It had to be. So, where was he?

She needed to put things back into focus. What had she been doing down the underpass? Where was Beth Lane? She vaguely remembered getting home. The extreme relief after the freezing conditions of the Underground entrance. Two people helping her out and up the steps. Quacker was the other one, probably.

Her phone lay on the carpet plugged in and charging. She teetered on the verge of a panic attack. The text to Haruto was still on the screen under texts. Sitting in the small rectangle. What if he'd seen it?

She pressed the phone icon at the bottom of the screen. Haruto Fraser. It rang a few times before he answered.

There was a silence as he shook himself out of sleep.

'Erm, why were you sleeping rough in Westminster Underground, Karen?' He sounded as cool and chilled as only Haruto could be. But there was an edge of impatience. 'Do you realise how much you drank last night?'

Her pulse picked up dramatically and she stumbled over her words. 'I was hoping Beth Lane would be there. Have you seen the film?' It was at that point she realised it was only five in the morning. 'Sorry, it's so early. Where's Beth? What's happened to her?'

'What's happened to you, Karen? You have got to get a grip or you won't make it. You know that, don't you? It's not Beth Lane nor Tessa Clark or Fatima Ahmed we're worried about. It's you. Your behaviour.'

'We?' Supposedly the grand 'we' was him and Quacker. They were now a couple. A tight little unit, it sounded. And she was well on the outer.

'You were muttering on about Zinah al-Rashid. You gave some of the rough sleepers a fright. It was bedlam down there. They expected a terrorist attack.'

'Yes, because everyone thinks it's all my fault this is happening. Because Tammy Bishop keeps writing me these damn letters saying she's no longer a threat. It's like I radicalised these women. Not Zinah al-Rashid. And they are in danger and not her. And I'm getting the blame. I went undercover and now I'm the one under suspicion.'

'You didn't have to do that.'

'What?'

'But you can never make work stop. That's why Quacker wanted to get you into the casinos. It's more like a nine to five. Just nine at night until five in the morning.' He gave a giggle, then a noisy yawn to emphasise the time.

She could feel the sinking in her stomach. 'Is that why you finished with me?'

'Karen? Why are you saying this? You worry me now. I think you should get more sleep.'

'I need to know the reason, Haruto.' Life was the pits. She'd planned the call and what she would say for days and here it was. Cold as ice. He didn't give a shit.

'You're obsessive, Karen. And that's not always a bad thing. You are one of the most brilliant people I have ever met. Perhaps you need someone who understands you better? How you are. The mood swings. They can be painful. Some of the things you say at times, you shouldn't.' She could tell he wasn't enjoying the conversation. 'Some of the things you do are fucking ridiculous.'

'I can change. I play the piano now to help me calm down when I know I'm getting a bit crazy.'

'I saw the piano. It's far too big for the flat. Why did you put it there?'

'Elspeth did. Not me. I was so low. It's tough to deal with how you broke up with me when I never thought you would leave me.' It was as much of an admission as she could make that he had torn her heart apart.

'I broke up with you? No Karen. You broke up with me.' The line was completely dead for what seemed like hours. She could hear him turn over in the bed somewhere. Where was he? Was he with someone? 'You broke up with me. We went through all that charade fixing a padlock to the bridge in Mainz. Why did you do all that?'

Her stomach involuntarily tightened into a knot. *Break up with him? What had she done?* 'Because I meant it.'

'You meant it at the time. When I suggested it. I know you did. But that's you, isn't it? Then you just change your mind and make fools of people. People who care for you. It's hurtful.'

'I didn't change my mind.'

'Then why did you remove it?'

CHAPTER FIFTY

'LABOUR MP MURDERED.'

Karen Andersen read the headline. The news was boggling. She had the Wednesday morning Daily Express open on the drop-down tray in front of her.

Eight hours earlier her boss had discovered her sleeping rough in Westminster while on a job for which she got no thanks, no acknowledgement and so she would do things her way. That's why at 10.30 Karen sat strapped in waiting to depart on the LH903 to Frankfurt.

The member of parliament for Cherrywood was dead. Beth Lane from Cherrywood was missing. A side column covered the campaign of terror against British Jihadi girls. The case Karen was working on, no doubt. She was stunned at the coincidence.

She slipped her phone off flight mode, careful not to be spotted by the cabin crew.

So why was Karen so reluctant to call Quacker and tell them where she was and why? Quacker would need to contact her. There was still time to talk to him before take-off. She'd even set out a list of bullet points. Things she had to clear.

Her thoughts were dashed by a brittle female voice. 'Put your blind up, please.' She'd been blocking the bright sun from her overtired eyes. 'Can you put your seat upright? And you need to put your table up.'

Karen Andersen knew the safety procedures. She was in an emergency exit row. She had to make a phone call. 'Just one second.'

'The table has to be up for an emergency evacuation. It's important that the passengers can get out easily.'

'And I'm by the window. And I'm about to raise my table.'

'Well then, I will just wait until you do that,' said the flight attendant. She hovered as if waiting for backup. 'And it's also important that the cabin crew can see outside. In case of a fire. Which is why I want your table up. Now!'

Karen held up her phone. 'Would you like to keep this for the rest of the trip? Just in case I don't put it on Airplane Mode. Then you'll be happy I've done everything you ordered me to?'

After this childish fit the attendant backed off and left to complete her rounds. Other passengers turned to stare and then smiled. Karen put the table up and even the paper aside in protest. Another cabin crew member arrived and told her it was all right to make calls for the time being. But the moment was gone. Quacker could wait.

Eventually the Cabin Crew Manager made the familiar, 'Sit back, relax, enjoy the flight.' They were on their way.

On her mobile a plethora of messages needed to be answered.

'You can't stop working,' Haruto had said. He'd been right. It'd been difficult enough to get a seat last minute. Quacker could definitely wait.

How could she advance the case while she was suspected of being sloppy? Quacker had raised what had happened in Germany. Haruto had told Quacker about their trip.

Haruto had accused Karen of ending their affair. Suggested she'd removed the padlock from the bridge. What was he playing at? Something had happened there. Bad vibes. Time to find out what had gone on. Time to do a one eighty and start afresh.

From Frankfurt Airport Karen took the twenty minute ride on the S-Bahn into the Hauptbahnhof in the City.

Lugging her heavy bag, she found the storage lockers adjacent to track 103. There were several primed and available. Closing the locker to 1630m, Karen withdrew the key.

Leaving the station, it was then a short walk towards Willy-Brandt-Platz on to Neue Mainzerstrasse, Untermainkal, Mainkal to the iron bridge. Her heart was in her mouth. What was she doing here?

It was the first time back in a year. It was not only a great place to view the historic part of downtown Frankfurt, but it was where couples got engaged. Lovers flocked there. It was where she and Haruto sealed their love by locking their padlock to the latticework.

She held the key in her hand. What would she do with it when she found it? Leave it or remove it? It was all over. So why had he brought it up? As Quacker had asked, 'Is Haruto trustworthy?' What had he been up to?

She saw the spires of the Dom and other churches in the background. She took out her phone and scrolled back to the picture she'd taken on the day. It showed the specific location they'd picked. A sensible move. There were thousands of locks. They'd photographed it so they could revisit and find it easily.

A musician played "True Love" on his accordion, a coin-filled cap open on the footpath in front of him. He was the same guy who had serenaded the morning they'd visited. He could have done the recital in his sleep. He had been part of the picture. Overhead a seagull squawked in disapproval.

She flicked open the photos. The two of them arm in arm. Kissing. Playfighting. A picture pointing to the lock. It was one of a bunch. Bright green. It stuck out against the three red ones and five others around it, which were plain brass.

The sun's rays briefly lit up the bridge. It spurred her on. Eventually, she came across it. The exact whereabouts. The ironwork was spot on. Shaped like a six leafed clover. She found the collection of padlocks. There were two red ones still in place. The brass ones were still intact. But there was no green lock. Their lock had been removed!

Karen bent down closer. She checked around the back, then moved on to the next set of locks. There had to be some mistake.

By now her mind was racing. Haruto had been right all along. He hadn't been lying. Their special lock had gone all right. And how could that have happened when Karen was the only one who had the key?

CHAPTER FIFTY-ONE

THE MEDIA COVERAGE of the killing of Huw Thomas on Wednesday morning got everyone talking straight away. BREAKING NEWS: LABOUR MP FOUND DEAD AT HOME. Quacker picked it up on Twitter. The first report took the line it was natural causes. Possibly a heart attack.

A journalist working to create more of a story put out something on self-harm. At thirty-eight past eleven, a newsflash came out that the death was being treated as 'suspicious'. At forty-eight past eleven, it had moved to: 'LABOUR MP FOUND STABBED TO DEATH IN CONSTITUENCY HOME.'

A local TV crew arrived first to capture the scene. Police and forensics crawled all over the red brick detached house in Cherrywood. Reporters and cameramen from all the media jostled to get shots, held at a distance by the yellow tape. Bit by bit the details of the discovery emerged. His cleaner had found him in the kitchen, lying in a pool of blood.

Quacker paced the room. He was pretty annoyed with Karen Andersen. He'd waited until ten in the morning to contact her to see how she was. He'd reckoned after half a night on the floor of an underpass, she needed the sleep. But now he was running out of patience. This huge story had broken, and she'd disappeared into the ether. All his calls went straight to voicemail. He'd left several messages. She'd dropped off the radar.

Along with the murder, they'd run a snippet on the Jihadi bride case. It had to be. Cyberbullying of Muslim women in London and the Midlands. Someone with Far Right connections was behind it. A woman in Acton who couldn't be named for safety reasons claimed a lanky guy verbally abused her daughter and then set the family home on fire. He'd been described as a tall, smartly dressed, white man. The TV had just reported that a resident living close by had seen someone who fitted this brief hanging about outside the Cherrywood MP's place the previous day.

The press as yet hadn't picked up on Beth Lane, who had described to Karen someone quite similar. The one they dubbed Orson. This is why Quacker had to speak to Andersen urgently.

He rang Haruto Fraser to ask him to whizz round to Devonshire and check up on her. He'd found her flat locked up. The neighbour, Elspeth Cochrane, said she'd seen her heading out earlier, but didn't know where she'd gone.

'Let's move on with this ourselves, shall we?' said Quacker, when Haruto pitched up at Acton. 'Just in case it is the same guy. Karen will get in touch eventually.'

In less than two minutes, Haruto had Huw Thomas's website up in front of him on his laptop.

'It's not long been updated,' said Haruto. His knowledge of JavaScript impressed Quacker who would happily admit his cyber craft was limited, to say the least. 'Huw Thomas states on this he's the pro-

Sharia spokesperson for Labour. But two days ago, the site had other text.'

'When was that exactly?'

'They made an entry on it on Saturday afternoon about some public meeting to be held. Nothing about Sharia. Nor the street patrols. It looks as if these were added later.'

'Any idea where Karen could have been off to?' asked Quacker. He was aware there'd been a big domestic issue.

'She's not answering my calls either.'

It left them both with an uneasy feeling.

CHAPTER FIFTY-TWO

THE CHERRYWOOD LABOUR Party Constituency Headquarters became the centre of operations following the death of their MP. Quacker called the office at half-past twelve and an assistant placed him on hold. He was told there were others ahead of him. The election agent, Mustafa al-Sayed, was handling the media, and Partridge Security would have to wait their turn. Eventually, Quacker got through.

'We were very good friends,' said Mr al-Sayed. 'A better friend he couldn't have been. The pain inside is something I can't explain.' He hypothesised at length. How his much-loved MP was killed for his admirable principles. He based this on the work he'd done recently. His contention was that it was connected with the defacing of the local mosque. He deplored how Huw Thomas had become a victim. Words failed him. 'But I can't be speaking to you fellows too much anyway. I am in the middle of enquiries everywhere at the moment. Turn on your TV and you will see me on the world news.'

Mustafa was right. He was the main broadcast event. He'd flown off the handle at several reporters who'd touched on a rift in the local office. But finally, he'd found one who wasn't so biased. 'Now will someone jolly well listen? Anyone who sticks up for Muslims gets it in the neck. This is only being picked up because Huw Thomas was so jolly famous.'

'Are you saying there are more incidents like these that don't make the press?' The reporter was listening closely, sensing a story line.

'The problem is with the reporting of events to do with race. Today people see all Asians as Muslims and all Muslims as terrorists,' Mustafa went on, basking in the attention.

'Not all of them, surely?'

'Yes, all. All. But police arrested more white guys last year for plotting bad things than they did Asians for plotting bad things. These racist thugs land at Birmingham Airport daily and hotfoot into Cherrywood straightaway. And you know what? No one does anything about it. That is the dilemma.'

'But, on his website, Huw Thomas supported a curfew? Which meant everyone had to be in their homes by a certain time?'

'He did indeed. Absolutely.'

'Bit extreme, wasn't it?'

'No, no, no. Not at all. You come and live here. See for yourself. Most of these fights and bottle-throwing events are alcohol-fuelled. You've got these people coming here from Eastern Europe. Getting straightaway on the turps. Then they go around causing trouble.'

'But isn't that a job for the police?'

'Sure. But the cuts have hit hard here. Where are the boys in blue? Nowhere to be seen. Back watching CCTV after the act. It means our local communities have to do their job for them. Huw was very supportive of that.'

The UK's Counter Terrorism Security Office agreed that this element of criminal activity was the fastest-growing area of their responsibility in protecting the public against harm. But they declined to comment on the case at this stage of the investigation.

The coverage continued right throughout Wednesday. At one time Huw Thomas would have been a contender for the most laid-back MP in Westminster. Now he was the most well-known for all the wrong reasons.

It'd been a sad day for the Cherrywood Labour team. Not only had they lost their great constituency representative, but also their accountant. Only days before he'd survived a vicious attack by white hooligans and had been suffering dizzy spells from the assault ever since. That morning apparently he'd fallen backwards down the office stairs and broken his neck.

Everyone was in double mourning.

CHAPTER FIFTY-THREE

BEA HARRINGTON SLUMPED into depression. Couldn't dress. Couldn't move. Couldn't even cry. She cowered in the bathroom. If only she could go to sleep and wake up to find Huw's murder had just been a nightmare. Erase the memory of the last twenty-four hours. Turn the clock back to two o'clock on Tuesday. But it was impossible.

Her brain churned. Soon it would surely explode. Why the hell had she asked him to leave? To pack up and get out? Forced him to drive back up north? What'd got into her? His unwillingness to support her over Tammy Bishop? To calm her fears? Or a rush of jealousy when she'd learnt he was seeing other women? Did it matter? She burnt with remorse and self-hatred.

I'll regret it as long as I live.

What's the use? Poor Huw was dead now, and it was all over the papers. He wasn't coming back, was he? Whatever they were going through divorce-wise, his estranged wife would be distraught. If not for herself, for his children.

I'm solely to blame, she told herself and curled up in a ball on the sofa.

It's my fault. They'd exchanged angry words but then it had blown into a full-on screaming match. Had it not been for their fight, he'd still be alive. She may even have cancelled two committee meetings. He'd be

229

in the kitchen right now. Probably making her some fucking coffee. Any excuse to shirk the Commons. Yup, that was Huw.

Bea turned on the television again. There was the same shot they'd showed ten times earlier of his house in Cherrywood. More flowers kept arriving. A policewoman was in charge of laying them on the pavement next to the gate.

You have to turn this bloody TV off. You have to get out of here.

But she couldn't under the grip of depression. She found the volume control on the remote and turned it down. It still didn't cut it off completely. She pressed mute. Finally it worked. Peace at last.

A new section of the film played, which initially made her think they'd swapped to another story. But it looked familiar. A full shot of Dolphin Square with her apartment in the middle of it rang big alarm bells.

She jabbed furiously at the remote before finding the mute button to turn the sound back on. 'Police are puzzling over the fact the MP shouldn't even have been in his constituency home last night. He should have been in London. Huw Thomas. Expected in parliament today to cast a vote. Instead, the subject of a major murder enquiry.'

Bea shook her head. Her legs went weak. She flicked off the screen.

It would only be a matter of time before they would be knocking on her door, wouldn't it? Or was she panicking for nothing? What had all this to do with her? Either way, she needed to come up with a plan and quickly.

What would she say about their living arrangement? Which angle were the media going to take on his relationship with her? It'd be too late once she'd spoken to the press to change story.

What if the Tammy Bishop matter became public?

Caffeine. That's what she needed! She shuffled back to the kitchen and snapped on the kettle. It was not time to be weak-kneed.

A sudden change occurred. This was all Huw's fault. He'd needn't have been so damn smug. Had he concerned himself with her situation for two minutes instead of his own, they'd never have argued. Her stomach rumbled. It was reading empty. She opened the fridge and saw his bottle of white wine from the night before still half full. She'd moved on to the Gordons until the tonic had run out.

She took out a stale croissant, ran it under the tap and put it in the oven. It would have to do because there was nothing else. And she couldn't go anywhere right now.

While the coffee was percolating, she walked to the back of the flat. The spare bedroom was like a ghost room. It was clear but for a suitcase propped against the wall. They'd agreed he could collect it once he'd decided where he was moving to. But otherwise, it was impeccable. He'd told her on his way that he'd left it tidy so she could advertise it online. His parting jibes.

Poor Huw.

She returned to the kitchen and switched on the smaller TV. A different channel was on. But there was no escape from the media coverage.

'Our top story today. The Labour MP for Cherrywood has been found dead at his constituency home.'

Constituency home. OK.

'The MP had a year ago split from his wife of twenty years. He was therefore not at his London address in Islington.' Islington. 'He was found with stab wounds to the neck and chest.'

The film crew showed the house from a different angle. The usual yellow tape around the crime scene. A close up of the hothouse roses. No mention of her. Of Dolphin Square. Good.

Next up on the television came Huw's agent from the constituency. Ali al-Sayed's father. Decent bloke. He was delivering straight into shot. Lamenting the death of their very popular MP.

So, what about the possible deselection at the next election? Had Huw been lying to her about all that? Or was Mustafa al-Sayed feeling as bad as her?

The unconvincing show of sympathy was drawn out as much as possible.

'This must be a terrible blow for you.' The reporter's microphone crept into shot for his response.

'The sad reality is I'm not surprised. Not in the very least. This is all about Islamophobia out of control. Huw stood up for us.' He told his story. Extremist thugs had assaulted his own wife and her friend in a chicken shop when they were both wearing the hijab. The assaulters, four white teenagers, had thrown chips and cans at them and yelled 'Go back to your bloody country'. Huw Thomas had sent them flowers. He ended, 'He was a lovely guy. That's the kindness he was known for right across the constituency.'

Bea took the croissant out of the oven. It'd come up well. Wetting it first was a trick she'd learnt years ago from the South of France.

God, keep France out of the news.

But Mustafa al-Sayed hadn't finished. He went on, 'This Far Right activity has been ramping up and nobody does anything about it.' The reporter was letting him flow. 'Even as we speak there are individuals on Twitter glorifying the killing of Huw Thomas. These people are sick.'

Bea flicked off the TV, and the flat was once again quiet. What to do next?

She opened her walnut writing bureau and selected a blank correspondence card and quickly scribbled a note of condolence to Huw's wife to put in the post. Cleared the decks. Tidied away the breakfast crumbs. At two forty-five that afternoon, Bea Harrington was finally ready to venture out for the first time that day. She had to resume some normal routine. Head into the Lords. Soldier on.

The journalist must have been waiting within the grounds for some hours. She had a cameraman with her. 'Baroness Harrington? Would it be possible to have a word?'

'Certainly. What's it about?'

What's it about? The words popped out of her mouth before she could stop them. Nerves. It made her sound as heartless as hell.

'Huw Thomas?'

'Yes, of course.' The damn woman was too close.

'Was it true the Labour MP, Huw Thomas, was living here?'

'Just while he was in London. We were great friends. I'm heartbroken.' She pushed forward and said, 'If you'll excuse me, I have to go.'

She hurried away and the crew continued their filming all the way out to Grosvenor Road. Bea flagged down a passing taxi. It was obvious she was also in the spotlight. She didn't want to go where there'd be a hundred other questions asked. So instead, she told the cabbie, 'Take me to Harrods, please.'

With Huw Thomas dead, there was no one to unwind to about Tammy Bishop. She tried to call the Private Investigator, Karen Andersen.

She couldn't think of anyone else.

CHAPTER FIFTY-FOUR

WEDNESDAY, 15 APRIL. It was around three o'clock European time when Karen Andersen returned to Frankfurt Hauptbahnhof. She had a few more hours left before she could check-in for her return flight. She was numb from a lack of sleep.

So, it had been true all along! Haruto Fraser hadn't made it up. Their love lock was gone. But something didn't fit. The only key had been in her bedside drawer all this while. So, how had it come about?

Why would someone bother to hacksaw through the tightened steel of the lock? And then what? To toss it into the river afterwards? And was it important?

She checked her phone. There were several messages. Everyone was trying to contact her. Haruto, Quacker. And now Bea Harrington wanted to rush a meeting on Tammy Bishop for some reason. What was that about? Before she could answer, there were facts to check. Backtracking required. What was the German connection Quacker spoke about? And why did Haruto dob her in it, if he had? It was about that time that things between had soured.

What did her stay in Mainz have to do with the assaults on the Jihadi girls? So what if some of the other sharers at the house where she had stayed last with Haruto had been members of a Far Right organisation? But what had they found out about her? Perhaps she hadn't leaked data, but it'd been stolen from her. If so, she had to face her fears and come clean with Quacker.

At the time neither Haruto nor Karen had struck it as a worry who the other guests were. In love, their thoughts were on each other. Perhaps in retrospect they should have been more vigilant. An eclectic mix of under forties from all across Europe. From circus performers to intellectuals and bankers. But had someone amongst them taken the opportunity to access her phone, her diaries? If so, they could have hacked the WhatsApp group and been tracking these women for twelve months, if not more.

She waited for the three-fifteen regional service to Mainz. The train moved in sedately down the track, stopping at every station. What would she unearth when she got there? If she ever did? They rumbled on at what seemed like inch by inch. She was undecided. Should she now go back or go forward?

Niederrad, Stadon.

The train stopped at Frankfurt Airport. It was too early for her flight home. Should she get off now and remain at the airport for her departure? She stood at the door, hesitating with indecision.

The padlock matter had shaken her up. But all that was in the past now to a certain extent. Not exactly earth-shattering. Not life and death. She had to focus on what was important.

Seated directly opposite Karen, a dark-haired man with a bushy beard was busy messaging three young blonde-haired girls at one time on Facebook, switching from one to the other. The Islamic call to prayer sounded as a ringtone and he answered with a big grin. Was he stalking them? Did they really know who they were chatting to?

Shades of Beth Lane's abduction. The coincidence between the two Cherrywood events. Was it the same guy? If so, he was growing more violent each time. No, now was not the time to do nothing. There was no choice. Karen had to continue on. Brace herself for loss of face.

She sank back into her seat.

The sky was turning pale orange as they pulled into Russelsheim. It took an eternity, Opelweek, stop. Gustavsbur, stop. Her fellow passengers got off at the Romishes Theater stop. Just as Karen drifted off, they arrived at Mainz Banhof with an abrupt jerk.

CHAPTER FIFTY-FIVE

KASPER ROSENTHAL LIVED in Rosenheim, an historic suburban area in the city of Mainz. He was a towering giant of a man with short, white-blonde hair and pale blue Germanic eyes.

His home, the place were Karen and Haruto had stayed the summer before, was a sprawling mini-mansion on a good street and in the heights overlooking the Rhine. Six bedrooms, three baths and a garden that had a swimming pool for the summer.

Fortunately for Karen he was at home to answer the door. But even if he hadn't been, what she'd been looking for earlier and expected to never see again was staring her in the face. The missing love lock. Their bright green love lock. It was being used to bolt a bicycle to a railing in the garden.

'Karen.' He spoke perfect English with a trace of a German accent. 'I was vondering when you would revisit us. That's your padlock from the Eiserbach Bridge. I am sure you recognise it.'

'I've just come from there in fact.' The thought that Herr Rosenthal would have removed the padlock forcibly just didn't compute with Karen. He glanced from the chained bike and back to Karen who held up the key. 'I have to ask how come, when I have the key?'

'Yes, Karen. You have ze key. But you don't have ze only one. Which is how the padlock is now back on the bicycle. But I don't think I should take the blame,' and his face turned pink with embarrassment. Guilty as hell, Karen thought.

It was just after four on Wednesday afternoon, but it was obvious from the hot buttery smells that dinner was already on the way. 'Why don't you come in? I think you deserve a proper explanation.'

She followed him into the enormous kitchen where he was in the middle of dunking a pork fillet in flour. 'You've travelled all the way from London just for this? Surely not.'

He swung open the king-sized silver fridge to find a beer for her.

'No thanks.'

'I'm having one. Now that you are here, that is. Otherwise, I would not drink at zis time of the day. Are you sure?'

'Yes, thanks.'

He ripped the top from a bottle of Paulaner. 'I was hoping you would never find out about this.'

'Find out about what? That you went all the way into Frankfurt to remove a padlock from a bridge and use it because you thought we'd never know?'

'Well, so many people say they will go back to the bridges to check on their lock. And they never do. But it wasn't me who did it, anyway.'

The story was that the padlock belonged to his on-off girlfriend Helga, who'd unlocked it. It had never been his property to give it to them in the first place.

'The day we went to the Eisherbach, I saw it on the sideboard. I like to please, you know? So, I gave it to you thinking it belonged to someone who'd been living here in the house but had left.'

'When in fact it was Helga's?'

'She was mad as hell about it. Because it was her padlock. Ooooh - ee. When she asked me what had happened to it, I told her. Why should I not?' He clapped his hands together. He seemed to find the whole situation hilarious. 'And she is a very good detective. Maybe better than you.' His tone was rather annoying. 'Can you believe she picked it out from all those hundreds and hundreds of padlocks!'

'Amazing. Did she by any chance use the photographs I so carefully took so that either Haruto or myself could find it again if we wanted to?' Karen had tagged Kasper in on the pictures. Now she was feeling a little dizzy from a combination of hunger and fatigue. 'And you are aware Haruto thinks I did it? I removed it?'

'That's good,' he said, paying no attention to her sarcasm. 'Very good. It's great he thinks that. It pays to keep a man keen, Karen.' He started to fry the pork fillets. The hissing sound as the pork cooked made conversation difficult for a time.

'But you are not here because of that. I can feel it in my bones.' He lifted the meat with a stainless-steel spatula, checked the pork was cooked and turned off the gas. 'You are here because Haruto caught Helga going through your things. And you want to know why, don't you?'

As soon as he said that, Karen felt a coldness pass through her. It was like shell-shock. The room was silent as a grave. She crossed her arms. 'Ok, go on then. So why? What was she looking for?'

'You can ask her about it yourself. She'll be here shortly for dinner. She still runs after me like a little puppy dog.'

'I can't stay unfortunately. I've got a plane to catch.'

Karen had to get back to Frankfurt. But she also didn't want to hang around Kasper any longer than needed. The house had become threatening in a strange way Karen couldn't identify. She made a quick apology about the railway station lockers being time limited and made her escape.

On the way back to Mainz Station she picked up vibes that someone was following her. Several times she turned, but couldn't see anyone.

It was now crucial to get back to London. She was urgently required. She was flat out. Running around in circles and getting nowhere fast. At twenty to six that evening, and with time running out, she raced to the locker at the Hauptbahnhof to pick up her bag. As she did so, she felt a tug at her arm. Someone who'd been chasing after her and was equally breathless held on to it with a vice-like grip.

'We need to talk. Just you and me.'

CHAPTER FIFTY-SIX

THERE HAS TO be a link!

The death of Huw Thomas. The assaults on the Jihadi brides. Tammy Bishop getting out of prison. Partridge Security spent the rest of the afternoon looking for some interdependence. The only word in from Karen Andersen, whose input was vital to the case, had been a text at around 1700 GMT. She was in Germany but would return later that night. Nothing more.

By then, both Partridge Security and Stop Hate agreed that it was wise to keep quiet about Beth Lane, to shield her from the press, who would delve deeper otherwise. She was vulnerable, possibly suicidal and still nowhere to be found.

But Beth's mother acted differently. Quacker had contacted her the day before to tell her that her daughter was missing. She'd then heard about the assassination in Cherrywood via her sister and TV reports. So, she'd bypassed them all and gone to the media herself. When the press searched the name 'Beth Lane' online, they came across the porn video.

It could have been a stellar story for them. Had Huw Thomas known about the sexual assault? As her local MP he might have done. And was the attacker a local?

It quickly emerged that Huw Thomas had held a surgery on the Saturday at the library where Beth Lane worked. Had his killer been there too?

'Thomas didn't give many constituency surgeries. It was odd that he should have one just before his murder,' said Quacker. 'And as a result, he wasn't well known by the locals, it seems.'

They began investigating the MP's background. Not giving surgeries wasn't such a big deal. Some MPs had had little or no contact with their voters for up to ten years. But the MP for the leafy vales of Cherrywood's voting record hadn't been great either. Haruto found a poll online that confirmed a woeful score of 59.6 per cent for absenteeism.

In response to the trashing, Thomas had posted on his Twitter: 'Only newbies trying to get a place in the cabinet turn up all the time.'

'He could be right,' said Quacker. 'And sometimes Members of Parliament don't vote on specific issues deliberately. So that doesn't necessarily mean too much. Opposition MPs are more likely to abstain for tactical reasons. Mostly that happens because of the many amendments put forward by Tories pressing the government to write in keeping with the views of the right-wing of the party.'

'But it might explain why he wasn't in parliament the day he was supposed to be,' said Haruto. 'And the fact that he was pretty laid back about his whole operation. There's a blog here from the right-wing saying his election agent, Mustafa al-Sayed, mostly ran the constituency because Huw was never around.'

'Which adds up with the radical claims on the website. Probably Mustafa's ideas, not Huw's, who seems to have left quite a lot more than just day to day running of things to him.'

The local newspaper had followed it up with an interview where Huw Thomas stood outside the House of Commons defending his position. 'Mustafa al-Sayed works for me. He is competent, loyal and puts in all the hours available to him. And I usually spend Thursday night and Friday back in my constituency in Cherrywood.

'But he was killed on a Tuesday,' Haruto added. 'Not a Thursday or Friday. That doesn't add up. Why wasn't he in London?'

But if anywhere needed leadership, it was Cherrywood. It typified the clash of two extreme philosophies, said the Daily Mail. An example of 'integration not working' in British cities. The Far Right and the Muslim community were at each other's throats, literally. And Cherrywood was being more and more Islamicised by the day.

There was no doubt in the minds of Haruto and Quacker that this surge in Islamification had something to do with the horrific murder of Huw Thomas.

However, there was also another component, the sex angle which the afternoon papers picked up on. The headline sure to sell copies, thought Quacker. WHO KILLED PARTY-LOVING LABOUR MP?

CHAPTER FIFTY-SEVEN

GLEN GIBB HATED the stuffy little basement. It was as if it had a strangle-hold on him. He couldn't breathe in there. Unsurprisingly, he got out of it as much and as often as he could. He planned to move out permanently very soon.

On Wednesday, 17 April, he would have headed out for sure. But the night before had caught up with him. He'd started feeling pretty hungover from the whiskey. And his eyes ached from a thousand views of Beth Lane spread-eagled, naked as a jaybird. Panic-struck.

Yes, he could have been off in the car, dressed smartly and looking for work. He'd even got some leads. He yearned to put this Islamic crap behind him. Give himself a much-needed break. But then there'd been the murder of Huw Thomas. Some nosy neighbour had seen him outside the house.

Was Huw Thomas off his rocker? Had he lost his marbles? He'd been the MP there for ten years. Never done bugger all. Then all of a sudden hyperactivity, like he had converted to Islam, promoting Sharia law and encouraging street patrols. Organising meetings at the mosque. Posting pictures of himself with the imam. Protesting about attacks on girls wearing the hijab. Double-crossing and a traitorous fraud. He was a threat to everything British. Didn't he realise what he was setting himself up for?

Glen Gibb almost let out a scream of frustration and anger. He was climbing up the wall and dying a slow death of boredom. But best to pull down the blinds. Retreat. Sometimes there was pleasure in darkness. And he'd been burning the candle at both ends maybe just that bit too long.

He hated this dump of a room even more than overpriced motels. But he had to be smart. Keep out of view. Just in case the police could build a case against him.

The upside was there was plenty on his laptop to entertain him, the naked shots of Beth right at the top of the list.

Let's go to the movies!

CHAPTER FIFTY-EIGHT

TAMMY BISHOP FINGERED and fiddled with the gold necklace nonstop. She'd not worn it for years. It was Wednesday, 17 April, the day of her release. She trembled uncontrollably. Don't get too excited and keep tugging at it, she told herself, or you'll break it.

Stepping out of prison was exhilarating and terrifying in one. The scariest experience ever. Why was it? The agonising wait for time to pass as the day approached, the excitement. But somehow, she'd expected to feel better than she did now the moment had arrived.

Putting on normal clothes was the first shock. She'd gained far more weight than she'd thought. The brown trousers that Karen Andersen had sent her didn't fit. A charity had donated a pair of size fourteen denim jeans, so she wore those. Anything to leave Bronzefield in something new.

The money felt different. Plastic, not paper. And smaller. But it would tide her by. The prison gave her a voucher for the cab to the station and also a train ticket from Staines to Acton Central. It was heart-breaking not to have her grandmother alive to greet her. But inshallah there'd be plenty of her nick-nacks to remember her by back home.

Inshallah? God willing? What was she thinking of? The phrases were on the brain. Like a song you can't get out of your head. Total reflex. Unplanned. Arabic, Islamic terms were a habit hard to shake. They were now haram. To be forbidden and wiped out from her new self.

The cab arrived. Alone in the taxi all was silent. Eerie after the constant yelling and intercom interruptions. The keys. The damn locks. The car made her feel sick. The motion and the smell. But she could also sense a smile forming and spreading.

The world is so different. Everything's changed. And me too!

She loved her new name. 'I'm Tammy Bishop,' she said to the taxi driver. She'd never ever go back to the old one. Zinah al-Rashid was obsolete. Stay firm. I've made it through the rough times. I'm as strong as an ox! I have a future of amazing possibilities. My mother is watching over me.

She sat back and mouthed along to the old seventies tune playing loudly inside her head. "I will survive!" She remembered it had been one of Bea Harrington's favourites, back when they were colleagues. Tammy got all worked up when she thought of her. The letter she'd sent. Yes, it was time they got together and talked.

She caught sight of a newspaper which the cabbie had put on the dashboard. What was going on in this new world? 'Can I see the paper, please?' she asked, super-sweetly.

'Keep it if you like.' The driver knew he had an ex-prisoner newly released in the back. It was his gift, the smallest of gestures.

There was plenty of reading matter. The Easter heatwave. The Brexit Extension. But the headline on the front page couldn't be missed. 'Labour MP Huw Thomas murdered'.

Speculation was rife and varied. This particular paper had taken up the sleazy side. Jealousy looked like being at the heart of his downfall. They claimed to have an exclusive on this scoop. How he'd been found wearing a pair of Snoopy sleeping shorts. He had a tattoo near his genitals with the letters B and W. The initials of a former reality star girlfriend.

'Great stuff, innit?' said the driver, over his shoulder. 'Poor bugger. He's not even cold on the slab yet and they've got all this shit on him.'

On the inside pages the paper had a potted history of the MP going right back to his school days. The old Etonian was a one-time record manager of a boy band called Love The Moon. He'd once owned a sixty-two-foot Swan, moored at St. Tropez in the South of France. His upcoming divorce to an heiress. And more recently his co-habitation with the Conservative peer, Baroness Harrington.

'They go on and on about his many affairs and all that,' said the cabby, as he turned into Gresham Road. 'But I think it was nothing to do with it. He was all lovey-dovey with the Jihadi lot. That was what I read somewhere else. Do you know the crowd? On about Allah all the time. Want to blow us up. Some people weren't too happy about it. The Far Right. So, I figure he was probably knocked off by one of those extremists. Don't you?'

CHAPTER FIFTY-NINE

HELGA HOM HAD followed Karen Andersen from Rosenheim to Frankfurt's Hauptbahnhof. She was tall, with jet-black short hair and unmistakable model looks

'Oh, my God, it's you,' Karen gasped in relief. 'What are you doing here?'

'Kasper will wonder where I am. He's been messaging. And he has a habit of appearing out of nowhere. I don't have a lot of time.' She had gone quite white with fear.

Karen had carefully reviewed the kitchen conversation on the ride back to Frankfurt. How Haruto had caught Helga in their room going through her things. And now it was all about to be confirmed first-hand.

They found a quiet spot in a cafe.

'Look, Helga, just tell me everything. Otherwise I can easily arrange a full raid on the house at Rosenheim. Believe me, I can.'

'I'm sorry about what happened. I went through your stuff because Kasper insisted. I would have done anything for him back then. Really, I would.'

'What were you looking for? What did you think you would find?' Karen didn't know whether she was ready to hear the truth, that she'd leaked data that could cost lives. 'I need you to tell me. I'm in so much trouble.'

'Any information on Islamic terrorists and their cells. Names. Contacts. The stuff you might have on your phone.'

'Why?'

'Kasper joined the AfD, the Alternative fur Deutschland, first off to protest over the refugee camps. He wanted them banned completely. He heard the politicians saying if Germans didn't like the number of immigrants, those Germans could leave. That made him crazy. And so then he set up his own organisation. It's teeny. But he is fanatical now, obsessed with it all. It's bad.'

'How bad?'

'He spends half his time reading right-wing papers. He goes on and on about the assassinations which were carried out by the Red Army during the War. His father was connected with the bombing of a Munich beer garden. And his brother was with the police and part of a group chat that used Nazi iconography. I came across it. And recently he's got worse.'

'Where do I come into this?'

'He found out what you do. A sort of undercover operation for a company that works for the British Home Office? There's a branch of right-wingers here that are linked to the English Concern Group. Have you heard of them? He was involved with them for a while. They knew about you and how you and Haruto were an item. So, he invited Haruto to stay with us on purpose. When Haruto found out what was going on, he challenged Kasper. It was the afternoon you'd gone into Frankfurt on your own. Kasper told Haruto to get out. That was when he cleared the room of your stuff and locked the door. I assumed you knew why.'

'No, I didn't. But why do you think Kasper wanted this information? What good could it have done him?'

'It was all over a woman called Carla Schmidt. She was a sportswoman until ISIS radicalised her. She'd married a fighter, then returned to Frankfurt when he died in Syria. Kasper told me he wanted to kill her. In fact, "exterminate them all" were the words he used. He loathes these Jihadi brides. Kasper had met an English man who had just come back from Syria looking for his brother. Turns out ISIS beheaded him. They'd discussed some form of reprisal which they could do together. Carla Schmidt changed her name and moved to the UK. I think Kasper hoped that if he got her details out of you, this guy would have done the job for him.'

'So that's how you turned up the names in the circle? From one of my burner phones?' Karen buried her head in her hands. That's how he would have got the details. Quacker was right. *How could she have been so damn careless?*

'But that's just it. I found nothing. You know that. There was no diary. No phones. Kasper was furious with me. But what did he expect? Being a private investigator and working for the Home Office, I knew you wouldn't leave stuff around like that.'

'You found nothing?' Karen closed her eyes. It was an unexpected release of tension. She'd achieved what she'd come for. Karen put an arm out and reassured Helga. 'But this sounds like the same one, the same guy we are after. Does the name Orson mean anything?'

'No. But no one uses their real names in these groups. I think he had some take up with horses. He talked about racing over the phone. Kasper called him GG I remember.'

'Please, is there any description of him?'

'I never met him. But Kasper has a selfie with him. They're the same height. If I can access his phone without him knowing, I can get it for you.'

Helga rose to her feet. There was only the matter of the bridge to sort out.

'What about the padlock? What was behind all that?' Karen asked.

'I bought it for Kasper and me. I wanted us to be together. But he didn't pick up on the hint. Or didn't want to. When I learnt he'd given it to you, it was humiliating. The last thing in the world I wanted was to leave it there. I'm very sorry. I should have told you, I know. I never thought you'd find out.'

'When did you take it off?'

'The next morning.'

Aha. All is clear at last.

Haruto had revisited the scene at some point and found it gone. He'd blamed Karen ever since.

'I should finish with Kasper, shouldn't I?' Her eyes filled. 'I just can't, Karen. I love him so much. But I wish he'd change. Do you think he will?' She wasn't expecting an answer.

They had already made their goodbyes. Karen had a flight to catch. Helga would return to Mainz and say she'd been studying. She was doing an MA in English. Kasper had messaged again to see where she was.

'Just one more thing,' asked Karen, as they left the cafe. 'Helga, have you ever heard anything about someone from the UK called Zinah al-Rashid? She's been in prison for terrorism offences. And she came

253

out today. Which is why I must get back to the UK in a hurry. We have to protect her from this nutter. She's turned informant and is at risk.'

'Yes. But Kasper won't touch her. He's only interested in women who have left Germany to go to the Caliphate. It's just Carla Schmidt he has in his sights.'

CHAPTER SIXTY

KAREN ANDERSEN SLID into the hard plastic airport chair. It was twenty-five to eight on Wednesday evening and she'd finally made the departures lounge for the flight to Heathrow, and enjoying the deep sense of relief at the outcome of the trip. She'd done her homework. It had provided more pieces of the puzzle that was Operation Orson. And last but not least, it was Helga who'd removed the love lock. Haruto hadn't lied to her.

She brought up the text she'd written to him from the helicopter and it was still sitting in drafts. With a triumphant jab of the finger she pressed delete.

Bea Harrington had texted Karen earlier to request a meeting. Now her name had popped up in the papers as an old flame of the murdered MP, Huw Thomas. Lufthansa had delayed the flight, so it was the perfect opportunity to check the net. The latest report on Huw Thomas covered his past life, the period when he'd been the manager of an eighties band called *Love The Moon*.

She entered the name of the band into the Google search bar and pressed enter. Instantly a message flagged up on Twitter from @BandyJoe, a keyboard player with steel hair, of a similar age to the MP. Below a picture of a Swan under full sail, the message read: #RIP Huw Thomas. The South of France. Good times with the lads and Marigold. #LoveTheMoon.

She felt a bolt of excitement. Something from Tammy Bishop's last letter rang a bell big time.

She'd asked Karen to investigate her mother's background. Miriam Bishop was a small-time eighties model who'd drowned in a boating accident in 1989.

'Now boarding section E.' Karen joined the last stragglers in the queue.

As she snapped her seat belt closed, Karen's thoughts turned again to the case. Who was Marigold? Could she be Tammy Bishop's mother? And if so, could Tammy have murdered Huw Thomas out of revenge. But, how? Tammy Bishop had only been out of prison a few hours. Anyway, that idea was a million miles from the theory the Far Right had been involved.

She texted Bea Harrington back: 'I'll meet you tomorrow morning. K.A.'

'I didn't mean to intrude on you two.' Elspeth Cochrane was centre sofa in Devonshire Road when Karen got in at ten that night. 'It's just that Haruto and I have been discussing the flowers that arrived here for Regine and that they were from her husband. You shouldn't feel bad she pulled the wool over your eyes, Karen. She did the same to me.'

'Ah.' Karen shot her a warning glance. Don't go on. But there was no stopping her.

'You know I think she thought they were from you Haruto.'

'How about a drink? I'm certainly up for one,' said Karen, seeing as Elspeth Cochrane looked like she'd had a few already.

'Let me get it.' Haruto leapt to his feet with a quick smile in Karen's direction whose tummy gave a little flutter.

Elspeth stood up and staggered towards the door.

'I'm off,' she said. She tapped Karen on the shoulder as she passed. It struck Karen she was one of the better people in life. She'd been there all day, concerned about Karen's sudden disappearance without notice. But also, she was rather courageous. Private investigators who work on terrorism cases are not the best people to live next door to, particularly ones who stuff up as much as I do, Karen thought somewhat ruefully.

'Thanks for coming by,' Karen murmured to Haruto after Elspeth had gone. There was much to catch up on, new things since the phone call earlier in the morning. 'You didn't have to.'

'I wanted to be with you,' said Haruto, sitting down closely beside her. 'Now you know for yourself what went on in Germany, it's easier for me to talk about it.'

'You should have told me before.'

'Perhaps. Kasper wasn't like that at all when I knew him before. People change.'

'But I didn't change. At least not my feelings for you. How could you think I had?' She was shaking with emotion as he took her in his arms. 'I never did.'

'God, I am so pleased about that,' he said. He kissed her on the forehead and held her close to him. 'I just wanted to cover things, and I wanted to take the blame if anything happened.'

'Thank you.'

'Well, I should never have taken up the invitation to Mainz. But I'd known Kasper for years. He was apolitical back then. Just a bloody big stud. I thought nothing of it other than he might hit on you.'

'Really?'

'His views were always on the side of Deutschland über alles, but never too much. I couldn't believe it when I heard them talking in the kitchen. They'd worked you out. How MI5 had involved you in a terrorism case. Kasper and I had a hell of a fight when I caught Helga in our bedroom.'

'Why didn't you tell me?'

'I didn't want you to know. Just in case it spoilt things between us. I'm sorry.'

'I'm sorry too.' But the relief was instantaneous. And possibly for both of them. A wave of powerful feelings. It'd all been a misunderstanding, driven by too much loyalty on both sides.

'So that's why we moved out of the house so quickly?'

'Karen, I loved you at the time. I wanted to protect you. Can you believe we were living right in the middle of a Nazi movement? It was all going on around us and we didn't notice a thing.'

At the time. 'Haruto, why did you tell Quacker about it?'

'In case there were any reprisals. So, I'd get the blame, not you. I didn't want him to think you were careless.'

'You think I am?'

'No, but I worry about you. Like you're always losing your keys, your phone.'

I loved you at the time. 'I have sixteen.' She fought back the tears.

'What?'

'I work them all. Different numbers, names. I need to go between them depending on the job.'

'Jesus.'

'I need to swap them all the time with so many different cases.' Her voice cracked. 'You said you loved me at the time?'

'I've got to get used to this too, you know.' Haruto shook his head.

'How long have you been here?'

'Three weeks.'

'Where are you staying?'

'I don't want to go into that at the moment. I wasn't expecting this at all.'

'But what were you doing at the Ritz?'

'I told Quacker about how I heard Kasper mention Ivan Koslov to Helga that day. He was hoping Koslov would fund his group. Until then the English Concern Group had no links with Mainz. Quacker knew Koslov went to the Ritz. So, it was his idea for me to work there. I think he just wanted to get us back together again too.'

They touched hands. There was a lot to take in. 'I never knew we were apart.' Which was a lie. It'd been her greatest fear. 'It seems Ivan Koslov knew all about me.' She filled Haruto in on the ride back from Wentworth. His behind-the-scenes knowledge of Basilah.

Karen and Haruto held each other. She'd never felt so close to him. Sweet, dependable Haruto. All the wonderful times they'd shared. She was desperate to get him back. But Haruto said that it was complicated, that there was someone else.

Haruto kissed her and Karen's tears tumbled out. They both understood without saying a word that there was something he had to take care of before that could happen. It was only right. He'd met a girl travelling. She meant nothing to him, but he'd have to tell her.

'There's something I want you to see before you go.' She fired up her computer, her heart still thumping with emotion. 'I think Tammy Bishop was involved in the death of Huw Thomas.'

'But she only got out of prison yesterday.'

'Not directly involved. But I feel she had something to do with it. Somehow. She wrote to me about a video her mother was in.'

The film had been hard to locate, but she'd finally tracked it down on YouTube.

He slid into the small chair next to her's at the desk. She played it for him, saying it wouldn't take long. She knew he had to leave.

'It looks like a late eighties thing. One of those videos they used back then to promote groups?'

'Run the clip back again for me, please,' he said, throwing an anxious glance at his watch. 'A bunch of weirdos dressed as fisherman singing and throwing nets about. So what is all this?' Two scantily clad mermaids on the foredeck were doing their best to seduce them. 'Can you believe they used to make this stuff?'

'It's only partly there. It cuts off halfway. The full film's been taken down. YouTube put up a notice. Too sexually graphic and suggestive.'

'It sure doesn't look that way in the least.'

'The real reason the film vanished? One of the actresses in the clip was found drowned in the sea the next morning in unexplained circumstances.'

'So Tammy Bishop's mother was that actress?'

'Yes, she's the girl on the deck. Tammy was just six at the time. I couldn't see any link until yesterday. There's a logo on the towel she's lying on. What do you make it out to be?'

They reran the film again to the part where the writing was visible. 'Love The Moon?'

'Huw Thomas managed a band. He owned a yacht called Love The Moon. It was in the paper. This is the boat.'

'This video must have been made thirty or forty years back.'

'The other girl with her is someone called Marigold. Someone Tammy Bishop is trying to trace. And I've found out exactly who she is.'

CHAPTER SIXTY-ONE

CAREFUL, BE OH SO careful now, Tammy dear.

It was nine-thirty on a damp Thursday morning. She'd been out of prison for less than twenty-four hours and already she was being tested.

Scorn on you! She watched a veiled woman out of the corner of her eye. Trying to buy a kitchen canister from a stall. Not an easy thing to do. Counting out the money underneath a black billowing robe. She stared at the black blob, black as the night, a black tent. Inside all that blackness was possibly a sweet, normal woman, a loving mother planning the perfect home for her beloved children. *Take off the robes! Free yourself.* That was me, once. But not anymore.

The psychiatrist in prison had goaded, 'When you get out of here you will be ready to serve again. You will study the Koran. You will re-support the Jihadist cause.' And now he was messaging nonstop. Why?

Her phone went. Another one, this time in Arabic script, followed up with in English, 'Sent in error.'

She responded, 'No problem.'

Then, 'How you doing?'

She answered back. 'I'm doing ok.'

He replied, 'Look out for Britain First or English Defence League. Silly people. But the young crowd believe them.'

Test me all you like. I'll not falter.

She didn't have a clue why she was wandering the markets and where she would go next. But the thought that Karen Andersen would arrive the following day brought a smile to her face. She was on a high and full of joy.

At last I will learn exactly what happed to Mummy.

Even though she'd not heard back from David Miller in prison, his moment would come. Why wouldn't he believe her? She yearned for his acceptance. She hadn't murdered their son. She hadn't murdered anyone.

It was all part of the test.

Girls were being targeted because of their pro-Islamic views. She'd read about the abuse in the paper. Too bad for them. And if she could help them, she would. She had changed.

Resist: I was one of the leading figures supporting ISIS. And I am no longer that person.

Resist: I'm bigger than Major Mariam al-Mansouri. I'm more stunning than the Kurdish Peshmerga. I don't need to wear 'military chic' to prove I'm strong and beautiful.

As she picked up a butter dish to buy, she assumed the woman behind the counter was glaring at her. Did she know she was just out of prison? Was she wearing a sign around her neck, 'Former Inmate?' It's not polite to stare, she was screaming in her head.

But why worry? She was proud as proud could be. She was someone special. She was peerless. They'd recognised her talents. The million-dollar question was, why are some people radicalised and not others? What turns an innocent person into a terrorist? She'd been there and back.

'It's a state. A process. A changing all the time.' Tammy Bishop would ride to the rescue. They'd flock to listen to her. She'd been lonely too long. It was the way she'd make new friends and earn the respect of others. She was a born winner, after all. It was her destiny.

Meandering through the market, she could not have been happier. The rain began to fall and she took shelter under a shop awning. But it was intermittent, and it didn't cloud her mood in the slightest. The only obstacle to her brighter future was someone she sensed was trying to bring her down. Drag her backwards. Clip her wings and depress her. Stop her on the path she had chosen.

Ali al-Rashid was a problem, pestering her all the time. His calls bugged her. When the next one came in, she blocked it.

CHAPTER SIXTY-TWO

AT FIVE TO eleven on Thursday morning, Karen Andersen sat waiting in a park annexed to the Houses of Commons as the rain drizzled down.

Bea Harrington, who'd arranged to meet her there, stomped up across the green getting her shoes very dirty. She wore dark glasses and carried a huge umbrella.

'Does the rain bother you? I rather like it myself,' she said, plonking down on the bench alongside Karen. 'I always feel good after an April shower. It's been nearly three years, hasn't it?'

The last time they'd met Tammy Bishop had been a conservative party candidate using the name of Tammy Kell. Bea Harrington had been her mentor. She'd betrayed the system by planning to use the access given to candidates to blow them all to smithereens. Her birth father, who'd joined the Caliphate, had radicalised her before getting himself killed. Now the onetime terrorist was out of prison and a free woman.

'She shouldn't have been let out,' was the first thing Bea Harrington said. 'You of all people will surely agree with me. Who makes these damn decisions?'

'If it had been mine, I wouldn't have recommended it.'

'So why the hell is she walking the sodding streets?'

'Most terror attacks are carried out by males. They're either working alone or part of a small group. They usually suicide during or after an attack unless the police get there first. Everyone wants to know why they did it. And they are no longer around to ask.'

'Bloody good thing too.'

'But that's why it's difficult to learn motivation. Pinpoint why a person becomes brainwashed. If we can learn how their ideas develop, then maybe we can stop them happening.'

'She's a criminal. You shouldn't be dealing with her. You can't trust a damn word she says. She caused Huw's death, you know?' She took in Karen's shocked expression. 'Well indirectly. Obviously. I'll get to that in a bit.'

'You said you couldn't talk to me at the House of Lords?' The rain pattered down on the umbrella. They both huddled under it, neither dressed right for the rain, shivering in the dampened breeze.

'Absolutely not. Too many ears. That place is a bloody disaster to go to after everything that's happened. You've no doubt read about me?' She wiped her nose.

'With Huw Thomas?'

'And they bug the flat. I'm sure they do. Otherwise, how could the journalists know the minute I'm about to walk down the effing drive? They are only after smut of course. There wasn't too much of all that at the end of it all, I'm sad to say. I'd suggest going somewhere out of the rain, but I can't think where. And I haven't long,' she added.

'It's ok. It'll be dropping off soon.' In fact, the bad weather showed no signs of abating, but time was pressing.

'You think it'll die down? Good. No, he was killed for his views. Poor Huw. I can't sleep at night thinking about it. He did put himself up for it. But look at all this shit.' Bea pulled out a soggy newspaper. The headline read: DID THE FAR RIGHT TARGET THE LABOUR MP? OR WAS IT A JEALOUS LOVER? 'I am sure they mean me. Not that I could kill a fly.'

Bea crumpled up and started to whisper. 'Keep that woman away from me, Karen. I really am not ready to face her at all you know.'

'Why does she want to see you so badly? Particularly when she accused your husband of molesting her. Was she telling the truth?' Karen raised two questioning eyebrows.

'I didn't think so at first. But maybe now I do. After I learnt James had been shagging the neighbour's daughter who I'd known since she was a bloody Brownie. Or so she says. Where we used to live. The constituency house. I sold the place for nothing just to get rid of it. To clear the debts and move on. Getting dog turds through the letterbox is not great for the carpet.'

Bea sat in silence and toyed with her hair. 'James had everybody fooled. Which is why when I ran into Huw Thomas again—'

'Again?'

'Westminster,' she trailed off for a few seconds. 'He was always the renegade. Attractive, for his age. Didn't give a shit. I was in the House of Lords by then. We met on a cross-party committee. I encouraged him with

267

this Sharia bloody problem. Can you believe it? And that was why he became a target. Wish I hadn't. He wasn't as extreme as the papers were making out. Not at first, anyway. But bit by bit I think they pushed him into it.'

'They pushed him?'

'His local office. The place is full of Muslims.' She began mopping her wet trousers with her scarf. 'Not stopping, is it? But, back to Huw. He took this thing over. You know the mantra. "Muslims respect Sharia law more than British justice as dispensed by the UK courts. If you want to have a civil diverse society, it has to work for all." Even the Archbishop of Canterbury piled in with it, didn't he?'

'I remember that,' Karen added.

'But anyway, Huw did as little as possible, as often as possible, and that went for everything. He was known for it. Preferred to be down here. With me. Once.' She reddened as if she was about to cry. 'Any excuse. Yes, he'd do the odd Friday up there. A Saturday surgery. When push came to shove. We spent more and more weekends together. Then he didn't come back at all the one before last. I thought it was another woman. But then he came out with all this crap about being deselected. Needed to ramp up his credentials.' She took out a cigarette and lit it. 'Posh guy, Eton educated, fighting for Muslims.'

'But it still doesn't explain what he was doing up there on that day. Why he would suddenly return to his house?'

'Because I asked him to leave,' Bea spluttered. She paused, sending a look to Karen as if she had been avoiding the issue but now wanted it out. 'I've not told

268

anyone this but you. It was all over Tammy Bishop. Or Zinah, what have you. I don't know what she calls herself to you. Anyway, she's been writing to me. She terrifies the life out of me. And Huw thought I was overreacting. That's why we fought that day. Frankly, I want nothing to do with her. I need you to keep her away from me. Please.'

CHAPTER SIXTY-THREE

QUACKER AND HARUTO had just finished lunch together at the Polish cafe in Kings Road, Hammersmith. They were discussing Mainz and the possibility it fitted with Operation Orson.

Haruto had tried twice to get through to Helga on the number Karen had given him. Each time it went straight to voicemail. He was reluctant to leave a message in case it put her in danger with Kasper.

'The guy she mentioned could fit the description. But there must be a hundred Far Righters who look just like him. And it still doesn't explain how he could get into the WhatsApp group.' Quacker looked down at his empty plate.

'It's Kasper who could help us. But we can't contact him directly. He'll know Karen's spoken to Helga. It sounds as if he's turned into a right arsehole these days.'

Haruto's phone lit up. Helga. She wanted to pass Haruto directly to Kasper. They were together.

'Haruto? It's ok to talk,' said Kasper. 'I know Helga has spoken to Karen about what happened. Hey, sorry about screwing up your affair.'

'It doesn't matter man,' said Haruto. 'Karen's cool.'

'Vee didn't know about ze assaults. Zis guy could be ze one you want, but I don't know.'

'It would help if you have a picture of him. We don't have much to go on at the moment. He might be nothing to do with it, of course.'

'I have it here on my phone. All he told me vas he ran a company that went down after ISIS killed his brother. He seemed pretty messed up about it.'

'Can you forward it to me?' The picture had two exceptionally tall men, one blonde and one dark-haired with a full beard drinking from beer steins. 'Did you speak any more about the work he did?'

'He just referred to it as the GG network. Something to do with building services.'

'What was he going to do for you?'

'Some blogging. I gave him a login. But he hasn't written anything.'

'So, what are you up to, man?'

'The organisation? Kasper Watch!'

'Yeah?'

'Well, it pools a list of people to check out. News updates. Just the radicals. We follow Facebook and Twitter. You know what ze Jihadis get up to. They troll, so we troll. If we don't, how do we protect ourselves?'

He then told Haruto his house in Rosenheim was now under watch as of that morning. 'Nothing to do with Karen.' Ivan Koslov had phoned the authorities and was reviewing the funding situation for Kasper's enterprise. He didn't want his organisation connected with the murder of an MP. 'It's nothing to do with us. If I could find this guy and he's been doing these things, I would take him down myself. I'd help you out. It's not us doing these attacks. You're talking Germany, not ze UK. We're peaceful mainly.'

Kasper Watch didn't endorse overt violence.

If Helga had exaggerated Kasper's radical profile, his behaviour didn't appear consistent. And they now had a photo of the activist who'd been in Germany. It would serve if only to cross him off the list of suspects. They'd check it out with Beth Lane when, and if, she reappeared. But Fatima Ahmed had faced him at the front door of her home. That was the best place to start.

At one-thirty Quacker and Haruto left Hammersmith heading for the Ahmeds' convenience store in Acton. But the shop was shut, with a note taped across the door. 'Closed for personal business.'

'Might just pop round to their home.' Quacker made a police check for the address.

CHAPTER SIXTY-FOUR

THE SALLE WHERE Karen Andersen fenced was holding a lunchtime match. Competition was something that helped her to focus. It was important to concentrate on the case and not herself, so she decided to go, taking the District Line from St. James Park to Hammersmith and walking the rest of the way.

She'd agreed to meet up with Haruto that afternoon. Almost everything she did now made her think about him. Sometimes she felt a surge of uncontrollable jealousy. Who was he with?

Will he leave her for me?

A fencing match is concluded when a contender gets to 45 points. So, the fact Karen's team was one point ahead at 5-4 was not much to get excited about. Could they hold on to the lead? The clash of foils grew louder. Unlikely. The opposition had dubbed her team the three dunces.

Karen sat at the side of the salle. She was next up. But random thoughts entered her head as the foil flew at her jacket. How had Orson hacked the WhatsApp group? Who was he? Tammy Bishop. Why did she terrify Bea Harrington? Would Haruto and Karen ever get back together?

The score was 18-20.

What was happening to her team? The three dunces? They were actually keeping up the pace. Zing! Clatter! Clank!

It was hard to find true love. Fatima Ahmed was being bullied into a forced marriage. She'd told the group she'd run away like Beth had done. And where on earth was Beth right now, anyway?

They were being battered about. Karen forced her mind back on to the match. But the creepy guy with the limp was on fire. He'd had a streak of six touches. The dunces were now back to 25-30.

Yup, it would soon be over. Massacred.

'Karen? You're on again.'

When the game was over, she'd better check on the WhatsApp group again.

The score was 35 against them. Ten more strikes and that'd be it.

She lunged at the white coat in front.

Touché.

A small cheer went up.

But she'd overlooked a clue. What was it? Why would Orson murder Huw Thomas?

She lunged again.

Another cheer.

She had to gain another nine hits to the body before the challenger opposite scored another five.

She'd never do it.

Know your opponent.

Another touch.

'Karen!'

Know your opponent. Why would it be Mr Far Right Lone Wolf? He was only into stalking Jihadi brides. Girls not guys. Why would he be outside?

Her opponent opposite fell back in a defensive strategy for the time being. He'd obviously not been expecting this level of attack and aggression.

274

What had come over her?

Another hit.

Now all she could see across the way was Orson. He shouted out as she hit.

She would not concede. She would not let him get away.

The fencing salle exploded, yelling her on. They were still going.

She would find out what happened.

Karen thrust forward in one twisting, triumphant stroke.

She'd done it. 45-44.

Touché.

Karen left the fencing salle on a high. It'd been a good move to go there. It was twenty past two in the afternoon and the rain had just stopped.

She turned on to Wood Lane and walked down towards the Underground. It was as she approached the station the unmistakably tall and willowy figure of Tammy Bishop was heading out of the Underground due south with a determined stride. She wore a full-length cloak and hijab but no face veil.

She thought, why am I not surprised? The sob story about her mother thirty years earlier had been a smokescreen. The perfect cover story. Something concocted to fool them. She'd schemed it all. How had they managed to be taken in again?

Karen about-faced and followed her. Tammy Bishop crossed and turned right into MacFarlane and left towards the Uxbridge Road. What was she up to? She immediately called Quacker.

'We've got a picture through of who we think could be Orson. We're headed to Fatima Ahmed's home to see whether she recognises the guy,' he said. 'But you stay with Bishop though. Check out where exactly she's going if you're sure you've got the right person.'

She could hear the blast of horns in the background. He was no doubt being driven by Haruto.

'I know it's her. I'm positive it's her.'

'She's in Islamic robes?'

'Head to toe.'

'Well, that part fits anyway.'

'That fits? Why is she wearing Islamic clothing when she's supposed to have renounced her support for ISIS?'

'Should explain a few things to you later. Any idea where she's headed?'

'I'm a hundred per cent certain where she's headed. The mosque.'

'Can you see who she meets there, if anyone?' Quacker didn't seem madly impressed. 'The Shepherd's Bush Mosque?'

But it wasn't at all the case. Instead, Tammy Bishop continued along Shepherd's Bush Green and turned west into Goldhawk Road. She spent a while in Pretty Textiles for You, examining silks and pieces of cotton. Next, she ducked into Textiles and Ribbons and emerged with a huge bag of what looked like Liberty fabrics. She crossed the busy road to enter the market under the railway arches where she ate what looked like falafel to Karen, affecting a greater interest in the hairdressing price list next door in the lightly falling rain.

It was while Tammy was engaged in buying Velcro from another stall, Quacker called back.

There'd been another house fire at the Ahmeds and this time a fatality. The method was similar to before, the Fire Chief had told him. Paraffin through the letterbox. Both front rooms destroyed. The daughter, Fatima Ahmed was dead. Her parents had not been present when the Far Right had hit for the second time. They were currently at Hammersmith Hospital with Victim Support who were doing their best to help them with their mental trauma.

'Fatima WhatsApped on the group yesterday,' Karen said. 'She refused to agree to an arranged marriage. It was probably the final straw. She was a classic honour killing waiting to happen. Orson just gave her parents the cover they needed to kill her.'

CHAPTER SIXTY-FIVE

KAREN'S FLAT IN Devonshire Road was a convenient place for the three of them to meet up. She abandoned shadowing Tammy Bishop and sprinted to the stop at Cathnor Road where she caught a 237 bus to Chiswick High Road. Quacker and Haruto had driven straight in from Acton. It was a quarter past three in the afternoon before the three of them got together.

They were all in shock over the death of Fatima Ahmed. Karen was eager to prove her point. She called up the WhatsApp group message where Fatima had posted her fears concerning her parents.

'An honour killing. Nothing to do with the Far Right.' said Karen. 'They'd threatened her before.'

'The fire will be investigated as a matter of course, so it will all come out eventually. It's unlikely they'll get off scot-free if that's the case. But we have to let police procedures take their course,' Quacker insisted, sitting down heavily beside Haruto on the sofa, before Karen had a chance. 'We've sent you a photo of the guy we think could be Orson. If so, it was very useful that you went back to Mainz.'

Karen's phone chimed as Haruto forwarded the photo. 'Both Beth Lane and Fatima described him as smartly dressed and clean-shaven. This doesn't fit with that at all.'

'You could be right. Anyway, we've got something to go on. And we don't want whoever it is getting near to Tammy Bishop, do we?'

'She should never have been released,' said Karen. 'She'll be plotting another attack for sure.'

'Not her, but someone else is,' replied Quacker. 'Which is why she's floating around dressed as she is. It was part of the agreement. We're hoping she'll pick up the vibes. Learn what is in the air. She still knows lots of people who support the cause.'

'And you're not concerned she won't be radicalised again? Or recruit Jihadi women?' It seemed to Karen a high-risk strategy.

'You're seeing her tomorrow, aren't you? I think it's important you stay in touch.'

Haruto got up to allow Karen to take his seat but she stopped him with a smile.

'She has a fascination with you because of how you outsmarted her that time when she was planning a suicide mission at the Conservative Party Conference!' Quacker chuckled.

'It's not one I share,' she said, tossing the fencing foil off an office chair and pulling it up to the centre of the room.

'But we know something is in the planning stage with ISIS. It's likely to be connected to sport in some way, according to the spooks. Rugby or football most likely. We've got so many fighters returning from the Islamic State, the security services have asked us to stay alert in particular at the mention of any reference to spectator events. She could be highly useful in that regard.'

'How many people know they've released her?'

'Only those she's written to and informed of the fact. We have to keep her low profile for obvious reasons. And her home address secret. And perhaps you'd better impress on her the danger she's in. Particularly as Orson has still not been apprehended.'

'Maybe she's bluffing,' suggested Karen. 'I know the way she works. She's a con. Claiming to have denounced her faith. Ready to take revenge on the girls she radicalised but who dobbed her in. Even the score. It could even be her who is behind all this intimidation. Perhaps she knows Orson. She's a liar. Writing to Fatima Ahmed's parents was classic. She would know they'd open all her mail.'

'Well, you can find out what her true thinking is. But let's say she's not guilty. I assume you intend to inform her about the attacks on the girls on the group? She might not even know about them.'

'I'll warn her not to post her address on WhatsApp in case Orson has hacked into it. But we can't trust her. I'm sure of it.'

'I agree with Karen. We can't trust her,' Haruto echoed. He allowed his eyes to dwell longer than necessary on Karen. She blushed. 'But perhaps run the picture past her?'

'I think first off we should shoot through and see if there's any more news on Beth Lane,' said Quacker. 'She could identify him. Don't you think, chaps?'

CHAPTER SIXTY-SIX

AT FIVE-THIRTY, Karen, Haruto and Quacker left Devonshire Road en route for Hounslow. It was where Beth Lane's mother lived. From the previous conversation Quacker had had with her over the phone, he'd got the impression she knew where her daughter was but wasn't letting on.

Haruto drove like a maniac, but Quacker seemed completely unphased. Sat comfortably alone in the back seat, scenes from Karen's last meeting with Beth kept flashing into her head. She saw again the girl in Costa's, eyes wide in fear, the horrified gasp on seeing the video of herself online and the terrified expression as she passed the information about Mia. The day running all over, from underground tunnels to the bank of the Thames looking for her.

Just as Haruto pulled up at the house the heavens opened up. What started out as a light shower had turned into another downpour. So they sat outside for five minutes to let it pass.

They approached the back door, Quacker leading the way. *Rat-tat-tat.* Immediately the door cracked open an inch.

'Mrs Lane? It's Donald Partridge. Wondering whether you'd heard from your daughter Beth at all?'

The door swung wide in response and there was Beth Lane herself. She glanced from Quacker to Haruto and then to Karen Andersen. 'It's me. I'm Beth.'

'I'm Donald Partridge. Private investigator.' Quacker extended his hand. 'Karen works for me. Haruto Fraser.'

'Can we come inside?' asked Karen.

'Why didn't you tell me you were an investigator?' she asked Karen.

Beth invited them in before running upstairs to find her mother, who worked from home making bridal gowns.

It was obvious Beth had been back there for a day or two. Two pairs of modern boots were lined up alongside boys' trainers and muddy wellingtons. Her mother had an allotment nearby, she explained when she returned to the room. The impact from the shocking video had worn off judging by Beth's mood and she seemed ready to talk about it.

'Was this guy who abducted me the same one who murdered that MP I read about, do you think?' she asked.

'Well, we're not sure. But it would help if you could look at a picture and tell us if you recognise him at all.'

They seated themselves around the kitchen table, the room reeking of cigarette smoke mixed with the smell of recently cooked sausage and chips. Haruto opened up the photo on his phone. Had she seen the man before?

'Was that him?' asked Karen.

'He looks familiar. But I'm not too sure.'

'You described the one you met as smartly dressed.' Karen wondered if she'd understood the question. 'The man in Cherrywood? Did he look like this?'

'Maybe somewhere else I've seen him.' Beth frowned.

'On the internet maybe?' Karen suggested.

'I don't do those sites much.' Beth gave an irritated sigh.

'Can you talk to us about what happened when you left the UK? I would just like you to tell Mr Partridge and Haruto what you told me. About why you didn't cross over and go on to Syria?'

'I went on WhatsApp to ask my future husband where he was. And he was so rude to me.' She was reluctant to go into further detail. But Karen had already filled them in. The fighter had wanted naked pictures of her. Then she'd ended up in a bus station messaging between Zinah al-Rashid in London and the Jihadi soldier who said he was in Raqqa. 'All I asked was for someone to cross with me and I would have gone.'

'These are the messages you sent.' Karen had kept a copy of them. 'Do you remember sending these?' She leant forward and showed her, reminding her of the time.

Zinah: You can have this perfect world, and it's there for you right now. But you have to try harder.

Jamillah: I want to serve Allah.

Zinah: The West has done too much damage already with its consumerism. It has tried to corrupt you too. There is plenty to overcome. By joining ISIS it shows real character and true commitment. You will become a perfect person.

A flush crept across Beth's face. 'It was years ago,' she said.

'So what did you do then?' Karen was hoping she'd tell them her story in her own words. It would be a miracle. But it was important to convince Quacker and Haruto of the extraordinary lengths these girls had gone to when ISIS brides were in fashion. Karen had to keep her chatting. 'You wanted to come back to the UK?'

'I wanted to go home. Yeah. But I couldn't.' She'd been stranded in the middle of a nightmare. 'I had to make out I'd gone there on holiday if I came back. So that's what I did.'

Mrs Lane was cool and reserved when she finally appeared in the kitchen. Karen could tell she felt awkward about not letting on about her daughter. She was sarcastic. 'So you found us all right?'

It was clear her mother didn't want to discuss Isis. She'd one hundred per cent bought into the holiday story or chose to believe it.

'Beth went on a holiday to Turkey. Do you want to see the pictures? Show them the pictures from Turkey! Why you lot are trying to make out it's more than that, I'll never know.'

Beth Lane obliged. She'd made up with her mother to save herself.

Yes, she'd taken lots of photos. The investigators knew the selfies were mostly to provide cover. It'd be the evidence she'd need to change her story when she got back. And now Mum was using it for it all it was worth.

Beth in Sanliurfa. The long ride in a Turkish dolmus to Adiyaman. The central hotel there had arranged the trip to Nemrut mountain. From then shots from when she'd gone to Katha via Harran.

'D'you do all this on your own?' Mrs Lane was smiling now. She was passing Beth's phone around. 'She was only seventeen, remember. I couldn't have done that when I was seventeen.'

Quacker had spotted a bearded individual in one of the photos. 'Who are the other people here?'

Beth took the phone back for a moment. 'Just a group of people I joined.' She couldn't remember all their names. Her face froze, eyes widened staring. 'That's him, isn't it?'

'May I?' Quacker looked at it again. He put it side by side with the photo from Mainz.

'Could this also be the man who took you?'

Beth, white and shaking, couldn't take her eyes from the photo, reliving it all. 'Yes. Yes it was. It was him.'

'What did you tell him about yourself? When you first met this man in that place in Turkey. Anything?'

'I don't remember. But I told him I was on holiday from England.'

'How long did you speak to him?'

'Only a matter of minutes. His phone was out of battery and he said he needed to text someone. His brother, I think he said. He asked to borrow mine.'

'Did you lend it?'

'Yes.'

'Then what happened?'

'He took it off to get a signal. But he gave it back.'

'It's likely he got into your phone and read all the WhatsApp messages. Got the mobile numbers of the other girls you were with on WhatsApp.'

Beth was still white and shaking. Karen could tell she was going back over all the minutiae. Trying to

285

remember and make sense of what happened. Wondering why she hadn't recognised him in the takeaway place or at the library. 'He looked different without the beard.'

'A pervert, him. Disgusting.' The mother's thoughts were still on the images she'd seen. 'We're keeping that door locked. No one goes out there or comes in it without that chain going on.'

'Do you remember his name? Do you remember anything else about him? You said he had a funny name like Orson. Was he anything to do with horses?'

'He said he was a gee-gee. Like a kids' name for a horse. He was so weird. I was terrified. A lot of what happened is a blur. I just don't remember it all.'

Haruto turned to Quacker. 'The GG network? Thought they were a building firm.'

'GG. Yes. That was it.'

CHAPTER SIXTY-SEVEN

A BREAK IN the case! Identifying Beth Lane's abductor was a massive step forward. Quacker, Haruto and Karen left the Lane household and regrouped in a Lebanese place two streets down from Hounslow Police Station. It was half-past six in the evening and they were buzzing. The data leak had taken place in Turkey.

They ran through the possibilities. Orson had infiltrated the WhatsApp group via Beth. Her messages had been a tough read for Orson coming from Syria searching for his brother. The Syrian fighter had demanded Beth send him naked pictures. So Orson had done the same to her in Cherrywood. It'd never been his intention to do more. Then when she'd stood him up, he'd published.

They'd managed to resolve the GG connection. Quacker summed it up. 'It sounds like a colloquial reference to horse racing but is in fact a construction company which went bust recently. This is the man,' he continued, tapping the table. 'Went to Mainz. Partied with Kasper Rosenthal. Hated British Jihadi brides. Is back in the UK. A lone wolf style attack.'

They were trying to make all the pieces fit together. But, as Karen reminded them, 'How does the murder of Huw Thomas follow on from that? Firstly, he's not an ex Jihadi bride. Secondly, the violence.'

There was a different pattern. But then patterns weren't always textbook perfect.

'Nor does it fit that he hasn't tried to contact you, Karen,' added Quacker. He leant forward to get a better view of the food being served at the next table. He had his eye on an array of baklavas. 'He's had a crack at just about everyone else. Tessa Clark? Him by the sounds of it. Beth Lane? Him. Fatima Ahmed? Maybe him, but we can't be sure. This Yasmin? We don't know. Mia? A terrible accident most likely. The German girl Kasper spoke about who moved to the UK?'

'Carla Schmidt? She wasn't part of the WhatsApp group,' Karen leant forward anxious not to miss a word.

'How did Kasper meet Orson in the first place? Do we know?'

'At a Far Right rally in Germany,' said Karen.

'It rules out Tammy Bishop as being behind it,' said Haruto.

Quacker sat back in his chair. 'Which puts her in the firing line for a visit.'

'But Karen is on the group as Basilah. She could be a target too.' Haruto looked Quacker straight in the eye.

Quacker came straight back with, 'You've not had anything since the flowers and those photographs you mentioned, have you, Karen?'

'The flowers!' Haruto smiled to himself.

'There was a rather magnificent bouquet which arrived at Karen's flat. No doubt she thought you'd sent it, Haruto!' Quacker gave a mischievous grin.

'We've covered that already,' said Karen. 'But they weren't from a stalker. They weren't even meant for me.'

It was as if Quacker couldn't let the subject drop. 'This'll amuse you, Haruto. They were sent to Regine Mendoza who had told her husband she was staying with Karen, when in fact she was all along carrying on with Ivan Koslov's bodyguard! A guy called Caves who used to work for me. The one you saw at the Ritz.'

Quacker wouldn't leave it. Karen felt a pang. Haruto had given no hint as to whether he had broken off with his new girlfriend or not.

Karen pulled up the photo of the flowers. 'There they are.'

'You took a picture of them?' Haruto seemed oblivious to their importance to her.

Tears filled her eyes. 'I rarely get sent flowers these days.'

Awkwardness stopped further conversation momentarily.

Then she saw the ticket.

She expanded the photo.

The message was signed with the letters GG.

Either Orson was on to her. Or Regine's husband, whoever he was, was the man they were after.

CHAPTER SIXTY-EIGHT

ON FRIDAY MORNING at half-past ten, as she ambled along the Embankment, Bea Harrington got a phone call from Karen Andersen. It dashed her spirits. For a full twenty-four hours she'd clung on to the idea the private investigator would not probe into the boating scandal. They'd not mentioned it at all yesterday. She had skilfully avoided the issue at least twice.

'I'm meeting Tammy Bishop very soon, as you know. I have to decide whether to tell her you were with her mother the night she died.'

It was a shock to the system. 'How did you find out?'

'Standard research. She will bring it up for sure.'

'There's nothing to tell. And what good would it do? It won't bring her back, will it?'

'It might help her to know the details.'

'Yes. Might help her, but it won't bloody well help me. She shouldn't be out, anyway.'

'She was released last Wednesday and she's back in London.'

'I'm not the only one who's angry about it. David Miller's sick to his stomach. Maybe now Bishop's out she could tell the father to his face just why she killed his son and then hid his body in her freezer.'

'I don't think that would be a very good idea at all,' said Karen.

'Where's she living, anyway? Some ghastly halfway house no doubt. They surely wouldn't let her go back to where she was before? Acton, wasn't it?'

'She has information which is vital to national security.' The address had been categorised as 'for approved eyes' only, to be considered highly secret. 'So I'm afraid I can't give that out. But I need to know whether you are happy for me to tell Tammy you were with Miriam on the boat?'

'Can you let me think about it?' she said, before closing off the conversation.

Her upbeat morning mood was shattered! She felt like screaming.

Call this justice?

Apparently it was okay for her to be scared stiff, but for some obscure reason not the other way around. The government must have a screw loose. It was ok for a bloody-near killer and mad woman to know where Bea Harrington lived. Bombard her with letters. Broadside her life once again. But not the reverse.

Now she had to be looking over her shoulder for not one but two people stalking her.

Why had Tammy Bishop altered her story? They had found the body of the twenty-one-year-old political activist Robin Miller in her freezer. Initially, she'd said she murdered him. It was all part of her Jihad nonsense. But then she'd retracted her statement. Said it had been made under pressure from ISIS. Very convenient. Spun the facts to get her out of prison. No murder, no charge. There'd been enough forensic to validate it, unfortunately.

But moving to a suicide story had shifted the blame for his death. It all went back to 2016. Political party intimidation had driven the young man to suicide. And the father, David Miller, still held a grudge against the Harringtons. He was driving her up the wall. He was always hanging round Westminster hoping to collar her on her way into the Lords. His London office was close by. It was only a matter of time before he popped out from behind a tree or a bench. Here. On the path beside the Thames.

Entering the cloakroom of the Lords, you can't miss the smell of old coats. Bea wrinkled her nose as she hung her umbrella on the designated hook. She waved to an acquaintance as a thought crossed her mind. She was friends with a woman who worked in the Candidates Department of the Conservative Party. They went back a long way. She'd suggest a glass of wine. She could use her influence. Tell her she'd received a letter from Tammy Bishop who used to be Tammy Kell. It'd come from prison. But the girl was now out and expecting a reply. Where did she live before? It was on file. Everything was held on file for years. It was private and confidential, but her friend had access to it.

Bea continued up the stairs with a spring in her step.

CHAPTER SIXTY-NINE

AT A QUARTER past eleven on Friday morning, 18 April, Karen drove down on her motorbike to meet up with Tammy Bishop. Karen had spent most of the morning trying to contact Regine Mendoza. None of them had an address for her. And calls to the Filipino went direct to voicemail.

On the issue of the boat, Karen had agreed to give Bea Harrington time to consider her options. It was only reasonable. Perhaps Tammy wasn't aware Bea was the model called Marigold. She didn't want her to know. She was panicking about Bishop turning up at her front door. Why was she so worried?

Bea's paranoia pointed to foul play. Maybe the drowning hadn't been an accident after all. Only 'Marigold' knew the truth, and she'd kept it to herself. If so, she had good reason to worry about how Tammy would react. Would she bear a grudge against Bea? Would she be out for revenge? It reminded Karen of the Marie Curie saying 'Nothing in life is to be feared. It is only to be understood.' And Tammy Bishop was hard to understand. That was the problem.

Similarly, Karen wouldn't let on she'd followed the reformed terrorist from White City to Shepherd's Bush.

'Hello, Tammy. Good to see you.' Karen just about managed to be civil to the woman who answered the door. She didn't want to appear confrontational, but she would take her on if needs be. There'd been endless repercussions in all directions from Tammy Bishop's WhatsApp group she set up four years back. A sexual assault. Two deaths. And from what Karen could see, Tammy was still only interested in herself. 'You've been writing me letters.'

Tammy Bishop replied, 'And you never answered any of them.' She turned and led Karen into the hall. Karen noticed her once lithe figure had morphed into prison plump during her spell inside. 'Excuse the dust and the cobwebs.' Minutes later she was sitting primly in her grandmother's living room. She stretched her arms wide apart. 'My inheritance. It's a wonderful house, isn't it?'

Karen perched on a functional chair opposite her. 'You've done very well for yourself.'

'I will get back into the clothes you bought for me. I promise.' There were shades of the old ambition which had impelled her towards politics, both UK and ISIS. At the same time. 'I can't stay this embarrassing weight forever. Do you think I should go on a fast? Takes ages to lose the pounds otherwise.'

'We need to talk about a few things other than diets Tammy. That's why I'm here.'

'Aha, but you look good. And I want to too. How do you do it? You don't have any tattoos, do you? Normally women who ride motorbikes cover themselves in ink. Very disfiguring.'

She was eager to show Karen around the property before their 'conversation'. Initially she was reluctant to show the lower basement and screwed her face up and posted herself hard against the front door to make the point. 'There's nothing to see down there and we would have to unlock it and that stuff,' she said.

'Are you going to use it again in the future?' Karen circled in a cat and mouse game. The floor below had been the headquarters for Tammy's former terrorist activities. Also, the place where Robin Miller had died and had his body stuffed in a freezer. She'd hidden the corpse rather than be caught out on her Jihadi involvement.

'Why wouldn't I want to use it again? It'll make a great studio. But I'll tell you about that later.'

'A studio? For what? Jihadi tapes?'

A turmoil of conflicting emotions chased their way across Tammy's face before resignation took over. She threw her hands up and gave a huge sigh. 'You want to see downstairs? I'll show you downstairs!'

With this, she seized a bunch of keys and led Karen out the main door. The downstairs was all bolted up like Fort Knox. But once inside it was clear someone had stripped it bare. Possibly when she'd been sent to prison. They stood in the centre of the space, taking in the vast emptiness. It smelt sickly sweet. Tammy was silent. She frowned as if she was reliving the moment.

'So this is where Robin Miller killed himself?' Karen hoped Tammy hadn't seen the wire on her.

'Yes.'

'He did kill himself, did he? Really?'

'The party drove him to it. They were a bunch of pricks over anyone who couldn't take the rough and tumble. Yup. I couldn't stop him.'

'So why did you say you did it?'

'To impress ISIS. I was very into them back then. You might remember that.'

'He came here to get a signature on a statement. Was that true?'

'Yes. He needed a witness. He was being badly bullied. I told him I doubted it would make much difference.'

'What did you do with the paperwork?'

'Recycle bin.'

'So he didn't find out you were with ISIS?'

'Funny that. I'd been sewing a suicide belt minutes before. But no. People only notice what matters to them, don't you think? He was completely taken up with his bullying stuff.' She wrapped her arms around herself against the chill. She nodded in the direction of the kitchen. 'He went in there to make coffee. Next thing I went in and found him dead on the floor. It didn't seem possible. He was only in there for a few minutes. You don't expect that sort of thing, do you?'

Karen followed her back upstairs into the cheerless, colourless front room. 'Thank you for coming,' she said brightly, 'I was afraid you wouldn't. When you didn't answer my letters, I thought you were ignoring me. But then few people did write back. You weren't the only one.'

'Why dd you write so many letters to people? What were you hoping would come of it?' Karen wanted to know.

'That I could put together a group of people I know and maybe have a party here sometime and build some sort of friendship group or something.' Karen recognised the same person she'd had to deal with before, deluded and a dreamer. 'Don't you think that would be a good idea?'

'You know what's been happening?' She told her all about Orson. Tessa Clark. Beth Lane. Fatima Ahmed. Had she heard? How she'd been burnt to death in a house fire very close by in Acton. Possibly an honour killing. Her face took on a grave expression.

'Parents can be very unpredictable, can't they? Some good, some bad. I keep thinking about mine. What would have happened if my mother had never lost her life? Would I have been a different person, do you think?'

CHAPTER SEVENTY

THE AGREEMENT WITH Tammy Bishop was that she was to help authorities identify Islamic terrorists buried dead within mainstream London society. Shed a light on the radicalisation of women. Give them a heads up on attacks if she heard of any. Spot signs of ISIS. Sus out anyone at risk of being recruited, particularly young and vulnerable girls. But her focus that Friday afternoon seemed entirely on events which had occurred in her personal past.

'I don't think Mummy's death was investigated properly.' Tammy kept bringing the topic back to her mother.

Karen could remember almost verbatim what they'd said about the matter almost three years ago now. At the time Tammy hadn't cared two hoots about Miriam or how she'd died. Why now? 'How did you find out about the accident?'

'I'm sure it was no accident.' Her face tightened. She fixed Karen with a stare.

'But has someone suggested that to you, or is it just your idea?' A loose window rattled with a breeze. It was bright sunshine outside, which lit up the cracks in the ceiling. The house needed work badly.

'Since going into prison I've suffered from insomnia. I told that to the psychiatrist. About being awake suddenly after dreaming about my mother. Everything about my mother. But jumbled up. You know how jumbled dreams are! And some stuff he suggested made sense.'

There was also nothing about insomnia in the psychiatric report let alone anything on a murder. Why would a psychiatrist put an idea like that in her mind?

'Apparently, he'd had cases before many a time.' She sighed. 'Anyway, about my mother. There was me all my life thinking she'd been a junkie. Nothing could be further than the truth. If there were drugs on her, someone must have planted them.' She got up and pirouetted off to get something non-alcoholic to drink. 'Can you believe that?'

She came back bearing two cold cokes on a small round plastic tray.

Karen wasn't sure what she believed. But she had to be careful and draw Tammy Bishop out any way she could, even if it meant pretending to go along with her conspiracy theories. 'It's possible. Someone may have lured her aboard. Forced her to take drugs and killed her when she resisted them. Then dumped her body overboard. It would look like she had drowned after an overdose.'

It worked. Tammy's eyes lit up. She seemed contented. 'Exactly! Now what can I help you with?'

'Plenty,' said Karen. 'I'm desperate for leads. We have to talk about what we call Operation Orson. That's part of your release conditions. And I need to know you're on the level with me now.'

'Why wouldn't I level with you, Karen?'

'You say you have renounced Islam? How are we to believe that?'

'Because it's the truth of course. I've completely given up on that faith.' Yes, she still wore the Islamic robes from time to time. That'd been the agreement. And yes, there was another terrorist attack imminent because she'd picked up something about it in prison.

It all fitted with what Quacker had outlined to Karen.

'Were you aware before I told you of what's been happening to the girls on the WhatsApp group?'

'No. Can you go over it all again?' She sat quietly sipping from the red can. She was on her best behaviour now, listening, attentive.

'Are you sorry about Fatima? Do you feel any remorse for her? If the Far Right didn't kill her then it was her own parents who did. Either way extremist Muslim beliefs caused her death.'

'I feel sad about what happened to her. Of course I do. But she would have followed her dream to marry a fighter and serve Islam. Even now. Tomorrow. The next day. She had it in her mind. I got to know the girls very well. And if she'd done that, her life would have been over.'

'But you radicalised her and put those ideas in her head.'

'Yes. And that was then. This is now. You have to send every ex-IS wife and Jihadi my way. That's what I agreed.' She lowered her eyelids over intensely blue eyes. A slow smile spread slowly across her face. 'I know just how to do it. I know. I know. Most conservative Muslim homes do not teach humanism and lay values. Everything other than their way is profanity. It's all 'Fear God. That overrides any other law. God's law prevails even over UK laws.'

'What do you think you can you do to help where others have failed?' Karen asked.

'Plenty. It's all about the glamorisation of jihad as spun by the extremists. Young people lap it up. Social media can do their best to clamp down but it'll just move to another platform. Who is able to stop that but me? I will find a way.'

'And you are not conning us again?

'ISIS deceived me. I misled you. Daesh are masters of deception. There are those amongst us now who are not who they are pretending to be.'

Karen was undecided. Was the woman she was with Zinah or Tammy? 'How did they brainwash you exactly?'

'We all believed that this life isn't real. It's the life after we die that's real. And we know in reality that nobody knows what happens in the afterlife. How do they get away with that? Because people are searching. Can't you see it all fitted for me because my mother was dead? And there was some continuity there. I wanted to believe I could be with her again.'

Tammy was moving the goalposts, veering it all in the direction she wanted things to go. Karen was growing woozy just listening to her. 'Can you look through the group again to see if anything jogs your memory?'

Karen handed her the phone with the WhatsApp group.

Another dreamy smile crossed Tammy's face as she ran through messages of three years back. 'I can't believe you were Basilah. And now we're on the same side, aren't we? I'll help all I can. I told everyone I would.'

Karen held up a photo of Orson for her. 'I had the sense someone was following me when I went past the mosque yesterday. But I've seen no one who looks anything like that.'

'He's clean-shaven these days. And dresses smartly. But it is likely he will try to contact you if he has any inkling who you are and where you are.' It was the fourth time she'd asked her. And it would be the last. 'And you haven't heard the name Orson or GG mentioned anywhere?'

'No. And while we are at it, nor this Carla Schmidt you talked about.'

'Well, she's not from the UK originally. She was on the radar of a German political group. She wouldn't be in this group.'

'I get that. I set this group up, remember. It was mine. I know every one of these women on here. Except for Yasmin.'

CHAPTER SEVENTY-ONE

THEY DESPERATELY NEEDED to contact Regine Mendoza. The only person who they reckoned may know where she lived was Ivan Caves. And with the possibility that GG was her husband, it was worth the time investment.

So at just past two o'clock on 18 April Haruto Fraser took up a position at one of the four roulette tables at the Ritz casino. He knew it was the one Ivan Koslov's bodyguard favoured. Perhaps he would show although it was ridiculously early. And hopefully Regine with him. That way they could trace the man who'd signed himself GG on her bunch of flowers and confirm he was her husband.

Haruto spent the first half-hour watching the roulette, long enough to survey the scene, follow the action. Trying to predict the pocket the ball would fall into. He knew he could use maths probability to beat the roulette wheel. It took a little work. It was how two MIT Professors had scooped up a fortune. But they'd done it with a computer. Now casinos banned devices. You had to do the numbers in your head.

Haruto had done it before. He noted carefully the outer rim to see in what segment the croupier released the ball into the wheel. Click, click. How it bounced onto the spinning track. Yup! It was roughly the same position for every spin. And it was essential to see where the throw started. No different from solving a complex case.

Haruto kept an eye on the door. When would they arrive? If they came at all. Maybe Koslov. Maybe Caves. Maybe together.

So far *nitchevo*. No matter.

But it was all about observing. Calculating where the ball would land. Combining the laws of physics and maths to increase the odds out of a given range of outcomes.

He checked his watch. How long to connect with the wheel? Then to make a complete revolution? If you knew that, you could work out the landing point. If!

It meant averaging the times over a hundred. But Haruto Fraser was a detailed person. The process took hours and filled in well with the tedium of waiting and watching.

Each croupier had their own throwing style.

Then there was the roulette wheel itself. How they spun it. There was always consistency between dealers. How fast they turned only differed by a small amount. It generally ended in the same section.

He stared at the wheel as the croupier released the nineteenth ball. He watched it hippety-hop up and down before it came to rest, whizzed around and dropped in the pocket. There was a pattern, yes. But this was the part with the most variance. The bounce coefficient.

Just as he was getting somewhere, Caves entered the casino, looking like he hadn't slept for a week.

But he was on his own.

Enough groundwork. *Time to play!*

Haruto placed a chip on five different numbers 6, 10, 28, 29 and 36. Slap bang in the middle.

The wheel spun. The ball engaged and settled. Number ten.

Haruto punched the air. 'System worked,' he said to Caves, who had decided to sit next to him in the near empty casino.

'You use a system?' The chauffer's eyes boggled. 'Wow.'

It'd succeeded. Ivan Caves was a hard man to get to talk. But following the second win with the number twenty-eight, there was plenty to chat about and Caves had just one thought in his mind, to get to know his new friend as soon as possible.

It was five o'clock and The Rivoli Bar was a convenient place for Haruto to share his winning secrets, although the numbers ten and twenty-eight had been the only winners. But he'd connected with Ivan Caves, and he was exploiting it for all it was worth.

Ivan Caves refused to drink alcohol. He had to remain sober in case his boss needed him to drive. But Haruto Fraser was getting the lowdown over two ginger beers.

Everything he heard confirmed what he'd been told. Caves had recently fallen head over heels in love with a Filipino woman called Regine. A whirlwind affair. He'd met her when she was singing at a club. They'd planned a future together, and he'd been saving up for a flat. He'd even deleted a picture of an old girlfriend he'd kept on his phone for five years.

'I still can't believe how she conned me,' he said, starting to churn over events. 'Just last weekend she tells me she's married. Why would I want to see her again? No future in it.'

But the very mention of Partridge Security by Haruto whipped him into a total frenzy. Quacker had fired him for no reason 'How is he, then? Tell him if he wants any info on Koslov to get screwed. I've got a good job with him. I'm not blowing that.'

'We have to know where Regine is living,' said Haruto. 'Can't you help us out with that at least, after what she's done to you?'

'What is this?' Caves was close to losing the plot, purple with emotion. His language wasn't exactly appropriate in the elegant Art Deco surroundings. The gold leaf and gold service.

'Karen Andersen can't reach her anymore. We are in need of your help.'

'So she was one of yours? Jeez. Never thought that' He shook his head. 'Regine's the first woman I've ever loved. You know that? Look, you can find your own stuff out on her. I can't help you. What's she done, anyway? I want nothing more to do with her. No. Not after she told me all these stories. She strung me along. We were serious too.' He looked wistfully at his phone. 'Now? Doesn't contact at all.'

On the promise of key information, as to why they needed to trace her, Haruto persuaded Ivan Caves to show him where Koslov put him up in The Ritz. It was a single room in the hotel, but Regine had been staying there and had left a few bits and pieces. There were the over-the-knee boots Karen had described. Mac

306

make-up. Several designer bags still in their protective sacks.

'Look at all these.' Caves held up one of the many handbags he'd bought her. 'Because if she isn't coming back, why hasn't she taken these?' Haruto assumed he was still clinging on to hope. Ivan threw it down on the bed in disgust. It burst open spilling contents. Along with a couple of flyers for singing engagements, there was an envelope addressed to a Mrs Gibb. Mrs Gibb who lived in Hemel Hempstead. 'So that's her, is it? She's Mrs Gibb?'

On the bedside table next to Ivan's bed sat a composite photo frame in pride of place. A picture of Regine and Ivan standing in front of Eros. A photo of them eating McDonalds together. One of Regine sitting in the driving seat of Koslov's Rolls Royce. Arms around each other. They looked like a smitten couple.

'Did she ever mention someone by the name of GG?'

'Yes, when I last spoke to her. That's him. That's the geezer she's married to. GG. She said he had a brother killed in Syria and after that he went odd or something. Anyway, I don't want any part of it. Married and all that. I'm done with her.'

But it was when Haruto told him about the assaults on the Islamic women and the possibility of GG being a murder suspect in the Huw Thomas killing that everything went crazy on the fourth floor of the Ritz.

'We have to go there. He might kill her,' he yelled in a fit of impetuous concern. He started yelling. 'Why didn't you tell me this before?'

He rushed out to get the keys. 'We'll take the Roller. It's right out the front parked there. I never know when the Boss might need to use it. He has an arrangement with the Ritz in case of emergency. This time I have one.'

CHAPTER SEVENTY-TWO

ON THE NIGHT of 18 April, Glen Gibb was at home in his basement flat. He hadn't been out for two days and it felt like a week cooped up there. But it was his secret hiding place. He could leave anytime he liked.

He'd been wondering what to do since Tuesday afternoon. The Labour MP had been found dead. Going to the authorities would get him arrested.

Keep alert. If you see anything suspicious. You are our eyes and ears.

There was something in the air. Another terrorist attack. They never left it too long before having another crack, the bastards.

Beth Lane and Tessa Clark were small fry. Mia dead. And Fatima too. Her parents had killed her. He'd followed everything. They were an evil bloody bunch. The arson attack in Acton had given them the perfect excuse to blame the Far Right. Planted the idea in their heads.

But what to do about Carla Schmidt? He knew she was a serious risk. If there'd been one thing he'd got out of Germany, it'd been that. Carla Schmidt was no longer Schmidt. That had been her married name, not her maiden name. And now she had adopted an Islamic one.

He'd noted her comings and goings over the weekend when he had been on the lookout for Beth Lane. That Carla spent a lot of time at the Cherrywood sports ground was no surprise. The former Jihadi bride had always had an interest in women's rugby, even coached on occasions the junior club players.

How to alert them? An email? An anonymous tip-off. A phone call? MI5 got them all the time. He called up his blogging account on Kaspers Watch.

It was time to get creative!

CHAPTER SEVENTY-THREE

THE MIDNIGHT BLUE Rolls sped up the road to Hemel Hempstead with Ivan Caves at the wheel and Haruto Fraser strapped in alongside him. It was hotly followed by Quacker in a Ford Fiesta and Karen Andersen on her Kawasaki.

The trio slowed as the rush hour traffic built up. The sat-nav track took them to a street in an old part of the town.

They had plenty of reason to get a move on. Caves had had no contact with Regine, nor Karen either. If GG, aka Orson, was Regine's husband and he'd learnt about the affair, she could be in danger. Was he holding her prisoner? They knew he was mentally unstable, capable of anything, even murder.

The house was in a terrace of modest Victorian cottages. A pot of pale-yellow flowers sat on the front steps. Cars lining the narrow street were a mixture of white vans and small get-arounds, mostly parked on the pavement. Typical of a commuter town with limited parking spaces. As such, typical middle class residents wandered along heading home at the end of the working week. The only ones who looked out of place that Friday was the posse of investigators.

'I'll lead the way,' said Quacker, flying out of his car. 'You can find somewhere to park.' Quacker didn't want Ivan messing up the operation. He was far too volatile.

But he'd led them there and wanted a piece of the action.

'I have to see she's all right.' He looked on edge, dead set and ready for trouble.

'Ivan, we're not the Flying Squad. Not even sure if this chap is dangerous or not. Chill it, please.'

Quacker finally calmed his troops. They had to act as one. Five minutes afterwards they filed up cautiously to the door.

But they needn't have bothered knocking. Regine opened the door straight away, eyes like saucers when she saw Ivan standing there. Regine's husband joined her. Yes, he was GG. They were his initials. He had a brother murdered by Daesh in Syria. Correct. But the man in the photograph who had kidnapped Beth Lane and was a suspect in the killing of Huw Thomas was tall. Gary Gibb stood barely an inch above his wife who herself was only 5 foot 2.

'Come in. We can't stand on the doorstep,' said Gibb. 'Nosy neighbours, you know.' He ignored the protests of his wife. He was right. It was making a scene in the street. Regine beat a hasty retreat into the kitchen, her hand over her mouth, leaving her husband to sort out the mess.

Gary Gibb was questioned on the flowers. Had he sent a bouquet of roses to Karen Andersen's place of work and abode, as Quacker put it?

'I did, I did,' he said. He was trying to take in who everyone was as Ivan Caves also squeezed into the narrow hallway. But just as Quacker was about to send him back to the car Regine reappeared.

'What are you doing here? Why you come here? He is a good man. My friend. You go.' She screamed at Ivan angrily.

'I'm more than your friend. I'm your husband, don't forget,' said Gary Gibb. He gave a little chuckle, raised his finger in warning. 'But let's all go inside and have a nice cup of tea. I know about everything that's been going on.'

Ivan, his face as puce as a plum, muttered away to himself in the background before turning on his heels and storming out the front door.

'A man who signs himself GG has been terrorising some Muslim girls and is also a suspect in a murder case. We have a photo of him. Obviously it is not your good self.' Quacker showed the picture.

Gary Gibb shook his head in dismay. 'I never thought he'd do anything like that. It's my brother. There are three of us, or were. Gregg was beheaded in Syria by those ISIS bastards. But what's this about a murder? I've never heard anything about that.'

They sat in the front room and Quacker went through it all. A wedding photograph sat on the mantlepiece showing the couple, Regine huddled up with her new husband. Over a reflective cigarette, Regine's husband said he knew all about the affair with Caves. He didn't seem too bothered. Regine got up at his insistence to see where her lover had gone to. She stared out the window.

'The Rolls. The car is blocking the street. Too big.'

'Go out and talk to him if you like,' said her husband. But Regine was in two minds.

'It's all my fault. I can't blame my Queen,' he said. He'd told her to leave him. He repeated this. It was

313

because of his black moods. It was not the life he'd promised her when they'd met in the Philippines. It was up to her what she wanted to do from now on since she'd found someone else.

'So there are three GGs in total?' asked Quacker, taking out a small notebook.

'Four. Dad was Garth Gibb. Now there are only two of us left. And we had racehorse names to match. Midnight Fire. That was Greg. Mummy's Boy and Also Ran, which was Glen. Cruel, wasn't it? I never used mine much. '

Also Ran!

'Regine traced me to Devonshire Road by my card,' Karen said, for Quacker and Haruto's benefit. 'Where did you get it from Regine?'

'Downstairs. When I was cleaning to sell.' The house was on the market. 'It was with the pictures of people with their heads off. It was horrible.'

Karen was now staring at the picture of the four men. The GG network, all together and complete. The bullying father, the bonded brothers.

'That's what they did to Midnight though,' said Mummy's Boy. 'It's not nice to see. Glen's not got over it properly. Nor have I. But what's this murder thing you mentioned? That's serious.'

'The Labour MP for Cherrywood was found dead in his home,' said Quacker.

'We know Cherrywood,' said Gary Gibb. 'Where we did some business before all this Islamification. But Glen wouldn't have had anything to do with that, I'm sure.'

'Someone saw your brother outside the house the afternoon of the killing,' said Quacker. 'The police want to talk to him about it.'

'I'm bloody sure they do,' said Gary. 'They'd love to pin something like that on him. But he wasn't there then. He was here. I know he's not too happy about these ISIS girls, mind. He has very strong opinions on girls who went to the Caliphate. But I expect he can clear that up for himself.'

'Do you know where he is?'

'Yes. He's here now. He's living with us. Just until we sell, that is. He's been downstairs for the last couple of days.'

Quacker was the first up. Then Haruto, then Karen. The three of them sprinted out the front door and around the back. There was a basement accessible from the rear of the building and that was where Also Ran had been living. But by the time they got there, he'd gone, disappeared.

At that point, as the team looked at each other wondering what to do next, they heard the sound of a car starting up outside. Also Ran had been downstairs listening all along and had picked up what was going on and decided to do a runner without further ado. He'd even got Ivan Caves to move his car to let him drive away.

CHAPTER SEVENTY-FOUR

AT TEN TO six on Friday night, Karen Andersen, astride her beloved motorbike sped down the M1 towards London. She had no option. Bea Harrington had an appointment at seven o'clock that evening, so Karen wanted to use the small window of opportunity to meet her.

It seemed unlikely now that GG had killed Huw Thomas and anyway he had an alibi. Also, his uncontrollable anger appeared to be just at Jihadi women. So the death may have had nothing to do with the Far Right movement. Nor Tammy Bishop either. Could Bea Harrington have done it? They'd had a row. He'd left the flat. Did she follow him? She was the only one who knew where he was headed that evening.

If Bea was the culprit, she hid it well and bubbled over with enthusiasm at the chance to show Karen over her apartment. 'At least no journos hiding in bushes. Not that there's anything for them here. Everyone at the Lords is locking themselves in cupboards, so to speak. Terrified in case they get caught up in it. As if. The funeral will be the next press junket. So what have you heard on the ghastly girl? You must be quick. I've got ten minutes and I have to shoot.'

It was a plush flat and smelt of fresh flowers and heavily perfumed candles. Bea Harrington wore a burgundy velvet dress. She was off to a reception.

'What did you and Huw argue about on Tuesday night? Can you tell me? It could help.'

'Can't think why. I didn't kill him. That idea is plain mad. You know that.'

'You discussed the Sharia stuff?'

'We were always scrapping about things like that. I even played a part in getting him into understanding all that nonsense. Huw Thomas wasn't that radical at all. But I looked at his website that day, and it was beyond a joke. Dangerous. Pushing all these Islamic extremes they come out with. This Far Right crowd will pick up on anyone who sticks their head above the parapet on Islam. I told him that.'

'Your fight? Was it over another woman, as they say in the press?' There was no point being unsubtle. The clock was ticking.

'Well, that's what kicked it off. Look, Huw had affairs galore. It wasn't all lovey-dovey between us. We enjoyed each other's company more than anything. I knew he'd never change. No, it was all over this psychiatrist thing. About nine months back I felt I needed to see someone, someone discreet. You have to be careful being in politics. Huw recommended him. Huw was ever protective of his friends. He didn't appreciate any slights on their character. And I made the mistake of suggesting the shrink he'd put on a pedestal wasn't trustworthy. He didn't handle it well.'

'What's his name?'

'Ali al-Sayed. I've been seeing him to help me get over James's suicide. These things you've kept bottled up for years just pour out, don't they? I'd told him about something in confidence. I got the feeling he passed it on.'

'What was it about?'

'Look, I'll tell you on one condition.'

'Which is?'

'You stop Tammy Bishop from fucking up my life again.'

'I will if I can.'

'If you can,' she added, in a low voice before pausing. For a second she looked like she was buckling under the weight of the world. 'There is something I need to get off my chest. And I don't have much time.' Bea gave a deep sigh. 'It's what happened that time on the yacht. I don't know how much you've found out already. Two of us took a modelling job down in St. Tropez and the other model drowned. I've always felt bad about it because I'd talked the girl into doing it. Nothing more. But I wish I'd never told the psychiatrist about it. It was a month back. I started having funny thoughts about him.'

'But this was years ago, wasn't it?'

'Exactly. But it was only two weeks after I told the psychiatrist about it I got this odd letter from Tammy Bishop. It was all Dandelion this, that and the other. "Dandelion" was the professional name of the model who drowned. We all had funny names like that back then. That's when I learnt to my horror Dandelion was Tammy's mother. Or so she claims. I didn't even know "D" had a child. She never mentioned her to me at all. She was just someone who signed with the same agency in Walpole Street as I did. She was desperate to be famous. We all were.'

'You're Marigold?'

'I wondered when you would work it out. Yes. Have you told her?'

'No. I said I'd wait for your decision on that.' Karen gave her an enquiring look.

'I've decided. Please don't. She said in her letter she would ask you to investigate the case. I can't do with opening that up again. It was awful, the whole thing. I couldn't bear it.'

'And you think the psychiatrist mentioned it to Tammy Bishop? But how?'

'I don't have a clue. That's what I wanted to find out from Huw. And he wasn't being very helpful. Quite the opposite in fact.'

'And the psychiatrist was someone Huw Thomas knew?'

'The son of a colleague of his. Mustafa. God, he's been all over the media, hasn't he? Ali is Mustafa's son. He works in Cherrywood and one day a fortnight in Harley Street. But he goes all over the country too I gather. Anyway, that was their relationship. He and his wife would even use Huw's house if he wasn't there. Their own place is being renovated or something. It was all to keep the bloody chap who ran his office happy. Huw handed him far too much power. Anything to get out of doing the work himself. Lazy people are like that.' She glanced at her watch. 'Now I've told you all this. You promised. You will keep her away from me, won't you?'

CHAPTER SEVENTY-FIVE

BEA HARRINGTON LET OUT a nervous laugh when David Miller finally collared her on the Embankment. She hadn't been expecting him on a Saturday. Her pulse started racing as he stepped out right in front of her. It was 19 April at nine-fifteen in the morning.

'Hello, David. It is David, isn't it?' she said. 'You've been waiting for this moment for quite some time, haven't you?' She continued walking and picked up the pace. Scared stiff. 'You well?'

'My office is close to here. I quite often see you going into the Lords.'

'I'm aware of that. And I rather wish you wouldn't keep stalking me as you do,' she said, sounding breathless. 'There's nothing I can help you with, I'm afraid.'

'None of you seem to care about my son anymore nor what happened to him.'

'I care a lot, but what can I do?'

'He was only twenty-one. Forgotten about.'

'I disagree with you there. There's been plenty in the press. It keeps popping up from time to time.' David Miller had been the instigator behind most of the articles, keeping the incident alive. Even if Robin Miller had killed himself the Conservative party should have done more. If not, they had a measure of responsibility after they'd let a potential terrorist penetrate the political system. 'You seem to forget, Mr

Miller, that my husband died too. He committed suicide. The drama over your son was a contributing factor. Believe me.'

'Look, I don't hold you personally responsible for any of this,' he said. They were elbow to elbow. 'The bullying report named your stepson, Oliver, as the person who threatened Robin. He is the one I'd like to talk to. Do you know where I could get hold of him?'

'I don't have the faintest idea. He's overseas somewhere. And you're probably right to want to. I agree, he's a bully alright. But he's not my child. And I never got along with him too well either. I am very sorry for you. I read the report into the bullying. It was a complete whitewash. Did you expect anything else?'

By agreeing with him Bea had taken the wind out of David Miller's sail. 'I know nothing will bring him back, but still I want justice. He deserves that.'

'Yes and I understand how you feel. I didn't know Robin well. It was my late husband he contacted. As if he had any influence over what was going on. But maybe he could have given my stepson Oliver a thumping over it. Or maybe done something more to help Robin's mental state. At least it wouldn't have given Tammy Bishop the excuse to do what she did.'

'Do you think she killed him?'

'Look at her track record. Recruited jihadi brides. Radicalised school children. Attempted a terrorist attack. She got away with all of that. She could get away with murder if she really wanted to. Why don't you leave me alone and talk to her yourself?'

'I would if I knew where she lived.'

Bea Harrington dug into her pocket and handed him the piece of paper. On it was the address of Tammy Bishop.

CHAPTER SEVENTY-SIX

THE FOLLOWING MORNING was a Saturday. 19 April. The Home Office website had raised the threat level for the UK from terrorism to severe. They didn't specify whether it would be either Islamic activity or the Far Right as the likely source.

At twenty to eight Haruto phoned Karen. He called from outside the place where he was staying with the girl he'd met on his travels. He told Karen that he'd tried to break off with her gently. But she'd gone crazy and even threatened him with a knife and he was now worried about her mental state. He was trying to calm her down.

At nine-fifteen Quacker rang to ask if Karen had checked her WhatsApp. All the messages still needed monitoring. Tammy Bishop had begun posting on it again under her alias Zinah al-Rashid. Despite having told Karen she'd not remembered Yasmin on the WhatsApp group, she was now in a full conversation with her.

Both Yasmin and Zinah were typing furiously between one and another. Both berated the Ahmeds for killing Fatima. They lambasted them. They should be punished. Locked away. Also, how could Beth Lane be so dim as to lend someone her phone in Turkey? Stupid is as stupid does. She was a half-wit. Zinah asked Yasmin where she was hanging out. The reply was, 'I don't give that out to anyone.' Zinah replied, 'Nor me.'

The communication stopped and the group was silent for an hour. Karen hopped on her bike and drove straight over to Acton Vale to confront her about the online chat. What was she up to?

When she got to Tammy Bishop's house, Karen couldn't miss all the chaos going on in the basement. Had she rented it out?

Karen bounced up the steps and banged on the bell. A youngish man, late twenties, Karen thought, opened the door to her.

'Are you to do with the shoot?' He hitched up his drainpipe jeans. He introduced himself as the first AD. The whole house was a hotbed of activity. A small media crew were buzzing about with silent efficiency. 'Is it Tammy Bishop you're after? You'll find her downstairs.'

Tammy Bishop had used the area to film her suicide tape three years back, but today it had become the backdrop for a late 80s TV show. Tammy was the star, dressed like something out of Dallas.

'We've been reconstructing this.' Tammy was trembling with excitement. She passed Karen a photo of Dandelion wearing a similar outfit. 'Don't you think we look alike?'

The director of the shoot found them. 'We're finished now. Got all we need.'

Karen and Tammy made their way back upstairs to the living room where the crew were flat out unplugging cables and wires.

'They've been all over the house,' said Tammy. 'I built the sets myself. Started on them after you'd gone yesterday. Took me all night. You can get everything down the Goldhawk Road in those little fabric shops.'

The whole idea was for a full-page spread in Woman's Life. The contract lay in full view on the centre table. 'This morning it's the photoshoot,' she explained. The article was underway. 'Reformed Terrorist Follows in Dead Mother's Footsteps'. Keeping out of the limelight had never been Tammy's intention.

'There's good money in modelling, don't you know?' She giggled like an excited child. The pathological symptom of her narcissistic condition was never far below the surface. The house had already become a shrine to Miriam Bishop. Framed pictures of her sat all along the mantlepiece.

'Do you want to see the photos?' She'd assembled a scrapbook of pictures and then recreated them with the photographic team. 'You're quite like Twiggy, aren't you, Karen? But with dark hair.'

'Why all this? Why now?' It was thirty years back. 'Tammy, why not move on?'

'You have to revisit the past to find the future. That's what my psychiatrist told me.' She shoved the book over to Karen. Staring out from the page was a young Bea Harrington. Marigold. 'Do you know who this is?'

Karen had promised not to say.

'You do, don't you?' she said. There was no escape. 'I think you do. She still looks the same, doesn't she? It's remarkable how I feel at the moment. I've been living with the guilt all my life. Shouldered the blame for her death. But I wasn't responsible. It was someone evil, a cunning and devious person.'

Tammy was going to be hard to dissuade from meeting Bea Harrington. Could she stop her? No wonder the paranoia. Tammy Bishop held her responsible for what happened to her mother Miriam. Karen had to somehow calm the situation.

'You don't have all the facts,' she said.

'I do. You were supposed to investigate for me. When you didn't answer my letters, I had to nut them out for myself. But I did it in the end.' She was being deliberately provocative. 'Psychiatrists can be good for certain things.'

'That's how you learnt about your mother's death?'

'Yup. Ali, my psychiatrist, found out that Miriam Bishop was my mother and she was "Dandelion" in her modelling career. Wasn't that clever? He also told me just how she died. It was like switching on a lightbulb when he did. My understanding until then was it was a suicide or a drug overdose.'

So Bea Harrington had been right. 'What else did you discuss?'

'My radicalisation mostly,' Tammy said. 'Western doctors don't understand how Sharia Law impacts on mental health. Ali al-Sayed read about me and made me his guinea pig.' Tammy was convinced the security services planned it. The psychiatrist was to vouch for her having changed. He would constantly question her faith. Had she really given up Islam? She ended with, 'He was a creep. I called him Pally Ali. Won't stop texting me.'

'When did he raise the subject of your mother?'

'A few weeks ago. He asked if she disgusted me. What with her being a model. And drinking and taking drugs. And that was the breakthrough for me. I didn't at all. Quite the opposite. And I now know who got her on to the boat. Who to hate. Not myself.' She was revving, higher and higher. 'Archie, my stepfather. He was a bully and so jealous. If he wasn't already dead, I'd kill him myself. It was his fault. Marigold introduced her to modelling. She pulled some strings. It made her feel special again. I wanted to thank her for it. Could you arrange for me to visit her?' She picked up a diary. 'She won't answer me.'

Karen felt the room spinning. She had an urge to escape the madness there and then, but she had to stick with it.

'You've been WhatsApping on the group. Why?'

'You told me someone's got into it. But you never said how. Why not? Because you didn't trust me, did you?'

Karen avoided the question.

Tammy continued. 'She didn't want to cross into Syria on her own, did she? She messaged on WhatsApp. There should have been others. She hadn't expected to travel alone. Of course I remember. It was me who was dealing with it.'

'Yes, I know,' said Karen. 'So she went on a trip to have a story ready for when she got back. Which was when she met Gibb—.'

'Who, by then, had learnt one of Greg's captors had a British jihadi bride called Basilah. She was at several executions I believe.' Tammy paused. 'You share the same Islamic name. Maybe this Glen Gibb thinks it's you, ' she continued, with a devilish twinkle.

'And he's hated British girls who want to wed fighters ever since,' said Karen. 'But how did you learn all this?'

'How he got into her phone? Or how he found Jamillah was a Jihadi bride to be? Or when he added himself to the group?' She sat back in her chair. 'Glen has used the cover of Yasmin the whole time.'

CHAPTER SEVENTY-SEVEN

KAREN ANDERSEN HAD a date with Haruto Fraser that night. That was if he could be sure his now ex-girlfriend would be calm enough to take the train to her sister's home in Cambridge as she'd promised to do. Somehow they both knew it wouldn't happen. But the anticipation alone helped her from going nuts.

She left Tammy Bishop at a quarter to eleven and drove straight to Quacker's house in Acton to share the news. Glen Gibb, who was Also Ran, who was GG, was also Yasmin.

They drank coffee and wondered what to do next. They considered one option, to try communicating with him on the WhatsApp group via Karen. He had to be taken in urgently.

'What is clear from what you say and what his brother Gary tells us, is that Glen's beef is only with the female Jihadis. It's a personal vendetta. There are scores of them. European women who've slipped back into mainstream society. Not just here. Holland, France, Sweden. So he could be dangerous. Who knows who could be next? Let's hope not you, Karen, God forbid.'

'I can't imagine he would think I'm the Basilah who was at his brother's execution.'

'Well, even if he does, it doesn't sound like he's on a killing spree,' Quacker commented. Sometimes he could be insensitive. 'Well, from what we've learnt, it seems unlikely he had anything to do with the killing of Huw Thomas.'

'But then what was he doing outside his house on Tuesday afternoon?' asked Karen.

'Tammy Bishop is taking a risk doing an article on her experience as a terrorist. What does she look like these days?' Quacker asked, taking in the photo Karen had kept on her phone.

'It seems a bit of a coincidence that Ali al-Sayed was the psychiatrist for both Tammy Bishop and Bea Harrington.'

'Not really,' said Quacker. 'Seeing as he's an expert in the field. And then known to Huw Thomas.'

They'd reviewed the boat story. It'd been a terrible accident but not one that is all that uncommon. Quacker continued, 'There are around three hundred and fifty thousand deaths worldwide by drowning a year. And if Dandelion's daughter holds no grudge against Lady H then that's all for the better isn't it?'

Karen wasn't convinced. Tammy Bishop said she didn't hate her at all. 'So I should tell Bea Harrington that Tammy's now all sweetness and light? Think she'll believe me?'

But before she could pick up the phone to her, events took a further change in direction.

Haruto ploughed through the door with his laptop open. He'd just received a message from Kasper Rosenthal. Glen Gibb had written a blog post, 'How the EU's policy allows terrorists to roam freely.' There was an image uploaded with it. The picture showed an Islamic couple entering a house. It didn't say where or when, but it was definitely in the UK.

Haruto called up the site. There was nothing distinguishable from it in the way of features in the background. The man had his back to the camera, and the woman wore the full burka. But Glen Gibb had tagged it, 'Carla Schmidt. Where is she now?'

'When was it taken? Can you tell?' Quacker asked.

Haruto reckoned he could work out the time by the angle of the sun. Not the place, of course.

'And what's that in the window?' Quacker pointed out a red political poster stuck to the glass. Barely visible.

'Could this possibly be the Huw Thomas house?' Karen asked.

'Maybe,' said Haruto, expanding it.

'It looks a little like the area where Mr Thomas lived,' said Quacker. 'But not his actual house. They've festooned it in yellow tape. It's still very much a crime scene.'

'So perhaps this was taken before the event. The day Huw Thomas was killed? And he's suggested this is Carla,' Haruto suggested.

'But Carla Schmidt was not on the group,' said Quacker.

'Glen Gibb knew about Carla from Kasper,' said Karen. 'Perhaps he found her.'

Haruto had a personal emergency at home and had to get away. This gave Karen the opportunity she needed to slip away too. As Haruto had pointed out, sometimes her hunches went unheard. And she couldn't afford to get this one wrong. Even if it meant a round trip of a hundred miles.

There was something she wanted to check out on her own before the date with Haruto, if it was ever going to take place. But she'd need to break the speed limit if she was to make it.

Karen Andersen's skin was tight against her forehead. She leaned into every curve, keeping the bike at maximum speed. The countryside was a blur as she sped up the M1, keeping a sharp eye on her rear vision mirror for police. It was a quarter to one on Saturday, 20 April.

About half an hour up the motorway she passed the sign for the turnoff to Hemel Hempstead. But she kept her head down. That's where they'd been the day before, where Glen Gibb had been living all long.

As she whizzed past, she thought about Regine Mendoza. How it all fitted that Also Ran had been her brother-in-law. The perfect set up for him. Located halfway between London and Cherrywood, he'd waged his vendetta between the two places.

Karen opened up the throttle all the way. She needed to get to Cherrywood as soon as possible. No amount of online searching or phoning around could tell her what she wanted to know. She had to eyeball it in person.

Selective snippets of conversation had been zinging through her head. From Bea Harrington. Tammy Bishop. From Kasper in Germany. Helga Hom. The Far Right. Islamic terrorism. Huw Thomas. Somehow they were all linked.

She turned off at the junction leading to where Huw Thomas had lived. The crime scene. There it was still sealed off with yellow tapes, as Quacker had pointed out. But Karen knew police still maintained a presence at the property, so she didn't loiter and cruised slowly past at fifteen miles per hour. Slow enough to confirm it was the same house in the picture of Carla Schmidt. The poster was there all right. Still stuck to the window exactly like in the photo. 'Vote Labour. Huw Thomas.'

She drove around the corner and stopped at a safe distance from sight of the police manning the house. She read through her original report. This was where GG had been seen. He'd taken a photo of Carla outside the house before he killed Huw Thomas. But why do that? Was he after Huw Thomas or her?

But Huw Thomas was supposed to be in London that day. If Glen had been stalking him, he would have known that. Therefore, he was hanging about for an opportunity to photograph the woman to do what he'd done to the others. He was consistent. He'd then post on the internet. Let the radical right do his dirty.

But who was Carla with? Her husband? Huw Thomas often let the psychiatrist, Ali al-Sayed, stay in the spare bedroom when he was away. That meant Carla Schmidt was Ali al-Sayed's wife. They were there at the Thomas residence when he returned.

Why had that not been mentioned before?

CHAPTER SEVENTY EIGHT

KAREN HAD TO get to the Cherrywood Labour Office and have a word with Mustafa al-Sayed as soon as possible. If Carla Schmidt was the person in the photograph, then Glen Gibb had her on his radar. At the very least, she must be warned. By Gibb's tone on the WhatsApp group, he was boiling over with rage and anger.

Karen shifted down into low gear as she approached the building and parked two hundred yards from short of the entrance. The main door of the dilapidated part headquarters was locked.

Of post war construction in the Attlee years when economy was everything, the building showed its age, tired and shabby. The walls covered with graffiti. Karen went around to the rear of the property. Somebody had broken one of the panel windows on the back door, possibly a local thug or one of the hooligans Mustafa al-Sayed had been describing on television.

Karen went back to her bike and took out the largest spanner she could find in the toolbox. The glass was already shattered, so what did it matter? She went back and gave it a tap and knocked out the remains of the glass pane. The opening was now large enough. She reached in and easily unlatched the door.

Inside, the office was in darkness, the blinds pulled down low. Karen took out her small LED pencil torch and swung the beam around the untidy office. There was evidence of recent occupation. Karen shivered in the damp room. But where were they now? At the far end of the ground floor there was a passage leading to the floor above. Karen found the key amongst a clump of them on a ledge near the door, which, after a bit of fiddling, opened to reveal a linoleum-tiled staircase as steep as a ladder.

Karen crept quietly up the stairs, her heart beating faster than normal. It was pitch black up there. Eerie. A gust through the broken window slammed the door shut behind her. She found the light switch which made all the difference. Inside a cupboard filled with blocks of plain paper, campaign leaflets and red rosettes. A gun-metal desk and chair were the only furniture in the room. *Why would they lock this place?*

Karen freed the stiff top drawer with a determined yank. Inside lay a solitary letter. Addressed to Huw Thomas at Dolphin Square. Without thinking of the consequences, she ripped it open. The letter was simple and to the point. Another death threat to the MP. Maybe the type he'd received before. But what was it doing there? Why hadn't it been handed to the police like the other one?

Engrossed, Karen wasn't aware she had company. 'What the hell are you doing in here? You have no right.'

Mustafa al-Sayed was easily recognisable from his TV appearances. He'd come across as an easy-going personality. But it was Saturday, just past three in the afternoon. Someone had broken into his ramshackle office. So he wasn't looking too happy. What was going on?

'I'm a private investigator.' Karen Andersen took out her card and offered it to him. She held up the death threat letter in the other.

'It doesn't matter who you are. What the bloody hell is going on?'

'Someone has been terrorising Muslim women. I'm on the investigation team. We think we know who it is but not where he is.'

'But does that give you the right to act like a cat burglar? Get out of here.'

'Wait. He may have sent this letter to Huw Thomas.'

'What letter?'

'This should be given to the police.'

'He didn't send them. I did.' He moved toward the desk and towards her. 'Don't you know anything about politics?' She was expecting him to lunge. But instead, he threw open another drawer and slapped a fresh wad on the top. 'Go ahead. There are more. You can take a look. You don't have to break into the bloody office to do so. Go ahead. Read them!'

Karen was edging her way over to the staircase. Mustafa was getting closer. She inched backwards around the room, feeling behind her. 'Why would you write those letters?'

'Why would I do it? It was not my idea. It was Huw's.'

She saw her crowbar still alongside the drawer. He saw it too. 'Is this what you used? Why couldn't you have rung?' He held it up and his eyes flared. 'Why do they send a damn girl to do this police work?' And watch how you are going, will you? We had a jolly member fall down the stairs and break his neck this week. They are as steep as hell.'

'Why would Huw Thomas write death threats to himself?'

'It was the one good idea he had. We were trying to build him up with the members. We thought it would show he was on their side. We had three ready to send from different addresses. But then this Far-Right guy killed him and we didn't get to do it.'

'Do you know someone called Carla Schmidt? '

'I have never heard of anyone called Carla Schmidt. Why should I?'

'The man we are on to has a vendetta against women who showed support for Isis. Or went to Syria.'

'Going to Syria doesn't make you a criminal. My son went to Syria. He was treating wounded Muslims. He's a psychiatrist. Maybe he is next on this guy's 'knocking-off' list.'

'Does he have a wife?'

'Yes.'

'Did he meet her in Syria?'

'No. On a Muslim website. It was my idea he got married. She is German. But what does that have to do with you?'

She took her phone. 'Glen Gibb took this picture on the day of the murder. Do you recognise these people?'

'It's my son and his wife.'

'So they were there on the night he was killed?'

'Possibly, yes. Because he was expected to be in town. But they would have left the very moment he came in. Not only to get out of the jolly way, but also because they are very religious. Chadia wears the veil and no man must see her face. That would even apply to our popular MP.'

The thought crossed them both at the same time.

'I know what you are thinking. But no, Ms Andersen. My son would not have been that disturbed to have killed someone because they saw her face.'

But maybe Huw Thomas saw something else.

CHAPTER SEVENTY-NINE

AT TWENTY TO four that afternoon, Karen Andersen left the Cherrywood Labour Party office heading for the housing estate where Ali al-Sayed and his wife lived.

Mustafa had given Karen his son's address. He'd not seen him for some days. He was sure they would clear everything up. But as she left she noticed how emotionally and physically drained he looked. Something was deeply troubling him.

It was all conjecture. But could Ali al-Sayed's wife possibly be Carla Schmidt? She reran the bizarre experience and what she'd uncovered. The fake death threats. That wasn't the concern. It was that Ali and his wife had been there that evening. And could it be that Huw Thomas had interrupted something he wasn't meant to see?

As expected, their house was empty. She did a quick canvass of the area looking for clues. 'Do you know where I can find the people who live next door?' Karen asked the gardener.

'No. I think he works in London sometimes. I never see her.'

But as neighbours go, no one seemed to know too much about them. They were more interested in talking about the massive sinkhole in the next street which had at long last been filled in. After all that time.

But eventually, she struck gold in the form of a local boy who was messing around on his bike. He'd been kicking a ball about on the green behind where Ali al-Sayed lived. Yes, he knew a German woman who'd played rugby with them from time to time, and had had a word with her earlier that day. 'She's playing at Twickenham today. And I'm not going to see her again. She's going way somewhere.'

Karen went back to her Kawasaki and was in the process of putting on her helmet when she saw Ali al-Sayed. He'd gone into the house leaving his BMW running and reappeared carrying a rucksack which he dumped on the back seat before heading off.

She mounted the bike, instinct sharpening just as Quacker rang.

'There's been a full-scale alert at Twickenham Stadium. And we've had Mustafa al-Sayed on the phone. You left him your Partridge card. He is very worried about his son. He thinks he might have become radicalised. Seems like your visit prompted him to come forward.'

'I'm at Ali's house now. Carla Schmidt is on her way to Twickenham. She's the one you want. I think she is planning an attack there. Not at the men's match. She will target the women's.'

CHAPTER EIGHTY

AT FIVE O'CLOCK that afternoon, Carla Jessen walked into the stadium dressing room. She glowed with pride at how well it had worked. Her determination to wear the German rugby uniform in this way had succeeded. The suicide belt in her sports bag would be fitted in the toilets.

Security was thick on the ground. With the UK terrorist level on red, police were everywhere and on high alert, on the watch for anything suspicious. Fans had to queue at the gate as everyone had to go through the stringent security checks. Even the catering staff were on the lookout. Word was out. Twickenham was a potential target for a terrorist attack. The big game, the men's, an international, Ireland versus England. No one was that interested in the warm-up event, the women's event. It didn't bring in the crowds, did it?

To Carla so much made sense now. Everything was for a reason. Who'd even heard of the German Women's Rugby Team? It had been around for nearly forty years. One of the well-respected teams with a huge following in Germany. So they rated second billing. Ha!

Carla's husband, Ali al-Sayed, was on his way. He'd be in London shortly. The arrangement was if he got through, they'd both explode the devices right in the middle of the crowd of non-believers. At the same time, to achieve maximum impact, the timer would set off the bomb in the car in Chudleigh Road.

She revved up, in charge. You can't serve two masters. Allah chooses only the best for his work. He'd found the special one for this mission. She would not fail Allah. *Allahu Akbar*.

Carla Schmidt had outfoxed them all. Run circles around the Far Right loser who'd stalked her. He'd blackmailed her with photos online. Yes, she'd been to Syria. She'd become the wife of a warrior. Now a proud martyr. He was in paradise.

Huw Thomas had discovered the truth. He'd returned to the house on Tuesday unexpectedly. He would have still been alive had he stayed up in his bedroom just that bit longer. The impatience of the non-believer! He'd come down too soon. A short tempered angry *kafir*. Infidel. He'd disturbed their operation. Seen the explosives. He deserved to die. It was very satisfying too pinning the blame on her blackmailer.

Then Nigel Harris. He'd suspected them all along. When Ali lured him upstairs in the Cherrywood office earlier in the day, he'd threatened him with exposure. So Ali had pushed him back down the stairs. *Allahu Akbar*.

A momentary surge of self-doubt shook Carla's confidence. No, no, no. She would serve Allah.

She was a reserve player, but being a standby was better. She'd be stadium side when she discharged the bomb. *Allahu Akbar*.

Was there a new girl on the team?

Why are you staring at me?

Who are you?

Carla's heart thumped in confusion.

Get your kit on now, she urged herself.

She bent down to tie the laces of her boots. *I must go to Allah in a respectful way.*

'Chadia al-Sayed?' She looked up, caught off guard by the use of her Islamic name. As she did so, police poured through every door and threw her on the ground.

CHAPTER EIGHTY-ONE

KAREN ANDERSEN RAN as fast as she could to her bike but by the time she roared off down the road Ali al-Sayed, in his glossy black A6 BMW, was turning into the corner ahead.

That Bimmer can move, Karen thought, as she opened the throttle wide.

'Can you keep us on the line and the car in sight?' Quacker had already brought the police into the loop.

'I might have lost him for the moment, but I'll do my best,' she said into her Bluetooth. But the BMW had blasted away.

'Head for the M6. That's probably the route he'll take.'

At the top of the street, she hit the heavy traffic. Swerving between the cars, she ignored the chorus of horns from angry drivers. At the next intersection she took a hard right into a 20 miles per hour zone. Karen swung the bike around the traffic, but she had to catch the BMW somehow.

Out of the low speed zone, the bike picked up as the traffic thinned out. Karen's speedometer read over eighty as she passed an oncoming bus with inches to spare.

She zigzagged around everything, squeezing between all the lumbering goods vehicles headed for the M6. Well ahead, she caught sight of the BMW's tail lights. Weaving through the jam.

'Quacker, I've got him I think,' Karen shouted into the speaker. 'Almost up to him now.' But the BMW had gone through an amber light and accelerated away again. It was now or never.

She opened the throttle and flew through the intersection as the light changed to red. The road was diesel-greasy and Karen slowed on the slippery surface as the Bimmer pulled well ahead again. She had to take care. But the BMW was pulling away fast and shortly it'd leave her far behind.

'Quacker, I'm losing him again.'

'We'll get the police to take over from here,' said Quacker. 'They are on to it. Do you read me, Karen?'

Karen ignored the instruction.

The high-powered vehicle hurtled down the road, Karen doing everything to keep it in sight. 'He's got rucksacks on the back seat. Could be explosives. Anything.' Her heart raced as she gave the bike its head.

The traffic slowed again and Ali's BMW came to a near stop. Karen cautiously squeezed her way along the dividing line between the conflicting traffic and came right up alongside the BMW.

Ali al-Sayed sat at the wheel cool and calm as Karen wrapped on the window. He went as if to lower the window, thinking he'd cut up the motorbike and needed to apologise. But Karen couldn't miss the two bags piled in the back.

He was suddenly aware she had taken them in. *What was going on? Who the fuck was this?*

Karen knocked on the window again as Ali closed it.

What to say. What if she'd got this wrong?

She shouted above the noise of the engines, 'Put your window down.'

Car horns blasted. Fucking bikes. Yelling.

And then Ali took off again, the BMW overtaking everything.

Skidding.

Karen Andersen in pursuit. Dodging in and out. A high-speed reckless mad pursuit.

Now sirens behind. In pursuit of the pursuer.

They reached the turnoff for the motorway and the BMW was blistering ahead.

'We're at the M6 now,' she said into her Bluetooth.

And then they were flying along the motorway. The BMW gaining, accelerating to 140 miles per hour, Karen yards behind.

Police sirens wailed out their warning ever louder as more cars joined the action.

Even above all the noise, Karen picked up the distinct flapping of the helicopter's blades above tracking al-Sayed's car down the M6.

The A6 veered around a van, undercutting it but just clipping the rear bumper in the process. The van spun into the right hand lane straight into an unsuspecting car, which smashed sideways into the safety barrier. Another car slammed into the van, and bounced and went sideways into Ali's BMW.

The convoy of patrol cars arrived in seconds filing down the safety lane towards the crash.

Karen had seen the initial impact and thrown her Kawasaki in a long slide into the near side lane.

Thwack, thwack, thwack. The helicopter hovered directly overhead.

The entire southbound motorway was closed.

No one was going anywhere this side of Christmas! Karen disentangled herself from the bike still shaking with adrenalin. The BBC news blared out the window of one of the damaged cars.

'All traffic has been stopped on the M6 heading south. Police have apprehended a man who has been found carrying explosives in his car. In a separate incident, security forces have detained a woman in the locker rooms at Twickenham Stadium on suspicion of terrorism charges.'

Karen called Bea Harrington straightaway. 'Listen, I thought you should know Tammy Bishop doesn't hold a grudge against you. Quite the opposite. And she has just helped us prevent a major terrorist atrocity.'

'Then I'll be more than happy to tell her all about what happened to her mother. I'll invite her over to the House of Lords.'

It was five forty-five on Saturday afternoon.

CHAPTER EIGHTY-TWO

TAMMY BISHOP WAS all tarted up in her eighties best. She wore a suit with big lapels, purple eye shadow, burgundy lip gloss. It wasn't a modern trend. But it was her trend. Her look. Dandelion style. Flower power.

Everything was brilliant! She was as happy and chirpy as birds in the spring! It was ten past six on the afternoon of Saturday. But the shops would soon close. So she had to get a move on.

She was filled with joy. News had come through that SO15 had prevented a Jihad attack at Twickenham and minutes ago she'd received a text from Bea Harrington inviting her to tea on Monday. Best of all, she had a date that night with a man.

How could things be better? When she'd opened an email from *Woman's Life*, it was confirmation that they'd approved her questionnaire. They loved her article.

'My confession: I've always blamed myself for my mother's death. Now I know who killed her.'

'I have not been a good person,' she'd said. 'But Mama's story should explain it. She was loving and gentle. Everything a six-year-old could wish for.' La de da de da. 'She was bullied by my stepfather who never let her go out without him present. But her special friend, Marigold, made her a star.'

She exuded the sweet, strong perfume of the eighties. She was off to buy two more bottles. One for herself and another for Bea Harrington. Either Obsession, Poison, Georgio. She hadn't yet decided. It would make a perfect gift to take to the House of Lords.

She left the house and locked her front door.

'Tammy Bishop?'

She turned as a man bounded up the steps. He wore conservative clothes, but he'd sprung her on her own doorstep. Possibly a journalist. Bloodshot eyes. Seemed close to tears. Stirred up about getting a scoop no doubt.

'I'm not giving any more interviews at the moment,' she said. 'I'm under contract to *Woman's Life*.'

He blocked her way. 'One question and one question only. I know that you'll lie. But I want an answer.'

'I'm running late for an appointment. Do you have a card?'

'I need to know why you murdered Robin Miller. Why you then made out he'd killed himself.'

'How did you get my address? It's not public.'

The first thrust from the long narrow knife drove Tammy back against the door. The second stab went deep into her abdomen. Tammy gave a long gurgling scream as the blade slashed deep across her throat.

'That's the last story you will ever spin.' He stood over the woman at his feet as she lay dying.

The man was emotionally and physically spent as he staggered from the scene.

At Acton Police Station he made the following statement to the duty officer in a calm but cold manner. 'My name is David Miller and I've just killed somebody. It's the woman who murdered my son.'

CHAPTER EIGHTY-THREE

GLEN GIBB GOT to the restaurant in good time. It was a seven-thirty booking, but he was there fifteen minutes early. Just in case she was there ahead of time too.

He'd driven into London as high as a kite. For once the news was positive. Both double-crossing Carla and her scheming husband were now in custody. And they had been stopped in time. Twickenham was safe and not a single soul injured.

This was to be the night of his life. Glen felt so good, positively glowing with pride. The morons of the secret services had, at last, caught on that Carla Schmidt was now Carla Jenner, the professional rugby player. And all thanks to his post on Kaspers Watch. How good was that? He deserved a medal.

As he soaked in the candlelit atmosphere he thought of his twin brother. Greg would be grinning down from Heaven if he could. And meeting a woman? He'd be right up for him on this date and almost present and next to him.

Steady boy, play it cool. Slow. Hold something back. Easy does it. Midnight was never on edge with women, he oozed self-confidence from every pore.

Was Glen nervous? In the normal run of things, he would have been shitting himself. But no. Instead Glen tingled with excitement. He was smugly confident. He was about to meet up with his soulmate.

He ordered a bottle of bubbly. It wouldn't hurt to have a glass before Tammy Bishop showed. Have it fizzing in the flute when she walked in would show style and sophistication.

On the spot, Glen Gibb made another life-changing decision. He'd drop the Also Ran nickname. Hated the sound of it. Detested it. It didn't suit the new him anymore.

Daydreaming about the thirty-four-year-old woman made his heart race and his eyes smile. Tammy Bishop. So this is how it felt, being love-struck.

What a woman. She was the one who had worked out Glen went by the name of Yasmin. Then she'd set up a separate WhatsApp stream. They'd been messaging back-and-forth straight for nearly twenty-four hours.

Tammy Bishop was a former Jihadi bride recruiter called Zinah al-Rashid. Glen was a man who bore a deep grudge against all the young women who went out there because of what they'd done to his brother. Hatred had consumed him for too long. She'd been on his list to target when they freed her. Wow. What a change!

Zinah was different now, changed out of sight. With the online conversation, they'd stumbled across something extraordinary. There was something special between them. With each exchange it got better and better. Lots of smiley faces and laughs. She'd written in fun, 'Me Zinah, you Yasmin.' He'd replied with Tarzan's cry *'Whoaoaoa.'* The cry of the jungle.

What a wondrous affair it would be. Glen had stared at the photos she'd sent him over and over again, fascinated, rapturously in love. She would be a big-time model. It was her ambition. Maybe he could help her. They had so, so much in common. Abusive childhoods. Feelings of inadequacy. And she'd never slept with a man. *I will be the first.*

Glen Gibb straightened his tie and took a sip of champagne. At long last someone understood him. Clearly understood him. She had a warm heart and was compassionate. She empathised with him. Why he'd been mad as hell with the Jihadi girls. Her kindness alone brought him to tears. He knew, just knew that they were completely right for each other. Marriage and children, why not?

She was running late. He took out his phone and WhatsApped her. 'Where are you, my darling Zinah?'

At a quarter past eight, when Tammy Bishop hadn't shown, Glen called her phone. A man's voice on the line.

"Can I speak to Tammy, please?' Glen tried to keep a confident tone. *Who on earth was this?*

'I'm sorry, Sir. I'm a police officer. Can you tell me who you are and what your relationship is with this lady?

'I'm her boyfriend. Where is she?'

'I'm afraid there's been a fatality.'

The rest of Saturday night passed in a blur, paying the bill, leaving the restaurant into the fading light. A major terrorist attack had been averted. The woman he'd fallen in love with had been stabbed to death. But on a Saturday night in London life swirled on around him as if nothing had happened. People bar hopped. It was a great bloody carnival. Pub crowds spilt onto the pavements. It was Party Central. A cacophony of disrespect deafened Glen as he walked the streets.

Glen just couldn't take it in. He read every message she'd sent, over and over again, and was no longer obsessed with Midnight, Greg, Jihadi brides, his tomb of a bedsit. Tammy Bishop had taken over his every breathing moment. He kept going over and over it all in his mind.

Her WhatsApp messages had saved him. It was like magic. He'd been saved by her love. She'd pulled him back from the brink of insanity. He treasured her for that. They would have married. Exchanged vows. She would have been his wife. Maybe they would have had children. If only he'd picked her up, none of this would have happened. If only, if only.

The kindly police officer had given as many details as they were allowed to release at that time. But the TV news networks were full of it, the Twickenham plot, and now the murder of Tammy Bishop. A former Jihadi bride recruiter who had been out of prison just four days.

The pain inside Glen's gut throbbed like a sword twisting and turning within him.

Tammy had told him about Karen Andersen. How Basilah on the WhatsApp group was, in fact, an undercover detective and they had become very close. The undercover detective had done it. Karen Andersen was the one who caused the death of his beautiful friend. She had betrayed her by leaking her address. It was supposed to remain secret.

For the second time someone called Basilah had destroyed his life. First in Syria. Now in the UK.

CHAPTER EIGHTY-FOUR

GLEN GIBB REACHED Devonshire Road at a little past eleven on the night of Saturday, 20 April. The Basilah home base, sandwiched between two shops, lay right before his eyes, a symbol of everything evil and the home of a fifth columnist. Karen Andersen, the contract killer.

If this was the centre of operations it took on a demeaning unimportance, a put down to Tammy. So this is where it all began? The plot to have Tammy Bishop killed? They'd cut her down to size. Now he would do the same to them.

Had they had it planned from the start? Probably to let Tammy out of prison so they could kill her. They knew David Miller was after her blood. He thought she'd murdered their son. Despite Tammy assuring them it was nothing to do with her. And she'd been telling the truth.

Glen could see Andersen's neighbour peering out from the drawn curtains on the first floor, possibly on the lookout for Karen to return. Karen Andersen, who'd been with the police congratulating themselves on the successful outcome of their plan.

Didn't they have any idea what they'd done? Why kill someone who could actually help them, an asset?

Glen Gibb had gone over everything in detail time and time again looking for a flaw. Once they were all asleep, in the early hours, he would go for the old neighbour. He'd enter her flat and behead her in her bed. Let the private investigator and British traitor sleep through it all. He wanted her to suffer slowly when she found out. And this was the best way he could do it. Keep the horror alive. To slowly go to hell with her guilt about what she had done.

Not that she would need to use much of her brain to work out who'd done it. It would be quite obvious. He would leave the head on her doorstep. And the photo of the ISIS beheading.

He could then forget about her once and for all. But she would never, ever forget him. How she'd broken his heart, betrayed and destroyed forever his chance of happiness.

Glen Gibb took a great gulp of brandy from his hip flask. He had to be patient. Bide his time.

Karen Andersen hadn't left the police station until after midnight. A detailed statement of it all painstakingly taken down by the duty officer. Twickenham. Tammy Bishop. The al-Sayeds. And to top it all off, she took home a speeding ticket for her efforts.

And she was alone. Haruto's new girlfriend had dug her heels in and refused to leave his place. Restless and upset, Karen turned over and settled her head into the pillow and tried to sleep.

Dozing she heard the distinctive sound of the downstairs front door closing. Karen sat bolt upright.

That was the front door. Elspeth wouldn't be going out at this time.

All was quiet now. Perhaps she'd imagined it all, going a bit crazy. No. Somebody was coming up the stairs to the flats. Heavy unmistakable footsteps. Not Elspeth's. Definitely not Elspeth's!

Karen reached under the bed for the claw hammer she always kept there amongst her shoes. It gave her a vague sense of security as a woman living alone.

Karen knew there was someone now standing outside on the landing. She stood up by her bed, undecided but ready with the hammer, heart beating fast.

Who on earth was it?

Karen called Haruto whispering, 'Please come over. Something is going on. I think Elspeth next door is in trouble.'

'I'm on my way. Be with you in twenty. Keep on the line.'

Had they overlooked something? They'd kept all focus since Friday on Carla Schmidt, which had proven to be the right move. True they hadn't stopped David Miller murdering Tammy Bishop because they thought the Far Right were the greatest threat to her. That was a mistake. So who was outside the door right now?

In the darkened room she slipped into a dress, ready for anything.

Karen continued through the list in her mind, recalled the others. There was Amirah. Humiliated but not hurt. Mia struck by a speeding car. Then Fatima, most likely an honour killing.

Glen Gibb. What about him?

Quacker had reassured her there. Glen Gibb was not a violent person. Karen wasn't so sure. He was a man on the edge. He'd left Hemel Hempstead saying he was going to kill Basilah. Did he mean it?

Kill me? Surely not?

Karen reached down to switch on the bedside light. Nothing doing.

The power to the flats must have been cut at the consumer units on the landing.

Glen Gibb. It was possible.

Once, he believed she was the Basilah who'd witnessed his brother's death.

But did he still believe that? If so, he might do the same to her. He was one of twins, DNA linked him to symmetry.

Have me find the head of someone very close.

If so, he would have made it his business to know everything about me.

Parents dead. Love life in tatters.

The only person physically and emotionally close is Elspeth Cochrane.

My neighbour.

Karen picked out a peculiar sound now. Couldn't identify it at first. And then she got it. It was when she'd had to free one of the windows with a chisel the previous winter. Wriggled it in between the frames. The same thing must be happening next door. He was using a bar to jemmy open Elspeth's door.

Karen tightened her grip on the hammer. She jumped in shock at the sound of Elspeth's door bursting open.

You must act, move, do something.

Without hesitation Karen crossed the landing and ran into Elspeth's flat through the wrecked front door.

Elspeth had slept through it all, but stirred now with the commotion. As the powerful beam from the street light lit up the room, Karen instantly recognised Gibb with his massive frame and rounded shoulders standing over the bed, knife in hand.

He shouted at Karen angrily. 'So! It's you, you piece of shit. Both of you are going to Hell.'

'Stop,' Karen screamed, 'You've got this all wrong.

'Liar, liar, you are all liars. I'm going to kill her first and you next.'

Elspeth sat up, still groggy with sleep, confused and terrified. Karen saw the flash of silver as Gibb lifted his arm high to stab the old lady. Karen swung the hammer at him with all the force she could muster. She almost missed him completely as Gibb's knife came slashing down on Elspeth, but hit his leg. Gibb screamed in pain. His knife sliced harmlessly into the bedding as he fell sideways. As he struggled to get up, Karen smashed the hammer at his hand still holding the knife. This time it hit the target. The knife clattered on the board flooring and Karen, with a swift movement, kicked it away under the bed.

Gibb reeled towards the stairs clutching his leg, stumbled and fell in agony all the way to the bottom. She heard the door close as he made his escape.

Minutes later, against a background of sirens Karen heard the treble impact as police broke through the front door.

'So what's all this then?' asked the welcome and burly police officer.

'The man who just left? He's just tried to kill both of us. His name is Glen Gibb.'

CHAPTER EIGHTY-FIVE

AT SIX O'CLOCK on Sunday morning, Quacker and three police officers banged on the door of the Gibb house in Hemel Hempstead. They demanded to see the annex where Glen Gibb had been living. They didn't find him in, nor were there any of the gore-filled photos Beth Lane had described.

They interviewed Gary and his wife Regine, who told them how distraught and broken-hearted Glen had been at the execution of his twin brother. And yes, he was fixated on pictures of ISIS beheadings. Gary had advised his wife to ditch them if she found them lying around.

'It's not good to look at images like that,' she said. 'It's bad for the mind.' There was another reason. They'd removed them in case they deterred a potential buyer for the house. Not wanting to put them in the bin, she'd stuffed them in her bag when visiting Karen Andersen at her Chiswick address. She'd accidentally left one packet there that day. Then, on cleaning up the flat, Regine had come across them in the drawer. She'd dumped them in the paper recycling bank outside the George IV pub on Chiswick High Road.

'We're concerned about how he could have had access to Devonshire Road,' said Quacker. 'And we know that last week you stayed there yourself. Did Karen Andersen give you a key?

'No. But I used hers to leave the flat to buy food and stuff. And while I was out I had a spare cut for me. She was away at a meeting.'

'And your brother-in-law knew you had this?'

'There are no secrets between us any more,' Gary Gibb told the police. 'Let's tell them everything, shall we? Regine here was seeing someone else and didn't want me to know about it. But that's all in the past. I'm a very reasonable man. I don't blame my wife. We were chatting about Ivan Caves when Glen had supper with us last Tuesday night.' He turned to his wife. 'I remember you saying you should return the spare key to Karen Andersen.'

Regine scuttled out for the key but it had gone.

Glen Gibb must have taken it. And he held Karen Andersen responsible for passing on Tammy Bishop's address.

CHAPTER EIGHTY-SIX

HOW HAD IT happened? Who had betrayed Tammy Bishop? Someone had passed David Miller details of where she lived. Glen Gibb had thought it was Karen Andersen. He had tried to murder her neighbour as an act of revenge and failed.

On Sunday afternoon, after they'd fitted new locks, Karen took to her bike. She whistled down the M25 and A3, deep into the Hampshire countryside reaching the marina at around a quarter to four.

Love The Moon was moored at the very end of the pontoon because of its size. The old sixty two foot wooden yacht showed its age with the teak deck in desperate need of maintenance.

Bea Harrington popped her head up through the main hatch. 'I'm downstairs. It's too fresh up there.'

Karen had been building up for a fight all the way down the A3. 'You told David Miller where Tammy Bishop was living,' She was certain Bea would deny it and was ready, red faced with anger.

'And I feel like shit about it.' Bea closed the overhead sliding hatch to reduce the cutting wind coming across the channel. 'If I had the courage, I'd do myself in. But the truth is I don't.'

It was the last thing Karen expected. She was shocked at how much Bea had changed in such a short time. Bare of all make-up, her skin had acquired a grey, ashen tone. Her eyes were sunken, pupils almost pin points. It struck Karen Bea must have undergone some massive shock. She seemed on the verge of a complete meltdown.

'You'd better come aboard,' she said, waving Karen on to the boat via the uncomfortably narrow gangplank. 'The constant clanging day and night from the main halyard on the boat next door drives me barmy.'

'Why did your husband buy this?' Karen had done her homework. She knew the register listed James Harrington as the owner. He'd bought it off Huw Thomas in 2001.

'God knows why. To show off probably. There are six cabins on this thing. It was how we met. Huw Thomas wanted to dump the big boat and enter politics as a 'man of the people'. It was too ostentatious. James was looking for an extravagant yacht because he'd just got divorced. I sold it to him.'

'Did he know about the incident when he bought it?'

'No. By then the drowning was old hat. Something like thirteen years had passed. Everyone had forgotten about it. James and I started going out together after that. Then we got married. He could never understand why I hated this thing. I barely set foot on it. I kept pleading with him to change the name, but no. He said it was bad luck to change the name of a boat. He was rather superstitious. I pretended I'd developed a fear of sailing. Now I've ended up with it, for my sins.'

Karen and Bea sat at the table in the main saloon, going through all that had happened years ago. Outside, the water gently lapped the boat. Miriam Bishop's death was no accident. They'd dropped the anchor in a bay near St Tropez. They should have been at their berth in the marina. An impromptu party. Everything got out of control. The lead singer of the band, high on coke, had tried to rape her. There'd been a struggle, and he'd killed her accidentally. He'd pushed her body overboard in a panic.

'I saw it all, everything. Said nothing. The band noticed she wasn't there the next morning. Raised the alarm. They were too drunk or too high to know what really went on.'

'It all happened in my cabin, poor thing. He smashed her head in no doubt. I washed the blood away. Can you believe that? Come. I'll show you.' She got up and led the way forward to her cabin and lifted the corner of the mattress. Bea's clothes were spread across the bunk. 'I'm staying here tonight.'

'Is that wise in your present state?' asked Karen.

'Yes, I know. But I'll be fine. The bedding's been replaced, but the blood soaked right through the cabin sole.'

'Huw Thomas knew?'

'He wasn't aboard that night. But, yes. It'd been his idea to get Dandelion along. He knew the singer fancied her, and he was trying to keep him onside. I didn't ask questions. I was crazy about Huw back then. I covered it up. I shouldn't have done that, should I? And before you ask, the guy who killed her has been dead for years. An overdose.'

'So that's why you were frightened of Tammy Bishop finding out?'

'I didn't want her opening it all up again.'

The incoming tide lapped peacefully against the hull pushing the yacht to and fro.

'Come on, I'll show you around her,' said Bea. Neglected and tired, she was a ghost ship, a shadow of her former glory. Karen couldn't see a single sign of a woman's touch. 'It's very blokey, isn't it? I had nothing to do with it. It's probably where James brought his women to impress them.'

'When will you go back to London?'

She slumped down on the saloon seat cushions. The yacht was now in murky darkness. 'Not tonight. I've sold it once before. I can do so again. I'll get on to the agents first thing in the morning if I make it. If I don't, it means Miriam's claimed me. After that, I'll make a statement at the police station about what happened to her all that time ago.'

CHAPTER EIGHTY-SEVEN

MUSTAFA AL-SAYED unlocked the door of the Cherrywood office. It was Tuesday, 23 April at nine o'clock. Time to get back to work.

Two hours later, after he'd taken delivery of printing supplies the Constituency Labour Party Chair drove over to the mosque. Since the thwarted Twickenham plot, worshippers had dropped off. Mobs of angry demonstrators had marched through the town, chanting in the streets. All Muslims were under suspicion. *Islamophobia has to stop, he thought to himself.*

Mustafa called his staff together at midday to update them on where he stood on the issue. He reiterated what he'd said on the TV the day before. It had mortified him to learn about Ali's radicalisation. He'd felt ashamed and apologetic. It was a disgrace to his family. Mustafa al-Sayed had long been aware his son held extreme religious views, but he believed he could handle the situation himself. Which is why he'd not reported his concerns to the authorities.

'I had absolutely no knowledge of what they were planning.' He was of the opinion the German-born Chadia had been the bad influence. They all nodded in agreement.

He informed them that he'd offered to stand down from his position but Labour Central had insisted he stay on. 'I am not my son's keeper.'

Ali al-Sayed had admitted to killing Huw Thomas. It happened when the MP returned to his home unplanned and had surprised Ali and his wife Chadia. He'd caught them red-handed, their plans, their evil intentions clear beyond doubt. And yes. The rumours were not unfounded. The prominent psychiatrist confessed to having met the reformed terrorist Tammy Bishop, in prison. He'd been hoping to reradicalise her.

'But democracy dies in darkness,' he told them. 'We must battle on. That means shining a light on the hate crimes. Upping the ante, if needs be. Exposing the white supremacists. Identify online abusers. Those are the ones who fan the flames which lead to these events.'

Which brought him to introduce their new member of the team. She'd just travelled up from London.

'Everyone, this is Beth Lane. She'll be on our communications team. She has a very harrowing story of her own. It will chill you to the core. And it happened to her here in Cherrywood by a representative of the Far Right. You can hear it all for yourself. And she can add valuable support at the upcoming by-election.'

CHAPTER EIGHTY-EIGHT

A FRESH UNDERTAKING! Let's get things going! Glen Gibb thought. London, Brussels. Brussels, Cologne. Another train from Cologne. Three changes and six and a half hours. It was Wednesday, 24 April.

He slung the bulky bag into the area reserved for luggage as the doors slammed shut.

The new Glen Gibb had shed his old image completely. Out with the smart suit, white shirt and red tie. In with the black jeans, black Fred Perry tee-shirt and black hoodie. He'd cut his hair and had them put in a few blonde highlights. The round-style glasses finished things off. His new look suited him well. It'd been a judicious move leaving the UK quickly.

And here was an opportunity for him to brush up on his rusty German.

He felt cautiously optimistic. For the first time in years he was looking on the shiny side of life. He'd get over Tammy Bishop's death in time. The burning anger was already fading and inside he felt a flush of optimism about things. He was moving on, just as she'd taught him to do. He loved the way she helped overcome the obsessive love of his twin brother. He could move on, start again, begin anew.

He took a long sip of his coffee. Bratwurst sausage in soggy bread. He should have picked up an English-speaking paper when he had the chance. Would the authorities be after him? He'd heard from Gary that the police had searched the annex. But what would they find? No photos. He'd destroyed those. Nothing much else.

But now he was on the run. How had that come about? Yes, he'd let himself into Karen Andersen's flat to give her the lesson of her life by decapitating her friend and neighbour. He'd been mostly out of control but it hadn't worked out.

Tammy Bishop could have been a major ally in the fight against Islamic ascendancy. He knew that. And even if it hadn't been Andersen herself, someone close to her had allowed her address to slip.

The whole of the Western world was being threatened by a Muslim takeover. The English Concern Group was a waste of space. Even though they had been made illegal by legislation, government needn't have bothered.

The green and grey livery train jerked to a stop at the Bahnhof. It was a twenty-minute pleasant walk to the address he'd written down on a piece of paper. A bike was parked outside the house, secured to the iron fencing by a bright green padlock.

He knocked confidently on the front door.

'Hello. Come in, Glen.' Kasper Rosenthal waved him into the spacious lobby. 'Your room is ready.'

CHAPTER EIGHTY-NINE

IT WAS FRIDAY morning, 26 April. Karen Andersen was having breakfast. The message scrawled across the side of the Weetabix box was a stark reminder of what had happened to Fatima, a poignant, bitter-sweet memory.

Providing material support for terrorism is a crime. But it wasn't Fatima's backing for ISIS that had brought shame on the family, but refusing to marry the Pakistani relative picked out for her.

The Ahmeds believed they'd get off the charge and displayed a cold indifference to the death of their daughter. An arrogant contempt for UK law. They knew less than five per cent of honour killing cases went to the Crown Court. Islamophobia was too much of a hot potato so the CPS avoided prosecution wherever possible. But Fatima's case would go ahead. She'd posted about her parents' threats and intimidation on WhatsApp. They'd threatened to burn her alive if she didn't go ahead with the marriage. It was a crucial piece of evidence and made for an open and shut case.

Rumour was that Glen Gibb had left the country now and it was unlikely his vendetta against ex-Jihadi brides would end just like that. He was fuelled with anger and resentment against the incompetence of the authorities too and their false accusations against him. The fires in Acton. The murder of the MP. Even the motorbike accident in which Mia had been killed. Would he continue hounding out ISIS sympathisers? It didn't matter because he now had a growing network of fans behind him.

They identified with his motivation and agreed on violence as the only response. Hadn't he stopped a terrorist attack? Whose side were the authorities on? Right Wing extremists loved his life story. GG, Also Ran, the victim who fought back and won. Overnight GG became an icon of lone wolf activism. He'd spawned his own breed of terrorism and he was a star.

Karen's head spun with these thoughts and all that had happened in just a few weeks. She cleared away the breakfast things and sat down at the piano and thumped out some easy-play Mozart to calm her jangling nerves. An aggressive knocking on the front door interrupted her piece before she even got to the third measure.

Damn. Some delivery or something.

The police had destroyed the intercom when they had barged in.

She ran down the stairs and flung open the door. Haruto stood there, shuffling awkwardly.

'Hi,' she said, a smile building.

'I thought I'd drop by to see what you were up to. You OK?'

'I'm OK, thanks.'

'Jeez, this door's a real mess.'

'Yes, they didn't muck about. Are you coming up, or is it difficult?'

He grinned. 'She's gone to her sister's. It's over.'

'Is she OK about it? And you?'

'Yup! And it's good to get the place back to myself, too.'

Without saying another word they climbed the stairs, two at a time.

Karen went straight out to the kitchen area to make the coffee. Haruto sat down at the piano and ran through a couple of jazz pieces Bill Evans style.

'I never knew you could play.'

'There's quite a bit you don't know about me,' he said, with a sparkle in his eye.

He took a padlock out of his pocket and handed it to her.

'What's that for?'

'You free for the weekend?'

'Yes.'

'There is another bridge I wanted to check out, if you're up for it.'

'Really?'

'This time not Mainz. And they've banned the padlocks in Berlin because of rust damage to the bridges. But maybe we could try Paris or Stockholm?'

'You don't have to do the padlock again. Not for me,' she murmured softly.

'Well, I don't think it's that cool any more, anyway. And love doesn't need chains.' He looked straight into her pale green eyes. 'It's locked in the heart.'

ACKNOWLEDGEMENTS

None of this would have been possible without the help of others. Firstly, my extraordinary husband Donald Burfitt-Dons of thirty seven years who loyally supported my 2015 candidacy in the UK General Election. The experience gave me a practical knowledge of party politics and provided adventures to write about in books such as *The Missing Activist* and now its sequel, *The Killing of the Cherrywood MP*. Without him I would not be able to research some of the far flung places we have travelled to together.

Thank you to my editor Alice Kingsnorth for her painstaking work and everyone at New Century who has helped to put the book on the reading circuit. Thanks must go to Simon McQuiggan and Muse Strategy for their design skill and assistance online. Also to the others who have advised me on contemporary security issues who would rather not be mentioned in print. And Google which is active in helping us promote cyber safety. For the advice on medical matters, I'm indebted to Dr Ivor Burfitt.

Heartfelt appreciation also to Reem I Abdelhadi for her patience with my Arabic and my fellow students at Ealing, Hammersmith and West London College who provided invaluable insight into the realities of life for Muslim women in the UK. Their private lives, secrets and taboos helped me enormously with Zinah and to bring Fatima, Amirah, Jamilah and Ahmed to life.

Grateful thanks to RUSI, the world's oldest independent think tank on international defence and security for their helpful research into jihadi brides.

Thank you to Hamish Brown MBE, Detective Mike "Duck" Proctor, the forensic psychologist Gill Merrill, sociologist Ian Flett, who advised on coping with stalking and bullying. They've supported my work with Act Against Bullying for nearly twenty years which shaped the background to the central character in the first book in the series, Robin Miller.

Finally, my beloved daughters Arabella Burfitt-Dons and Brooke Williams, son-in-law Rhys Williams and the new addition to our family, my granddaughter Dempsie Lee.

Lightning Source UK Ltd.
Milton Keynes UK
UKHW010811031121
393297UK00002B/102